"T⸺ ⸺⸺⸺⸺ ⸺⸺⸺⸺⸺⸺⸺⸺⸺⸺⸺ writ⸺
and this one is astonishingly good... ⸺ ⸺⸺⸺ s writing
is accomplished and very engaging."
Kate Saunders, The Times

"Matters of personal identity underlie an exhilarating
ride through LA's seamier side in the company of a
hard-bitten yet highly engaging protagonist."
Ross Gilfillan, The Daily Mail

"A poignant novel about identity, and a love/hate letter to LA."
Glamour Magazine

"An elegant noirish mystery."
Amanda Craig, The Independent

"A gently transgressive, transatlantic quest that conjures
up both the languid heat of LA and the confusions
of a young woman on the cusp."
The Lady

"Anna Stothard's dark debut *Isabel and
Rocco*, written while the author was still at school, was a
McEwan-esque tale about two teenage siblings left to fend
for themselves. Her second novel, set amongst the navel-gazers
of California, proves no less precocious."
Emma Hagestadt, The Independent

THE ART OF LEAVING

ANNA STOTHARD

ALMA BOOKS

ALMA BOOKS LTD
London House
243–253 Lower Mortlake Road
Richmond
Surrey TW9 2LL
United Kingdom
www.almabooks.com

The Art of Leaving first published by Alma Books Limited in 2013

Cover image © Mohamad Itani/Trevillion Images
Cover design © Rose Cooper

Printed in Great Britain by CPI Group (UK) Ltd, Croydon CR0 4YY

ISBN: 978-1-84688-237-1

To J.

Luke appeared in the bedroom doorframe naked apart from one sock wrinkled around his ankle. His stubble was wet from drinking out of the tap, and you could see a little clotted blood on his top lip, split in a scuffle at a party earlier in the night. He was oddly accident-prone, with a tendency to start fires, break vases and try to stop fights.

"How's your lip?" Eva said, slipping off her shoes.

"Fine." He touched the cut with the tip of his tongue. It took Luke half a second to undress, so he always ended up sitting in bed like a ringmaster while Eva performed a faux-nonchalant dance around him, angling herself behind cupboards and doors to avoid him seeing her at unflattering stages of nakedness. She could feel Luke watching as she took off her dress, revealing a flash of skin-coloured tights before she grabbed a towel off the floor and sat down with her back to him. A flustered moth struggled around the bedside lamp, throwing itself at the bulb.

Eva's favourite moment of any party, even good ones, was taking off her shoes afterwards. Luke joked that she was the person you'd want to be near during a fire or a terrorist attack, because the first thing she did when she entered any room was to suss out the potential exits, ready to evacuate. In photographs she was always glancing in the wrong direction, standing on an edge or in a corner looking as if she were about to step out of frame. Luke, by contrast, existed in every space as if he had always been there and would remain there for ever. He was the centre of every photograph, squarely at the front of every crowd.

Luke had slept with a remarkable number of women for a man with a large crooked nose, a lopsided jaw and hawkish grey eyes set too deeply in his head. He had black hair that clumped like wire in whatever position he happened to have slept the previous night and looked even worse if he tried to brush it. When he was ten years old he was attacked by a dog in a field near his father's farm in Devon, and would have died if it wasn't for a passing rambler who dragged the animal off Luke's face. Scars from later mishaps also mapped his skin, but mostly it was scars from the reconstructive surgery he had when he was ten – little pale hemlines under both his ears and across his left eyebrow, which in her unkind moments made Eva think of a mask: he was constructed, sewn together over his bones, and she wondered how he would have looked otherwise. He would still have had a long Roman nose and animal shoulders slightly too broad for his body. Still, he acted as if he were the best-looking man in any room. Former flings of his occasionally tried to make friends with Eva at parties, smiling at her as if colluding about a shared fashion mistake. "How *is* Luke?" they'd say, cocking their heads meaningfully to the side.

Eva yawned and climbed tipsily into bed. Luke stared at her for a moment longer, clearly trying to decide if he was too drunk to have sex or not. If she'd tilted her head slightly towards him he would have made a go for it, but instead she reached towards the pint glass of stale water by her side of the bed.

"Lights off?" Eva said, her back to him.

"Sure," he mumbled. The moth transferred its quest for brightness from Eva's bedside lamp towards the streetlight under the curtain. The creature hovered there in the slim wash of fake sunshine, and Eva resisted the urge to get up and kill it. Instead she stared at Luke's profile in the shadows and wondered how she was ever going to leave him, now they lived together.

* * *

The next morning, Eva and Luke walked silently through Regent's Park in the rain. The sky was grey and the trees made a jagged horizon around the grass. Some of the metal struts were broken in Eva's umbrella, collapsing the slick skin on two segments so droplets spun backwards at her ankles. Luke's navy-blue golf umbrella advertised his law firm, and he held it very straight.

Eva and Luke were the only people on York Bridge that morning, heading towards the Inner Circle of Regent's Park. They'd walked from their flat on Silver Place through exhausted morning Soho, past locked-up strip clubs and slot-machine arcades just blinking into life again, dodging shoppers in the rain, all the way across to the buzz of Marylebone Road. Luke's split lip looked worse than it had done when they went to bed, swollen and bruised purple like the mouth of a child who'd been gorging on blueberries. With the scars, too, he looked unwholesome that morning. He touched his cut with his free hand every so often as they stepped through the gate into Queen Mary's Garden with its row upon row of rose beds. Despite it being the first day of August, unseasonable rain and cold meant only a few petals were still intact in their knots of pollen. The beds were labelled with metal signs: Alchemist, Eden, Honey, Colette, Anne Boleyn.

"War of the roses," said Luke at the sight of the dilapidated flower beds in soggy semi-circles around them, each flower clenched against the weather.

They continued past the open-air theatre and made it back out onto the boating lake. They crossed the bridge into the main expanse of green, football goalposts forming empty square brackets across the grass. There was hardly anyone around – a few dog-walkers, two kids playing football a couple of pitches down and a clump of people with umbrellas in the far distance. From where Eva and Luke were walking, the umbrellas seemed to be doing a synchronized dance, all leaning backwards or turning at the same time. Eva thought maybe they were a devoted yoga or karate class practising in the rain, but as she and Luke walked forward the group revealed themselves as a band of bird-watchers. Each umbrella was arched over a pair of binoculars or a long-snouted camera, all perfectly still until the snouts and goggle eyes swooped together in slow unison.

Little birds bounced out of the trees with the raindrops – more visible than usual, Eva thought, but maybe it was just because she was looking. They were mostly hunched-shoulder crows with shiny coats, sulking in the tangle of tree branches. Then a bird with wings the shape of oars peeled off from out of a tree, swooping, before curling upwards again and landing tauntingly on a higher tree, where it was more visible and less reachable. The troop of bird-watchers turned their heads following the bird's flight.

"What is it? A buzzard?" said Luke.

"A golden eagle named Regina," said a man in a long coat standing nearby. "She escaped from the zoo this morning."

Crows squawked from the smaller trees, not sure about this new creature on their turf. The crows couldn't keep still, conversing in throaty, beaky noises, like courtiers arranging carriages and crinolines for their exotic new queen. Eva didn't know if eagles ate crows, but if she were a crow she'd be evacuating the area around about now. She thought of all the times she'd stood on King Edward's Bridge looking down on Regent's Canal, flanked by the Snowdon Aviary on one side and the bearded-pig enclosure in the main zoo on the other. She always wondered what the cynical urban ducks, pigeons and grubby seagulls made of their exotic cousins behind the aviary grill. You often saw little free birds swooping around the peaks and troughs of the skeletal aviary, talking with or perhaps taunting the foreign captives inside.

Regina remained on the top of the tree, ignoring the zookeeper's plaintive whistle and the sodden, deflated grey rabbit being used as bait. The man who had explained about the zoo offered Eva his binoculars, and she lifted them to her eyes – focusing on blurred twigs, sky, dead crinkled leaves – then she caught a foot in the corner of the lens and found her way to Regina's wide shoulders and haughty body. The bird was shades of brown with wings tucked up tight at her shoulders. A thuggish neck turned into an elegant face, almost debonair up there on the top of the world, turning every so often to view a different angle. Eva could see a hooked beak with a half-smile, and eyes hooded with angry feathered eyebrows.

"She looks like Queen Victoria when she was old," said Eva, passing the binoculars to Luke – and, as he looked, Regina's twig vibrated and she took off from her perch. The bird-watcher tore his binoculars back from Luke, but in a blink Regina swooped into the middle of a nearby football field and put claws to earth for just half a second before hurtling herself back up again and landing in a much lower tree on the other side of the football pitches. The zookeeper's shoulders slumped. Everyone turned to follow Regina with their eyes, binoculars or cameras.

"Flirt," said Luke, tilting his head to the side and smiling. Eva looked at Luke's profile – jagged nose and strong jaw, split lip and thin, sometimes mean-looking mouth. Though they'd been going out for three years, until a few months ago he'd lived alone in Hackney. The furniture in his flat had been entirely white and it always made Eva think of a set-designer's diorama of a young lawyer's bachelor pad, complete with Japanese prints in the bedroom and abstract photographs of bridges and boats in the living room. In early May, though, a pipe burst in the flat above his, and Luke turned up at Eva's front door hugging a box of damp classical-music records, a bottle of old red wine that his father had given him for his eighteenth birthday and a suitcase full of shoes. When Luke put his boxes down in the hall Eva noticed that her boyfriend's rushed midnight packing included such essentials as a shoe-cleaning kit and a Gordon Ramsay cookery book, which just didn't seem right. The next day he made a second trip and returned with a vast flat-screen television, a vegetable steamer and his minimalist Japanese paintings that explored different shades of "white". Soon Eva's bookshelves contained *Blackstone's Criminal Practice*, *The Dictionary of Law*, *Contract: Cases and Materials*. If Luke were planning on finding a new place of his own any time soon, a friend had pointed out to Eva with a smile, he probably wouldn't have spent an entire afternoon alphabetizing their books.

Eva was oblivious to quite how hard Luke worked until he moved in with her. She knew he would stay days at a time in Holiday Inns near Northern Crown Courts, Skyping her from empty business centres at midnight, but she only understood the scale of his commitments once he took over her living-room table with his papers and spent most nights working there into the early hours, listening to Rachmaninov and Mozart on his mother's old vinyl player. Eva would occasionally just sit on the sofa and watch him work, fascinated by the exactness of his movements, so different from the clumsiness of his body at other times. Laid out on the top right of the table he always had a red biro, a sharp 2B pencil, a rubber and a fountain pen Eva had bought him for his twenty-ninth birthday. He was fond of Post-it notes, but only the traditional-sized yellow variety, which he covered in his illegible handwriting and then smoothed lovingly onto typed pages before lifting the stack vertical and tapping out uneven edges, sinking any last stragglers with his oversized thumb. Eva's quiet flat suddenly bustled with bike messengers turning up at five or six in the morning carrying briefs for Luke to read before work, clerks and colleagues phoning him at all hours.

One afternoon a few weeks after he moved in, Eva picked up bank statements and takeaway menus from the mat at Silver Place and saw a plain white postcard peaking out among the multicoloured coupons and flyers. It was addressed to Luke in neat capital letters, so she idly flipped the card over in her hand. On the back, a quote was written in the same tidy hand as the address: "'Cover her face; mine eyes dazzle. She died young' – John Webster". Eva stopped on the landing. She read the note a few more times on the stairs and then again in their flat, turning it over and running her fingers along the sharp card edges, then along the deep indentations of the ink. Later that evening, when she put the card in front of Luke, he just shrugged. Apparently everyone in his chambers had been receiving threatening postcards, with quotes and obscure intimidations, since defending and acquitting a doctor who performed very late abortions. Luke sipped his wine and put the oven on for dinner, mumbling that pissing people off was the nature of his job. Eva raised one eyebrow, perplexed, and added his reaction to a list of curiosities about this gatecrasher in her flat – a list that included him practising opening statements at full volume in the shower and reading legal textbooks with a slight smile on his face while waiting for water to boil or on hold to customer services.

It had never crossed Eva's mind that he'd want to move into her chaotic Soho flat. 4D Silver Place used to belong to Eva's grandmother, who'd died of a stroke when Eva was eighteen and had left the flat to her. It was on the top two floors of the building: a small entrance hall and a washing machine on the lower level, then five cluttered rooms with cigarette-stained wallpaper up above – two small bedrooms, a living room, a kitchen and a bathroom – none of which had been redecorated for decades. They were packed, still, with Seventies rugs and raggedly upholstered furniture. The living room and the main bedroom both had windows looking straight out onto the grey-brick building opposite, barely five metres away across the slim Soho alley of globed street lamps with hanging baskets of half-dead ivy. It was never entirely dark in the flat, because those lamps glowed twenty-four hours a day, along with flickering traces of neon from a nearby bar. As Soho alleys go, Silver Place was sedate. It was only a few roads down from Walker's Court, where the sex cinemas were packed together and girls in leather skirts stood on either end haggling over the price of blow jobs, but Silver Place had two media companies, a second-hand bookshop, a café, a bar called The Pink Angel and a hair salon.

Eva had been renting out the spare room of Silver Place for seven years, each lodger leaving something of themselves in the hallway or cupboards. There were shoes and tubs of paint, piles of loose paper, plastic bags full of tangled cables and back-up drives of potentially crucial documents. Eva's grandmother had had a soft spot for anything to do with magicians or illusionists, so the flat was scattered with postcards of sideshow acts, slides of magic shows, "How to" guides for amateur illusionists, playing cards allegedly signed by magicians that nobody except Eva's grandmother had ever heard of. A vintage advertising poster from a 1904 magic show staring Harry Houdini used to have pride of place in the entrance hall, but when Luke moved in he persuaded Eva to hang it in the bathroom instead: *"Europe's Eclipsing Sensation, the World's Handcuff King and Escape Artist,"* the lurid yellow-and-pink poster proclaimed above the toilet. *"Nothing on Earth Can Hold Houdini a Prisoner."* Now the Japanese paintings exploring different shades of "white" hung incongruously in the entrance hall. This messy world was not the natural habitat of a barrister who owned two cashmere coats, folded his boxer shorts and put shoehorns in his footwear at night, yet there he was with Eva in Silver Place, three months into their cohabitation and counting.

In the Saturday morning drizzle Luke and Eva walked at a slight distance behind the zookeepers, who picked up their dead rabbit and followed the escaped eagle towards her new perch. Eva willed the bird to bend its craggy knees and lift off again, farther away. A crow passed over Eva's head, from one small tree to another, and she jumped. Luke's eyes remained rooted to Regina in the distance as they followed the keepers. At the edges of the park, other people were standing still under their umbrellas and watching at a distance. Eva wiped rain from her face, and that morning's Nurofen suddenly wore off. Everyone looked glumly at the sky. The crowd seemed to have expanded – at least twenty damp coats had appeared: twenty half-circles of umbrellas above twenty stooped shoulders – but Eva could have sworn Regina was staring straight at her.

"She won't be able to survive in the wild," said someone nearby. "She'll be attacking the dogs soon."

"Regent's Park is hardly wild," said Luke.

"She'll die, though," said the man. "She's a zoo bird."

"She nearly went for a poodle, earlier," tutted a middle-aged woman.

"They were cleaning her cage. Guess she was done with the zoo?" said someone else. "Fair enough."

Luke touched his mouth and winced, as if he'd forgotten about his face for a moment and had just remembered its swollen top-lip bruise. He put his tongue out and lifted the tip onto his broken flesh, revealing the milky-coloured underside of his tongue. Eva thought back to how, early on in their relationship, he'd tried to teach her to touch her nose with her tongue and failed.

* * *

The engagement party the previous evening had been at a crammed pub with sticky wooden floors in Soho. Eva had arrived late, and wet, wearing clothes she'd thought were passable when she was in Silver Place but seemed all wrong when she saw her reflection in the mirrors behind the bar. Eva always looked as if she had one foot in yesterday and one in tomorrow, messily caught between moments. She had shoulder-length chestnut hair, nearly translucent skin with a scattering of freckles, petite features with a gap-toothed smile and green eyes that always appeared dazed. People often asked her if she was lost, or if she was OK.

The party was for one of Luke's friends – most parties they went to were thrown by Luke's friends; he was more sociable than she was. When Eva stepped through into the pub, Luke was already there in the middle of the bar talking to the hostess, a precise-looking work colleague of his named Catherine. Luke was wearing a grey suit, a rumpled tie snaking out of his trouser pocket. His thick black facial hair grew so quickly that he was always unshaven by the end of each day, as well as exhausted. Catherine grinned as Eva approached.

"What did you do, *aim for* the puddles?" she said to Eva. "I was just showing Luke my ring. Isn't it *exciting*?" She held out a big ring on her skinny finger.

"Congratulations," Eva said. "Lovely." She glanced over Catherine's shoulder into the throbbing party and already wished that she didn't have to go through the middle of the evening just to get to the relieving walk home.

On the top level of the two-floor pub, the thud of a DJ deck occasionally spat out bleary-eyed, disorientated dancers to stoop over plastic glasses of warm beer on the stairs. On the ground floor, hog roast and apple sauce appeared on paper plates from the kitchen. Trays of tequila were dotted around, and Eva absent-mindedly drank the occasional shot, which cheered her up. Eventually a few people she knew turned up: a boy she went to university with, a girl who worked in a Soho bookshop, a few friends from school who had become enmeshed with Luke's friends over the years. She spoke briefly to some Parisian ex-fling of Luke's – "How *is* Luke?" the fling said – and smiled blandly when people offered "congratulations" about her and Luke's recent co-habitation. At around eleven o'clock the rain let up slightly, and in the multitude of bodies Eva realized she hadn't seen Luke in a while. They had a habit of peeling away from each other at parties, only reattaching at intervals.

She forced her way out towards the garden at the back of the pub to get some air. Guests were already lounging against a lopsided chain-link fence or perched on a mouldy picnic table, ashing in the skeleton of a rusty barbeque or in empty terracotta flowerpots. The garden faced out on a gloomy Soho backstreet, with a row of grey apartment buildings that joined Old Compton Street to the left and a thinner street with a row of rundown shops to the right. Eva

couldn't see Luke, so she stepped over to the fence, pleased
to find a space in the party where she could breathe. On the
pavement beyond the fence, a bald elderly man did up his
shoelaces and an adolescent boy put his arm around a girl in
a purple velour tracksuit, making for a blinking kebab-shop
sign. Above the apartment block opposite, she could see a
couple of cranes – one red, one chrome – bent over Soho
like they were feeding on some of the smaller buildings. An
aeroplane passed over the top, and Eva wondered where it
was heading. Two drunken women giggled on the main
road, a police car passed slowly by and a tall man wearing
hot pants picked up cigarette butts outside doorsteps. Eva
scanned a row of dilapidated shops to her right, and in the
darkness she saw the familiar slope of Luke's shoulders
twenty metres away across the road. He had his back to
the pub, and a woman in a red jacket was just that moment turning away from a conversation with him. Mostly
obscured from view by Luke's shoulders, all Eva saw was
a red sleeve and a flash of blond hair disappearing around
the street corner.

Eva often found herself watching Luke in "deep" conversation with other women at parties. They took him to
quiet spaces, to hallways or patios, and confessed to him.
Women thought, because Luke looked a bit peculiar, that
they didn't find him attractive, and then they were left confused because in fact he was. They confessed to him about
secret broodiness or problems with their mothers, and he
always listened well and they left unnerved.

Eva squinted across through the layers of darkness towards the street corner. The woman was gone now, but for

a moment or two Luke was still just standing there in the spitting rain. The air smelt of wet rust, and Eva arched her foot inside the sole of her stilettos. She watched him. Until Luke, Eva had never been in a relationship that lasted more than six months: she'd broken up with men in train stations and outside libraries, on cathedral steps and crouched over late-night McDonald's milkshakes. Before Luke, she'd considered herself talented at leaving people and places. The first smile of a love affair was mostly fiction and blind hope, but you knew where you were with goodbye: you knew that mistakes would dissolve, doors would open, and then everything would be possible again. Even while loving Luke – while actually experiencing the emotion of love – she often caught herself considering their eventual parting. It was the ending, Eva maintained, that gave meaning to a story.

She'd attempted to leave Luke twice in three years, but failed in different ways both times. She'd broken up with him easily enough, but neither exit lasted long. Once he was gone she'd been struck by unexpected panic: she didn't want to be with him, but she missed him. She could list a million reasons why she needed to leave him: she wasn't ready for this sort of commitment, and he always wore matching socks (even to the shop for milk in the morning), and for his twenty-ninth birthday he asked for a saucepan set from his mother. They didn't read the same books. She read fiction with the occasional historical biography thrown in to make her feel intellectual, and he only ever read books on law or austere-looking hardbacks with catchy titles such as *The Siege of Kohima 1944 – The Story of the Last Great*

Stand of Empire. He was passionate about good food, while Eva was happier with a toasted cheese sandwich. He wouldn't eat all day if he knew he was going somewhere good for dinner, and it sent him insane that Eva ate the bread in restaurants and then wasn't interested in the meal. He dressed well, and Eva dressed badly. He was sociable. Eva wasn't. He rarely worked less than twelve-hour days, Eva had a job in a publishing company where she spent most of the week staring absently out of a window. He was engaged with the world. She was mostly, and as much as possible, not. He folded anything that could conceivably be folded, even her knickers sometimes if she left them out, while Eva consistently abandoned her clothes in a puddle at her ankles. He loved fireworks. She associated them with getting the flu. Every fifth of November he insisted on standing in the freezing cold on Primrose Hill watching stuttering colours in the sky while she grumbled and wanted to go home into the warmth. She would often watch him at parties, or at the living-room table reading witness statements, and feel only the slightest connection, like he was someone she felt she ought to recognize but couldn't quite place.

Of course they must have had a few things in common, to come this far. They could both tell you the Scrabble score of any word in half a second, for example. But that wasn't really enough for a lifetime. They were (suddenly, it seemed to Eva) at the stage where everyone around them were making concrete decisions, solidifying into people with mortgages and rings and ten-year plans, but Eva wasn't sure she was ready to give up on the idea that she could do anything and be anyone she might imagine. As wedding invitations multiplied ominously on the mantel-piece and conversations between friends often turned to house prices, Eva couldn't help thinking she could do with one more blast of a clean slate, the adrenalin rush of one more first time before "for ever" started.

After three years of half-thinking about leaving, though, she was not only still with Luke, but she was standing at an engagement party watching him at a distance and feeling something resembling longing. Eva turned away from him and glanced at a terracotta pot full of mud, a globe of rain trying its best to hang on to the metal back of a chair, a girl in a minidress moments from vomiting in a flower pot, and when Eva looked back to the street corner Luke wasn't there any more. She turned on her heels and walked over to the pub's garden door to find him. Eva's younger self would have been disgusted by this stasis.

Eva stood on tiptoe at the edge of the crowd while Luke came through the front door from the street. He often looked terribly sad when he thought nobody was watching him. She wanted to climb into his mind, sort through his troubles and unclutter him. She waved over the crowd's head, but he was staring firmly in a different direction. He began to make his way across to the back of the room, where the paper plates of hog roast were being served. Eva sunk down from her tiptoes and decided he would guess where she was – away from all the people – and come find her.

"Hi, stranger," he said as he came out five minutes later, just as expected, with a limp paper plate of hog roast and apple sauce. He kissed her on the mouth and she smiled, pleased to see him.

"You having fun?"

"Sort of," said Luke. They paused.

"Is a hog roast a whole pig?" Eva asked, although she was thinking of the slash of red and blond at the street corner.

"A young pig, usually," he said, putting a bite in his mouth. Luke's mum and dad had divorced when he was six. His father moved to Devon to run a small farm and abattoir, while his mother married an investment banker and moved to Chelsea. It was peculiar that his mother and father had ever married, but it made perfect sense that, when briefly together, they'd created Luke. He had his father's big hands – butcher's hands – and the same square jaw, but their mannerisms were different. He had his mother's dark sense of humour and elegance. Eva had always loved Luke's huge hands.

"What's the best bit of a pig?" Eva said. She had a split-second image of Luke's worn-out father standing in Smithfield market in front of a butcher's stall covered in sliced-up animal flesh, showing her a pig's heart the first time she met him. "It's the same size as a human heart," Luke's dad had said, proudly, placing the glob of purple muscle into Eva's cupped hands.

"I like the shoulder, personally." Luke finished chewing his mouthful, then after he swallowed he leant over and abruptly licked Eva's bare shoulder with his tongue. He looked thoughtful and smacked his lips as if he were a wine taster, or a judge on *MasterChef*. He pretended to taste Eva's skin in his mouth. "A bit salty though, that one. Dirty aftertaste."

In the dark a swarm of bats flew off the apartment building in the street beyond the garden and disappeared.

"Acid rainfall," Eva said. "I'm not organic."

"The belly of the pig is the most versatile and tender cut. The extra fat means you can leave it roasting for hours without ruining the meat's texture. The fat ensures a gummy skin which will give the roast some wonderful crackling." Eva slipped one of her shoes on and off and bent her aching foot against the sole of the shoe again while he spoke.

She had an urge to touch the outline of Luke's jagged face. "The pig trotter is often discarded, but many chefs are today serving meals based around it," Luke continued. "It's credit-crunch meat. Trendy and cheap. Shall we get another drink?"

"Let's head off soon," said Eva.

"Just one more drink, then home? One more song?" Luke said, even though he was clearly exhausted. "I'll bring drinks out here." Eva didn't answer, just let him kiss her and turn away: in her head she was already halfway home, dodging second-hand raindrops from awnings in Soho, waving away minicabs, running her fingers along the edge of door keys in her pocket.

Luke disappeared off into the party. Eva waited for him outside. A woman came and struck up conversation about the history of glam rock, and Eva nodded along for a while, interjecting the occasional question about David Bowie. A girl who used to work at Eva's office appeared in the garden and started debating with the glam rocker about the best places in London to buy facial glitter. Ten minutes later Luke still wasn't back, so Eva made her excuses and squelched over the garden, back towards the party.

"Have you seen Luke?" Eva said to one of his friends. Many more people appeared to have turned up at the pub while Eva was in the garden, and everyone was dancing. You could almost see a layer of steam blowing off above their heads.

"Think he's maybe at the front?" shouted the friend, and Eva shouldered through dancing girls with dilated eyes and the men waiting to pounce on them. Through the front pub windows, Eva saw Luke standing on the street outside holding the base of a cold bottle of beer to his lip. Groups were smoking or calling taxis, but Luke was alone, frowning. Eva paused before walking over to him. She watched him peel away the base of the beer bottle to reveal a button of glossy blood on his lip. When sober, Luke seemed exactly the sort of person who would never end up in bar brawls – decorous, well-groomed, controlled – but when he was drunk he was often in the wrong place at the wrong time. A handful of times since Eva and Luke met, she'd ended up holding ice cubes and TCP-soaked cotton wool to his hands or head while he told her he was trying to stop the fight, had nothing to do with the fight, hadn't meant to fight.

"What happened?" Eva stepped out of the pub door, shocked, and making Luke jump.

"Some drunk dancing guy elbowed me in the mouth at the bar," Luke said.

"Which guy?" Eva said, turning back to the throng of dancing men with half-moons and triangles of sweat under their arms and backs. She went over to Luke and peered at his cut, around the size of a tadpole. She kissed him on the cheek. "Does it hurt?"

"Some idiot drinking Jägerbombs," said Luke. "Fuck."

"Let's go home," said Eva, holding his shoulder.

* * *

Eva first met Luke two years before they started going out, when he turned up on some distant mutual friend's recommendation to look at the spare room in Eva's flat. He was meant to see the room at six p.m., but by the time Luke rang the doorbell it was half-past nine, and to express her irritation Eva opened the door wearing ragged pyjama bottoms and old hotel slippers as if she was just about to go to bed. The buzzer was broken, so she had to go downstairs to the street to let him in. He'd clearly come straight from the office and was wearing a sharp suit with a grey silk handkerchief only just sticking out of the jacket pocket. His face was almost expressionless, as if in the middle of a poker game he knew he was going to win. Eva noticed several almost imperceptible scars on his right eyebrow and the edges of his jaw. Behind him, in the alley, Eva saw frizzy black hair, a streak of lipstick, a tight skirt stretching and contracting as the girl's heeled shoes angrily paced the cobbles. The girl was shouting into her mobile phone: "Those are not the photographs I asked for – you're an embarrassment, this is a disaster, a disaster, a disaster. You're going to have to get the new ones biked over."

"I'm here about the room? Sorry I'm late," Luke had said to Eva in a low-pitched and level voice, ignoring the shouting girl behind him, instead tilting his head to the side and looking at Eva's cotton plaid pyjamas up and down.

"Is she coming in?" Eva said. The girl standing outside on the street had one stiletto-heeled foot raised up behind her thigh now. Balancing on one leg she looked like some tropical animal, her face in shadow, her long neck bent backwards – a flamingo, perhaps.

"No, she's having a crisis," said Luke as the girl in the tight skirt gave him a quick wave with long fingers. The yellow light of a street lamp revealed almond-shaped eyes and a big mouth with oversized teeth. Her black fringe was cut bluntly across her forehead like an expensive doll's, sticking out a bit because it was so frizzy. At first glance she was gawky rather than pretty, and Eva didn't get a chance for a second glance before the girl's chin curved away from the door, back to her heated telephone conversation. "Better to leave her alone when she's like this," he said. "My name's Luke."

"Eva," she said. Luke followed her up four flights of carpeted stairs to her flat. Before he even stepped inside, Eva knew he wouldn't rent the room in her moth-infested Soho flat with its chocolate-brown easy chairs and Seventies shag carpets.

"Washing machine," Eva said, beginning her tour, turning away from him and pointing to the groaning appliance.

"Is it meant to make so much noise?" he said, and Eva didn't answer. She decided she didn't care for this interloper with his expensive clothes. Without a word, she continued up the stairs that went from the flat's front door to the rest of the rooms above, past her grandmother's collection of little clay and porcelain monkeys that were arranged on the first landing window sill. Eva was always meaning to redecorate, but in truth she found the figurine monkeys, art-deco lamps and illusionists' memorabilia comforting. During Eva's childhood her parents moved house eight times, through four countries, but Eva always spent the summer holidays in Silver Place. When she was fifteen, her parents moved to Singapore, and Eva persuaded them to let her move in for good with her grandmother.

The dusty staircase changed direction in the middle and doubled back on itself – seven more steps up to the second floor, where Luke frowned at the sight of the lurid Houdini poster. Eva pointed to the tiny rectangular kitchenette, which was directly in front of the staircase. It had cracked green tiles and was scattered with Diet Coke cans and pizza boxes.

"Kitchen," Eva said, and watched a moth for a second as it flew into the hall light. There had always been moths in Silver Place. Over the years, they had flown out of Eva's hair or clothes on various embarrassing occasions – once on the Tube during rush hour when a young mother looked appalled and squeezed her pram all the way to the other end of the carriage, once during a lecture on Victorian sensation novels at UCL, and once on a first date with a boy whose name Eva couldn't remember, because he obviously never called again after Eva sexily let down her hair in his car and a moth flew out into his face.

Luke pretended to ignore the moth in the hallway, and Eva didn't go after it. He glanced back through into the living room, which had a big window that looked down onto the alleyway and across into other people's windows. Eva and Luke could both still hear the rhythm of the flamingo girl's high heels clacking on the cobbles down below. From the window Eva saw the girl was smoking a cigarette now, holding it at arm's length to ash in the road. When Eva turned back at Luke, she saw him frowning at her cigarette-stained floral wallpaper.

"This is Ben's room, the one who's moving out next week," Eva said, opening the room to the right of the stairs. It had been Eva's when she was younger, but her teenage world of books and museum postcards was almost unrecognizable now. Ben's bed and floor were always covered in a swamp of boxer shorts, sunglasses, computer games, contracts and aeroplane tickets. He was older than Eva and worked for MTV as an "emerging-market strategy director", so spent most of his life on planes to and from Eastern Europe. "Ben travels with work a lot, so he's hardly ever here. I haven't seen him in weeks," Eva said.

"You know the moths probably lay eggs in there," Luke said, noting the faded carpet with its bare moth-eaten patches under his brogues. "You should get it replaced."

"I got it cleaned by moth-exterminators last year – thanks, though," Eva replied.

Luke didn't say anything, and then Eva realized he wasn't behind her. He had opened the fourth door, at the end of the short corridor, which was Eva's bedroom.

"That room's mine," Eva said quickly. She followed Luke to the mouth of her bedroom. Without invitation he stepped inside the low room, which looked far too small for him. Clothes were flung everywhere, dripping out of the wardrobe and drawers – a wrinkled sundress, a pair of toothpaste-stained jeans, an oversized T-shirt muddled amongst blankets on the unmade bed. This was the only room that Eva had sort of redecorated when her grandmother died.

She'd bought a red carpet from a charity shop, put some pictures up on the wall, a few framed photographs on her desk and dressing table. Luke took another step inside Eva's bedroom and Eva didn't stop him, although she wished she wasn't wearing her pyjamas now. In terms of the power dynamic his suit clearly trumped her cotton plaid pyjama trousers and slippers. The elastic of the belt was even a bit worn, and she had to keep checking that they weren't slipping down. She might have been tense about this City-boy stranger being in her bedroom, only his clothes and face were both faintly ridiculous. As he walked over to Eva's desk, he glanced down at notes for an essay on *Beowulf*, but active on Eva's laptop, embarrassingly, was a game of Internet Scrabble. Eva had been just about to put the word "RACCOON" on two purple double-word scores when Luke rang the doorbell.

"Raccoon," Luke said, raising his heavy black eyebrows and looking pleased with himself. "You have the letters for raccoon, you know."

"Yes, I know," Eva said, in a tone that was meant to be icy, but didn't quite go the distance, because obviously he'd just found her playing Internet Scrabble on a Friday night, so she couldn't be too haughty. Eva narrowed her eyes and guessed that this grey-eyed and immaculate man was the sort who put his feet up on other people's furniture without asking.

"I think that's the grand tour over, then," said Eva, hoping to prompt an exit, still hovering around the edge of her bedroom, while the stranger remained in the middle of it. Luke didn't take the hint, but peered at a photograph of twelve-year-old Eva standing with her father and mother next to an aeroplane. The three of them looked self-conscious on the runway, palm trees in the background.

"You have *exactly* the same frown in that photo as you do now," Luke said, which clearly wasn't a compliment. Eva had a restless, sad expression in the childhood photo, her hair nearly down to the end of her spine and held back from her freckled face by an Alice band. To Eva's right her father had his arms crossed over his chest, his frowning green eyes staring upwards at a space just above the camera as if already imagining the intense relief of getting off the ground. He liked to be airborne, to be moving. He wore his smart Singapore Airlines pilot uniform with his hat in his hand, showing the precipice of his receding hairline. Eva always found it hard to believe that her parents first met anywhere as still and solid as in an Essex community library (where her mother was a volunteer and her father, on a training course nearby, was looking for *An Illustrated Encyclopedia of Fighters and Bombers*). By the time Eva was born, they were already golden-tanned, having lived in Laos and Thailand for years. Eva was born in the Bangkok International Hospital and grew up all over the place – Beijing, Bali, Hong Kong, wherever her father was stationed. It wasn't a requirement of her father's job that they move so regularly, but her parents didn't like staying in one place for too long. In Eva's family photograph, her mother was throwing a worried sideways glance at her husband.

"Your dad's a pilot, then?" said Luke.

"Yes," said Eva, blankly, because that was blindingly obvious from the photo. Turning away from the picture, Luke gazed down through the bedroom window onto the alley below, where his friend was waiting. He put his right hand up to his face and rubbed his eyes. Deep pinches of skin formed between his eyebrows when he frowned. Someone once told Eva they were called "Darwin's grief lines", because Darwin discovered that monkeys and humans had similar expressions when they were sad. It gave a sense of what Luke would look like when he was old.

Eva shivered. One minute he was a City boy of the sort Eva tried to avoid in cocktail bars and pubs, the next minute he was being curious and over-intimate in her bedroom. The sun was going down, and Luke was silhouetted in front of the window. His shoulders were stooped and the handkerchief in his pocket had wilted. He sat on Eva's bed, and his suit wrinkled around his arms. It seemed presumptuous to sit down, especially on the bed rather than the office chair, but for some reason Eva didn't say anything. It was as if he'd melted, slowly, since arriving at Eva's front door eight minutes ago and now his head was far too heavy for his shoulders.

"Won't your girlfriend be getting a bit bored down there?" Eva prompted.

He didn't say anything for a few moments.

"It's my sister," he replied eventually, eyes flicking to the window again. Eva had moved from the door into the room. She'd stepped past where he was sitting on her bed and was now standing near the window. She regarded Luke's sister, leaning on the lamp-post with her BlackBerry cupped between her hands, grinning slightly at some joke or plan she was typing on it.

"But yeah, I should go anyway," he added. Luke stood up again. It wasn't a big room, but Eva and Luke were standing on opposite sides. Eva was backed up almost to the window and he was at the door. He glanced uncertainly towards the window.

"I'm guessing this isn't really your sort of flat," Eva said.

There was a long pause, where he looked at his big hands and then back up at Eva, shifting his feet, and although Eva felt sorry for him because of his beleaguered expression, she wished he was already gone, or hadn't come in the first place. He had a latent aggressiveness to him, like he was reining himself in. He was making her anxious.

"I don't suppose you'd, like, maybe want to come out for dinner with me or something some time? Maybe play a game of Scrabble?" he said. "Against me instead of your computer?"

"I have a boyfriend," said Eva – which was true, although of course the relationship was ending: Eva's relationships spent much of their life in the process of ending.

"Right," he said. "*OK* then. OK."

"OK," Eva said.

"Sorry for being late. I wouldn't have been if I'd known."

"Known what?" Eva said.

"That you'd be ready for bed at nine o'clock on a Friday?" he said, after a pause.

"Half-past nine," Eva corrected.

"Right," he said. "Well. Nice to meet you."

A minute later they were downstairs on the small first-floor hallway, while the floorboards vibrated from the washing machine. Eva opened the door for him, and when he slipped past her she felt a shudder, like nervousness, which she took to be dislike.

"Have a good weekend," Eva said politely, then she let him walk down the red-carpeted stairs on his own, down to the street, while she went back into the flat and sat down at her computer in front of her Scrabble and her English essay.

"What do you think about getting very drunk tonight?" Eva listened to Luke say to his sister in the alley under the window.

"*Of course*," said the sister.

* * *

Two years later Eva was making a sandwich in a friend's kitchen near King's Cross, avoiding the music of a party in the other room. Eva hadn't been there long, but was already plotting her exit. The key to leaving a party was not to make a fuss and not to be seen. You sneak out as quietly as possible so the host imagines that you stayed much longer than you really did. While Eva was waiting for an opportune exit moment she was making a sandwich out of leftovers from a barbeque. As she buttered a slightly stale bun, a tall, broad man with spiky hair came into the kitchen and started winding around, also making a sandwich. Eva didn't recognize him and continued to spread butter, then cut a tomato into slivers. The man took a hamburger bun out of its packet and grabbed a plate from the cupboard above Eva's head.

"Would you pass me a knife?" the man had said to Eva as he put the plate down. She opened a drawer and handed him a knife. As she did so, she noticed that he had scars on his jaw line and also that he looked vaguely familiar, but she couldn't work out why, so she went back to her sandwich.

"Tomato?" she said to him after a moment, offering him the second half of the tomato she'd just sliced for her own sandwich.

"Thanks. Pass the chicken – is that chicken?" he said. She gave him the leftover barbequed chicken from a greasy plate, watching him now, and sure that she knew him from somewhere. "So who is it you know at this party?" he said.

They made sandwiches and continued their clipped conversation, trying not to touch each other in the small kitchen. She could feel him watching her and kept glancing sideways at him, trying to place his face. She felt oddly comfortable with him, perhaps just because she in fact had met him before, but in the moment it seemed more complicated. She didn't mind the feeling of his eyes on her. (Afterwards he said he knew exactly who she was when he saw her: "Scrabble girl" – but she wasn't sure that was true.) The entirely odd kiss happened somewhere between buttering the buns and placing slices of wet tomatoes carefully on top of the butter. When she was taking out tomato ketchup from the fridge and he was putting back the pack of butter, Eva turned slightly so they somehow found that their mouths were nearly aligned. There was a pause, and neither of them moved.

They'd hardly said five sentences to each other and then, when their faces were inches apart, Eva finally remembered the rude lawyer who sat on her bed and studied her family photographs and told her she should clean her carpets more regularly. He smiled uncertainly at her, then a kiss on the corner of her mouth turned momentarily into a real kiss before breaking off into another hesitant smile. The whole thing lasted all of fifteen seconds.

"You taste like Coca-Cola," Luke said afterwards. They simultaneously moved apart – Eva stepped back almost into the open fridge door, him onto a stray piece of tomato. Music resounded in the living room nearby. They both looked away from each other.

On the night bus later, as London fled past below her – Euston Road, Gower Street, snaking towards home – Eva imagined being on a veranda with this new stranger, possibly in Spain for some reason, drinking exceptionally cold white wine and telling him that she couldn't stay with him any more. In her daydream he was wearing a sun-faded T-shirt and dark linen trousers and the sun was hitting the side of his face as their imaginary relationship clattered to an end. Eva closed her eyes and saw the muscles of Luke's jaw twitching like something beginning to tear. His face appeared to be grimacing with the remarkable effort of not reacting and it reminded Eva of how people look the moment after they fall over in public, a mixture of broken pride and attempted indifference. Eva hardly even knew Luke when she first kissed him, let alone loved him, but she couldn't help inventing a story about what it might be like to fall *out* of love with him.

EVA: I don't love you any more.
LUKE: Is there someone else?
EVA: No.
LUKE: It's just me, then?

EVA: I'm so sorry.

LUKE: You're sorry you don't love me, or sorry for wasting my time? How long have you been thinking this?

EVA: Since the very first moment we kissed.

LUKE: But I've been happy.

EVA: I don't want to spend the rest of my life waking up next to you.

LUKE: *Did you ever love me?*

EVA: Yes.

It did cross Eva's mind that perhaps there was something wrong with her to think of endings so often during beginnings. As the bus curved to her stop near Tottenham Court Road station, she tried to think of beautiful beginnings in great novels, the timeless romantic catalysts, eyes meeting across crowded rooms.

The Great Gatsby? She couldn't remember the first time Gatsby saw Daisy. "*I'll call you up,*" Eva thought of Nick saying to Gatsby though. "*Do, old sport,*" says Gatsby. "*I suppose Daisy'll call too.*" But of course Daisy doesn't call. When does the narrator first see Holly in *Breakfast at Tiffany's*? Eva couldn't remember, but she did remember Holly dropping her cat amongst garbage cans. "*Go, scram!*" Holly says. A minute later she returns, shouting, "*You. Cat. Where are you? Here, cat.*" But it's no use by then. Of course in the movie the cat comes back and Audrey kisses the unnamed narrator in the rain – which says a lot about what people want from an ending – but not a lot about the art of leaving.

* * *

August of that rain-sodden summer of early cohabitation was Eva's four-year anniversary at Echo Books, the independent publishing company where she'd started working after she finished her English degree and couldn't decide what to do with her life. She began at Echo as a publicity assistant, then became an editor because she was no good at publicity and had a tendency to send curt emails to important people. Echo Books published glossy-covered romantic novels, and there were so many unsold books in the Fitzrovia office that Eva used them to lodge her windows and doors open, to stabilize the wonky furniture, even to soak up leaks under the kitchen sink. It was meant to be an interim job just to get her through before she found what she wanted to do, but time had ticked on – plodding commas, dotted *i*'s, all the minutiae of stories. The job wasn't so bad as jobs go: she had a window to stare out of when she was bored, time to herself, and the rhythmic exactness of editing calmed her down.

The rooms smelt of space heaters and acrid book dust. The books piled in her little top-floor office had titles such as *The Hunger of Strangers* and *Ophelia's Garden*, but their pages were crinkly-damp and yellowing. In the hallway outside her office was a broken skylight that dribbled onto the carpet when it rained outside. Sharing the top floor with Eva and the broken skylight was the company accountant and a store cupboard where the printer lived, inexplicably positioned on the top of an ancient filing cabinet so that anyone below six foot had to climb on a library stool to reach the paper. There were several older printers up there, too: abandoned plastic creatures with broken bodies and cracked cables, blanketed in dust. Some had an origami crunch of yellowing paper still stuck in their mouths, frozen in the moment of death. The office used to have a cleaner who hoovered and emptied the bins, but she'd left a year ago and hadn't been replaced. Since then, the staff tended to meet authors and journalists at cafés to avoid anyone seeing mouse droppings in the corridors and buckets of rainwater in the hallway. Every day Eva read other peoples' romantic fantasies and corrected the grammar of their Ottoman sultans and plumbers and pastry chefs, and time passed. She read about tropical islands and nunneries. She found that apostrophes and commas became particularly chaotic during sex scenes, and she amended nipples belonging to a single woman rather than many, broke up breathless paragraphs with at least the occasional comma or full stop, kept tenses consistent as heroes and heroines reached their sexual climax. She was queen of grammar, a pedantic headmistress of gutter language.

Between pages, sometimes even between paragraphs (and increasingly, as the years plodded on, between sentences), Eva stared absently out of the window onto Goodge Street below and watched the world go by. There was a homeless man who sat on a bench opposite and offered advice to passing strangers: *Beware rubbish trucks! A woman should never be seen without a hat! Don't slouch! The Apocalypse will come on a Tuesday!* Eva had become quite fond of the prophet with his red umbrella in the rain and his broken sunglasses in the sun and his shopping trolley full of plastic bags in all weather. She bought him sandwiches once or twice a week, and he always told her she should smile more. Behind his grey-coated figure was the pink façade of a cupcake shop, an Oxfam, a dry-cleaner's, a hair salon and a restaurant offering a £3.50 Chinese-Thai buffet. Then between the hair salon and the Chinese restaurant was a red door with a burnt-out 1950s-type neon sign above naming it "The Scorpio Club", where there was always – as far as Eva could see – a man with a crew cut sitting outside. His face looked as if it had been made in Plasticine and then pinched together between two fingers, his wide nose nearly touching his damp upper lip. The Eastern European bouncer and the homeless prophet had a difficult relationship. Sometimes the bouncer shared his cigarettes, sometimes he hissed abusive-sounding things in Russian or Polish or whatever language he spoke, but mostly the two constant features of Eva's Goodge Street view ignored each other.

The Scorpio was allegedly a lap-dancing club, but Eva had never seen anyone except the crew-cut Eastern European man go in or out. Nine-to-five probably wasn't their prime business slot, so it wasn't surprising. What was peculiar, though, was how diligently this gatekeeper guarded the door throughout these off-peak hours. The club was three grey-brick floors with two windows on each level, all lined with greenish-grey curtains that rarely opened and were never illuminated. Bits and pieces were scattered over some of the sills: a pot plant, the occasional mug or magazine, an ashtray or a wineglass implying life inside. The only exit Eva had ever witnessed from the club was quite early on in her publishing career, when a white rabbit with black paws once bounded out of the door and onto the pavement. Eva watched from her office window – surprised – as the bunny stopped on the street, turned its squat little head left and then right with a dimwitted expression on his furry face, as if deciding which way would be best. While the rabbit was making this key decision the doorman scooped the animal nonchalantly off the pavement into his muscular arms, handing the defeated creature back through the door. Briefly, inside the corridor, Eva saw a plump elderly woman wearing a red scarf tied around her head. She bundled the struggling bunny into the folds of her clothes, turning away from the light.

Soon after the animal's escape attempt, Eva caught her first glimpse of a woman with a long bony face and deep-set eyes at the top right-hand side of the club. On an unseasonably sunny autumn day, when children were kicking leaves and the lunch-break crowd in yeti layers of scarves and hats were huddled over soup or sandwiches on street benches, Eva raised her eyes from whatever manuscript she was correcting and saw the shadow of a girl peaking through the curtain gap at the window directly opposite her office window, wearing a leopard-print spaghetti top. It wasn't the elderly woman who cradled the rabbit, but someone much younger. As soon as Eva looked up, the figure brushed her limp golden hair off her face using her whole hand and disappeared from view.

The second time Eva saw the figure was mid-summer, and a troop of Hare Krishnas were making their way down Goodge Street chanting the Maha Mantra, those soothing baby syllables, nodding their bald heads and giving away leaflets to women smoking cigarettes outside Tesco's and

Oxfam. Eva watched the smiling Hare Krishnas and then raised her eyes absently upwards, towards the darkened windows of the Scorpio Club. As the Hare Krishnas chanted, Eva saw through the curtains that the bony-faced girl in the window directly opposite was also focused on the chanting troop. Eva smiled. After a moment, the Scorpio girl seemed to sense Eva's presence and looked up. Catching Eva's eye, she again put her whole hand like a claw over the crown of her head to push her hair back, turning to step away from the window. Eva kept smiling through the two sheets of glass and the rising cloud of summer central London smog, but the curtains had already twitched down, half-closed again with darkness beyond.

When Eva wasn't correcting grammar or staring out of the window, she often read unsolicited manuscripts from what was meanly called the "slush" pile. She felt excited every time she peeled open an envelope, but a few minutes later she'd be scanning unpunctuated page-long sentences about bawdy maids with hearts of gold and nuns wearing silk stockings. Often the manuscripts came with cover letters about the authors' own romantic lives or difficult histories. Eva didn't suppose it was a nice thing to rate people's emotional problems in terms of their literary output, but in her experience recovering alcoholics wrote the most boring sentences in the world, closely followed by recovering heroin addicts. Victims of abuse seemed to be quite poetic souls, even in the genre of saccharine romantic novels. Manic depressives were patchy. Accountants were mad. Sometimes the authors would send gifts with their manuscripts: a stick of gum, a hand-rolled cigarette. Some

enclosed the odd photograph: a half-naked girl with col-
lagen lips on a New York train carriage was Eva's personal
favourite, closely followed by a man dressed up as Father
Christmas squatting over a toilet seat with a face the same
colour as his bunched-up trousers. Eva wasn't sure how this
was supposed to be persuasive, especially since Echo Books
only published shiny-covered and lightly erotic romantic
novels for women.

She saw the Scorpio girl for the third time at the beginning
of August, as she was changing her clothes for a book-launch
party. Usually Eva was given the odd recycled party invite by
her boss, a seventy-two-year-old woman with long, bright
white hair down to the end of her spine who called everyone
"my dear" in a BBC accent, but from time to time she was
invited in her own right by some PR department trying to
pad out an event. Eva would trot off to people-watch and
drink free white wine for half an hour – often without talking to anyone at all.

Eva put on lipstick by her office window, getting the last
buzz of sunlight through the chain mail of rain outside. It
was spitting and grey out there. When she'd puckered, Eva
looked up from the reflection of her mouth in her powder
compact and saw the girl at the opposite window again,
this time wearing a tattered dressing gown instead of a
leopard-print top. It was about six o'clock, and the space
between the two windows was blurry with rain, but in near
silhouette Eva noticed a high forehead and sunken eyes – a
tiny, knotted mouth. The Scorpio girl looked directly at
Eva. She waited for the girl to turn away, but instead Eva

could have sworn that the figure opened her mouth to say something. The girl stared straight ahead, right at Eva, and her mouth definitely moved. Perhaps it was a conversation she was having with someone obscured from Eva's view by the curtains, or perhaps she was singing to herself. Whatever the Scorpio girl did at the window, it was quick. Eva blinked, and when she opened her eyes again the figure from the window across the street was gone.

After seeing the Scorpio girl for the third time, Eva had that same feeling as when she passed a single magpie in the park or caught the eye of a black cat. She couldn't help a skittish feeling under her skin even though she knew magpies and black cats and girls at windows were harmless. So Eva was already on edge when she turned up at the party on St James's Street later that evening. The venue was a gentlemen's club called Brooks's, with ornate ceilings and a history of aristocratic debauchery written in spills and bodily expulsions on the carpeted floor. There were portraits on the walls, and big windows with heavy velvet curtains. It was the launch for a society journalist who had collected all his columns into a book titled *Foreign Affairs*. The invitation, with her name specifically written on the envelope, had been on Eva's desk for three days, but she couldn't see anyone she knew there. The party consisted mostly of drunk journalists from a former age. The women had embalmed faces – taut eyes and foreheads. But the mummified women looked better than the others, with their finely crackled layers of hopeful foundation. Eva skirted around the side of the party. To the right was a portrait of a bulbous-faced

man in a judge's wig with a wrinkled mouth and eyebrows
that jutted far out from his eye sockets. Standing in a circle
in front of her were similar types to the man in the painting,
except for the wig. One had a latticework of broken capil-
laries on his cheeks stretching out on the thin skin of his
nose, another had a double-droop of bags under his eyes.
They all grinned and drank.

Eva sipped her wine and noticed a younger woman standing near a table piled with books. The woman seemed to
know the author and was speaking animatedly to him
in the corner. Her lips were painted the same shade of
pink as the flowers on her long-sleeved dress, and she was
fidgeting from foot to foot, tucking her hair behind her
ears and smoothing her dress over her thighs. Her thick
blond hair was parted neatly to one side so it fell with an
almost metallic sheen across one side of her face. If you
could have mapped the landing of each glance thrown from
around the room, a tangled nucleus would have formed
where the woman was talking to the elderly author. Fur-
tive looks shot towards the woman and away again, skimming, taking in a bit at a time: a shoulder, the curve of a
breast, the arch of a foot, until each guest probably had
a twenty-piece puzzle of the woman's body and face to
take home with them.

Eva checked her phone. Half-past seven. Perhaps Luke
would be leaving chambers early and they could have dinner and continue the game of Scrabble they had started,
hungover, the previous Sunday after watching Regina roam
free in the park. They had a habit of playing Scrabble games
that lasted weeks, leaving the board on the living-room

coffee table for whenever either of them had a moment to spare. He was a tactical player, a fan of high-point letters straddling numerous words, while Eva would always put a proper word down if she could, even for fewer points. She was about to put down "TUMBLE" (ten points), which she was looking forward to. She would miss their Scrabble games, she knew, when she left him.

Eva discarded her empty glass on a nearby stained table-cloth and began the slow slink out of the room towards the coat racks near the bathrooms.

The Brooks's Club Ladies toilets had brownish wall tiles lit by a single bright strip light on the ceiling. It was empty, and Eva dug out some lipstick from the bottom of her bag, fingering bits of fluff off the greasy tip before hinging her hips on the sink and leaning into the mirror. In the reflection, Eva noticed that the toilet cubicle behind her was locked, and then there was a sigh from behind the door.

"He said he only loved me *sometimes*," the voice in the toilet cubicle said. "How could he say that to me? He makes everything sound like such a drag. But I have to go," the voice said. "I have to get back to this awful party."

Eva finished with her lipstick, put the cap back on, and went into the farthest toilet cubicle, clanking the door shut and coughing to announce her presence, so that the voice might continue its conversation out of the toilets, out of earshot. The voice paused. Eva peed.

"But he broke up with me *during* sex last New Year's eve, did I tell you that? Literally during sex, when he was inside me," the voice continued. "He was on top and he just suddenly stopped and stared down at me and said he 'couldn't do this any more'. I was all, like, 'don't worry, we've both been drinking', and he was like, 'no, I mean this, *us*, I can't pretend to be happy with you any more'."

Eva raised her eyebrows to herself and wondered how to escape this situation.

"It was pretty humiliating," said the voice. "But for him to say he only loves me *sometimes,* geez." The voice paused. "OK, OK. Look, I'll see you later. I really have to get back to this stupid party. I'm waiting for someone."

There was another pause, and it went on for so long that Eva couldn't do anything to escape except flush and pull up her tights, noting a ladder at the ankle, then come out of the bathroom. As she washed her hands, the other woman also came out of her toilet cubicle and caught Eva's eye in the mirror with a sort of shock. The woman, the shiny-haired blonde she had seen near the author, quickly rallied and gave Eva a sad, apologetic half-smile. She was holding her shoes in her hands and so was smaller than she'd appeared before − five foot three, perhaps − smaller than Eva. Her eyes were red-rimmed with emotion now, and although she wasn't actually crying she'd smudged her eyes. She put her heels on the floor and slipped her feet into them, rising up again to nearly Eva's height.

"You're not *leaving*, are you?" the woman said to Eva quickly, talking into the surface of the mirror rather than to Eva's face. "The party's just started. I didn't even see you in there. You are absolutely not allowed to leave. We need you to bring the average age down."

"Sorry," said Eva, smiling tightly into the mirror and washing her hands.

"I just need to break up with him, that's all," the blonde nodded backwards at the toilet cubicle, referring to her earlier conversation. "He said he only loved me *sometimes*. Isn't that horrible?"

"Maybe he was just being honest. Nobody is actively besotted all the time."

"Perhaps," said the woman, tilting her head to the side. She touched her wet eyes, but didn't smooth out the mess. "What's your name?"

"Eva."

"Grace," the woman smiled with a little nod, and while Eva dried her hands under the blow-heater, Grace washed her hands and spoke above the buzz of heat. "The next evening – New Year's Day, after he broke up with me... this is last New Year's, so a while ago, right? – I chucked him out of the flat and he slept on a park bench and got mild pneumonia, and his teeth were chattering when he knocked on my door and he'd bought me flowers, and I had this bookshelf I wanted put up in the living room and one thing led to another and we never mentioned the episode again. One of us should have left ages ago. It's never been him, not really. You know? We all have doubts. I know *all about* doubts." Grace wiped dampness from under her eyes and further smudged her make-up. Her dress had long sleeves with tight-buttoned cuffs over petite wrists, which looked somehow fragile. "I don't blame him for having doubts," Grace ploughed on, "but if he's going to keep changing his mind, then I'd rather he kept his doubts to himself. You know?"

Eva flicked the last moisture off her hands and picked up her bag from next to the sink. "I hope it all works out for you," Eva said with a forced smile, stepping towards the bathroom door and glancing back at Grace, this time not through the medium of the pockmarked mirror. She had an elfin profile, as if drawn with a very soft pencil. Her pink lips had faded slightly since Eva saw her first in the party, but a sediment of colour still stained their edges. Her skin was olive and smooth even in the glaring bathroom light.

"I'm doing the publicity for *Foreign Affairs*. Are you a journalist?" Grace said, even though Eva now had her hand on the bathroom door, ready to leave.

"I'm an editor, at Echo Books," Eva said, as one of the embalmed women walked past her into the bathroom.

"We all used to read them at school!" said Grace, smiling. "*Kiss Me Deadly*, I remember that was an Echo. *Unstoppable Love*, that was another."

"Good luck with the party." Eva stepped out of the bathroom as the embalmed woman stepped in.

"I hate leaving parties," said Grace, following behind Eva. "I always think something amazing will happen the moment I'm gone. At dinner parties I have this annoying habit – Justin hates it – I gather my bag and coat and then insist on having one last, intimate conversation with everyone." She laughed, a little too loud, as if she were forcing herself. "Justin says I always spend half of every party dressed in my coat and scarf." Eva smiled back at Grace in the hallway. She was standing next to the stairs, and Grace hovered near the entrance to the party room, staring at Eva.

"Bye, have a good evening," Eva said. She turned towards the stairs, not looking back to see if the wide-eyed stranger was still watching her. She exhaled as soon as she was away from Grace and could see the building's exit.

* * *

After that evening at Brooks's Eva still felt as if she'd locked eyes with a black cat. She assumed it was because of the girl at the window of the Scorpio Club. Eva picked up a soggy copy of *The Evening Standard* from the pavement as she walked home from Green Park: up St James's Street into Piccadilly, and then through the tight labyrinth of Soho streets, spilling bars and dirty shiny puddles, past the Chinese newsagent with red-paper fans and dragon masks in the window, the XXX bookshop, the trendy frozen-yogurt shop that turned up last year. On the front of the *Standard* was a picture of Regina, swooping. "FREE AS A BIRD" read the headline. "Hundreds of Londoners gathered to watch celebrity zoo bird Regina evade capture for the third day in a row." Eva ripped out the page and put it in her coat pocket. She tilted her head up as if she might see Regina with her curved beak and furrowed eyes, disdainfully skimming over London. Eva imagined Regina riding the smog down between buildings, attacking babies in prams, or digging her claws in the hair of lovers as they meandered hand in hand through the evening. Without stopping in Silver Place, Eva took her night walk a little further, towards the corner of Charlotte Street and Goodge Street. She paused there between a photographic shop and a boarded-up pub with the homeless prophet fast asleep in the doorway, blankets and jumpers wrapped around his dirty face. The club's gatekeeper sat quietly on his stool outside the red door, chain-smoking. His squished face was pensive that evening. Eva took a few steps forward until she was five doors away from the Echo Books office, frowning up at the deserted windows of the Scorpio and seeing nothing behind the ragged curtains except shifting, formless slices of shadow. It was pitch black, as always, beyond the curtains.

For ten minutes nothing moved behind the glass, so she took a step even closer and squinted until the vague shadows formed shapes: bunny rabbits, smoke, birds, fingers? When Eva's grandmother was dying, she would sit up in her bed at University College Hospital and crossly insist that she desired "not to be here more" or "be stitched here more" or "not to be exit, my love". "I'm all scooped out, my loved one," she'd say to Eva, her wrinkled forehead creasing. "Pleased to freedom, now, little girl, I want to finish utterly, please, my loved one, please."

May Elliott, who was Eva's paternal grandmother, was a wiry woman who didn't believe in depression or tiredness, who worked in ammunition factories throughout the War and hadn't been able to hear out of her left ear since a bomb fell on the grocery shop next to where she lived. Her husband was in the RAF and died in the autumn of 1940, when his wife was newly pregnant. Eva's grandmother quoted poetry with the flair of a university professor, although she'd had very little formal education; she told wonderful stories, but couldn't tell jokes, because she'd crack up laughing before the

51

punchline. Eva had a passable relationship with her parents, but it was her grandmother who meant the most to her. Where Eva always wanted to be, quite exclusively throughout her nomadic childhood, was tucked up in Soho, being told stories: of Khufu and the Magicians, King Solomon of Ancient Israel, Clever Aja of the Ashante people in Ghana, the adventures of Merlin. Sometimes – even now – when she was trying to sleep, Eva thought of the wax crocodile that turned into a living reptile when he smelt sin; the flautist who charmed the princess; the king who danced his sorceress lover to death as a punishment for daring to read his mind. Some of May Elliott's favourite stories had been "true" ones from newspaper clippings or the biographies of magicians: performers being attacked by tigers, members of the audience having heart attacks during some trick, diabolical hypnotists putting false memories into the minds of volunteers.

As she stared up at the windows, Eva remembered the story of a beautiful magician's assistant named Sophia who disappeared, according to her gran, in a puff of smoke during a Las Vegas magic show one summer in the early Sixties. Sophia and her lover, Dante, had been travelling the world and performing together since they were children. The "vanishing assistant" trick was a simple matter of false mirrors and gymnastics, only in this instance Sophia never did reappear, and Dante the Mysterious went insane with grief and guilt and longing. People gossiped that Sophia ran away with a rival magician, but Dante could not believe this. Instead he spent the rest of his life searching the globe for a place he'd heard about in whispers and horror stories from other travelling virtuosos: a supernatural waiting room where all the glamorous and exiled magician's assistants, half-translucent white doves, ghostly gormless rabbits, gold coins and oversized playing cards appeared when they disappeared from magic shows around the world.

In May Elliott's bedtime story, Dante never found the beautiful Sophia, but as Eva stared up at the windows of the Scorpio she imagined that it might be Sophia, the magician's assistant, who occasionally came to the window there. There were no trafficked Yugoslavian teenagers behind the curtains, just a room where magicians' props and assistants materialized in the moment they vanished from the stage. Sometimes the objects and creatures got stuck or banished in limbo and never took their rightful place in reality again, which was why sunken-cheeked Sophia was still crouched in there, waiting to be saved by her magician lover. The inhuman shadows Eva could see drifting behind the curtains above her were twenty-first-century Las Vegas tiger cubs, or doves from birthday parties in church halls, all trapped with Sophia in the Scorpio Club. Eva smiled and caught the eye of the bouncer on his chair across the road. The man didn't smile back, just took a long drag of his cigarette and frowned at the gum-speckled pavement at his feet.

Eva closed her eyes for a second in the street and thought about being a child and watching planes taking off. She thought of televisions going black, cars falling off cliffs, *Casablanca's* Humphrey Bogart drawling the words "*We'll always have Paris*" into the insipid, doe-eyed face of Ingrid Bergman (you can almost see her love turning into nostalgia if you look very closely at her eyes). Eva thought of her grandmother looking confused the days before she died, and about Paul Simon's 'Fifty Ways to Leave Your Lover', where the chorus only really mentions seven. She imagined Regina's oar-like wings riding over Regent's Park, Bonnie and Clyde glancing at each other before machine-gun bullets rain at the end of Arthur Penn's film, and Luke's face staring up from the bottom of the stairs at Silver Place every morning while Eva stood at the top and waved goodbye.

* * *

It is impossible to understand a person fully until the moment you leave them. Before the very last moment, everything is still in a state of flux. Each time Eva thought she knew Luke, some new version of him reared its head, and the unrest made her nauseous, made her itch. When he came home late, still bristling with arguments and smelling of adrenalin, she occasionally had the sensation of a stranger walking around in her flat. In the late-evening interim period between being "ambitious barrister" and "boyfriend" he seemed like he wasn't a person at all, just an exhausted face and a suit. Perhaps Eva's natural state of restlessness stopped her from understanding Luke, or perhaps Luke really was difficult to know. He certainly wasn't good at talking about anything that he could not control. He had studied history at university and read history books eagerly, yet the nuances and imperfections of his own history appeared to hold no interest for him. He lived in the moment, squarely looking to the future.

The first night she ever spent with Luke, she provided a narrative of her life for him: the different schools she'd been to, a summary of the friends she'd had, the countries she'd lived in – leaving Bangkok aged four, Beijing aged eight, Indonesia when she was ten. She described the street of identical modern villas in Kuta, where the houses all appeared slightly shrunken, as if the architects had shaved a few inches from every surface and hoped nobody would notice. She told him about her huge collection of dolls and the games she played with them: toy soldiers searched for the Holy Grail, Barbies went on quests for pots of gold, Cindy ruled the world with psychic powers. She told him how she'd collected maps, too, which her father brought back from all the places he flew to: Meda and Kuching, Phuket and Hanoi. In a box under her bed she'd kept fold-out laminated city maps, aviation maps, world maps, bus maps, Tube maps, political maps, road maps and climate maps. Before Luke she had never told anyone about those maps. Her father used to joke that she'd be an explorer when she grew up. She just liked the exactness of cartography, though, all the vastness of the world contained in careful and accurate drawings.

She even tried to explain to Luke her interest in endings. He sat up on his elbows and stared at her with a look of such absolute clarity that she could feel her edges firming up, strands of herself resolving under his gaze. She told him how, when she left Beijing, she had childishly assumed that all the skyscrapers and pollution would simply cease to exist once her eyes couldn't see them. She and her mother had stood at her bedroom window saying goodbye to the city. "Goodbye bicycles," her mother cooed while Eva sobbed, "goodbye courtyard, goodbye taxis, goodbye neighbours, goodbye laundry line, goodbye landlord's cat." As they loaded their bags into a friend's car and drove to the airport, the apartment building ceased to exist; as the plane lifted off, the whole ragged city was wiped off the face of Eva's earth.

"Are you going to leave me?" Luke had said, kissing her stomach.

"Not right now," Eva had smiled. "But think about the end of *Casablanca*. The end sums up the whole movie: '*We'll always have Paris*' is the best bit. Or Hitchcock's *The Birds*, when Melanie and Mitch drive off into the sunset surrounded by a swarm of birds."

"I think I like the middle of movies more."

"*Nobody* likes the middle of movies more," Eva had said, laughing. "The middle is just the lead-up to the end. *Chinatown*: '*Forget it Jake, it's Chinatown*'. *The Silence of the Lambs*, Hannibal Lecter is '*having an old friend for dinner*'. The whole point of stories is their end."

"*Play it again, Sam*," Luke said. "That's the middle of *Casablanca*."

"You're misquoting it. It's: '*Play it once, Sam, for old times' sake*.' You'd remember it right if it was the last line of the film."

When Luke got out of bed to fill up their wineglasses, Eva idly scanned the bookshelves to the right of his bed, judging his taste: history books, law textbooks, some Hemingway, Steinbeck, Ballard. In the bottom right-hand corner of the shelf she noted an album with worn edges, and glanced back at the door before sliding it into her hands. They'd known each other a month before then. She knew he was accident-prone and kind, funny and intelligent, but she didn't know enough details of his life before her. She stood in her knickers and flicked through to a snap of thirteen-year-old Luke with thick-framed glasses and acne, an earnest look on his scarred teenage face, as if quietly solving calculus problems in his head to pass the time. Ten-year-old Luke collecting a prize during assembly. A photograph of his pretty mother with a "No. 1 Mum" mug; Luke and his father on a camping trip.

She squinted at a photo of Luke in shorts and a football bib on a wooden bench, his arm slung protectively across the shoulders of a girl with heavy red hair that fell in two thick curtains over a timid, freckled teenage face. Her eyes were extremely green, little whirlpools. She wore a blue dress and matching ballet slippers.

Eva turned the album towards him with a nervous smile when Luke had come back into the room.

"First love?"

He paused in the doorway for a moment. She thought he might be angry at her for looking at the album. He turned his face away from Eva and put the two glasses of wine on the bedside table among books and pens.

"Yes, she was a girlfriend – Mary." As he took his hands away from the wineglasses, he nearly knocked one off the edge.

"She doesn't look very happy in this picture."

"She wasn't always very happy, I suppose."

"How old is she in this picture?"

"Sixteen?"

"She looks younger."

Behind the bench in the photograph, kids were playing five-a-side in a fenced playing field and a boy in a baseball cap was running towards the camera with a fist raised, as if punching the sky. The image was so over-exposed that the sun looked more like the white of a bomb about to hit the lovers. On that early night together Luke took the album out of Eva's hands before she reached the end of it. He folded it closed and slipped his hand distractingly under the elastic of her knickers.

"Stop snooping," he said, kissing her and then handing her a glass. For a moment Eva and Luke were kids, teenagers, adults all at once: versions of themselves reconciling briefly.

* * *

If Eva had to put a pin on the exact moment the road split that rainy summer after Luke moved into Silver Place, it wouldn't be the glaringly lit bathroom at Brooks's listening to a stranger's problems, or the vicious postcard Luke received, but sitting at a restaurant window table looking out on Gerrard Street in Chinatown two weeks after first meeting Grace. Eva had just bought a moth-extermination kit, ready to wage war once more on a patch of larvae that she'd discovered in a small corner of her living-room carpet. She had a toxic spray in a bag at her feet and a packet of triangular yellow "traps" that allegedly gave off a whiff of female moth pheromone to attract the male moths to a gluey death and stop the mating cycle. She sat staring out of the greasy Chinatown window at shoppers buying melons, jack-fruits and guava under an awning across the damp cobbled road while wet free newspapers flapped and escaped in the wind. There were sopping duck bodies hanging by their legs in front of her face at the window, pigeons flicking a crisp packet back and forth on the street outside. Eva thought about the pleasure she was going to get from sucking the moth larvae up into the vacuum later. She could go home and do it now: she didn't have to wait. She didn't know the people she was waiting for, even, or at least not well enough to mind standing them up. The first time Grace had called the Echo Books office, Eva had taken a moment to work out who she was. "Remember me from Brooks's? The girl you met in the bathroom? I got your office number off the net," Grace said. "Just tell me to sod off if you're busy, only I'm in Soho this evening and I saw your office is near there, so I thought I'd try my luck with you. Want to have a drink?"

Eva instinctively replied that she was working late, but the next week Grace called again: she had a client meeting in Soho that afternoon and had a hankering for Chinese, so would Eva and her boyfriend perhaps like to have dinner with her and her boyfriend?

Waiting at the restaurant with moth pheromones at her feet, Eva bit her thumbnail, tearing the skin, and watched Grace appear between hanging duck carcasses outside the restaurant, ten minutes late, wearing over-the-knee boots and a belted black raincoat, her hair caught up in a smooth 1950s-style blonde conch-shell bun with a silk band. She billowed into the restaurant full of smiles, taking off her raincoat to reveal a figure-hugging black dress, with coloured bangles up her wrists. The bangles jumped as she moved her hands to tuck a strand of loose hair behind her ears. As at the Brooks's party, everyone in the room stole a glance at her. There was something both trashy and elegant about how Grace dressed. By contrast Eva felt inconspicuous in her messy jeans and faded T-shirt. A few steps behind Grace was a beautiful, preppy-looking man in his late thirties with ashy hair and chrome glasses resting on the bridge of his nose. His tanned skin was slightly gaunt and faded, his broad shoulders looked sunken, as if he'd been brought up on sunshine and barbequed meat but then pulled down by London's winters.

"Justin, honey, this is my new friend Eva I told you about," Grace said as she sat down on the circular table by the window.

"Lovely to meet you, Eva," said Justin, separating his chopsticks and smiling.

"Is your boyfriend coming for dinner?" Grace said, flicking a napkin onto her lap and opening the menu.

"I told him where we are. He's planning to come by after work, but he's having a tough week," Eva said.

"What does he do?"

"Barrister."

"I see. Do you live nearby?" said Grace.

"Yes, just off Lexington Street."

"Justin works near Soho," said Grace. "Bluetone Productions on New Burlington Place. You've probably walked past it a million times. He's making a documentary on the history of sunshine at the moment – from the Big Bang to skin cancer. That's right, isn't it?"

"We're filming an episode on worship right now. Aztecs to sunbeds."

"He's been travelling a lot this year," said Grace. "Chinese mythology, solar myths in African tribes..."

"What do you do, Eva?" said Justin with a steady gaze.

"I'm an editor."

They ordered enough wine, crispy pancakes and dim sum for Luke in case he turned up, but in the end he didn't join them for dinner that night. Eva texted him to ask if he was coming and he didn't write back, so she figured he was still as busy as he had been all week. Eva, Grace and Justin talked about novels and star consolations, London museums, office chairs, the rain and whatever else relative strangers make tipsy conversation about over greasy Chinese food on a damp Friday night. Grace and Justin had met at a Christmas party organized by his production company. She'd bought him a martini and they'd been together since, living together for the last year. There was something frantic in the curve of Grace's mouth, something aggressive in the way she smiled. Justin, on the other hand, had an almost irritating, yogic sort of calm. His voice was authoritative without being insistent, and feelings – smiles, frowns – appeared on his face slowly.

"Shall we play 'two truths and a lie'?" Grace said, but didn't wait for an answer, just glared at the remains of her crispy pancakes and then up at Eva, who sipped her wine and resisted the urge to bite her thumbnail. "I went to a psychic this morning and he told me that keeping secrets was bad for my health," Grace started. "I once made a model Eiffel tower out of matchsticks. I'm double-jointed in five places."

"Mmm. You don't strike me as a patient person. I doubt you ever made an Eiffel tower out of matchsticks," said Eva, after a pause. "That's the lie."

"You're double-jointed," said Justin.

"I'm only double-jointed in *three* places, actually," smiled Grace. "You should know that, Justin, honey." Grace and Justin stared at each other.

"The eight-year-old Buddha reincarnation stole my iPhone last year in Himachai in India," Justin said. "I'm scared of the sea. Grace isn't wearing any underwear tonight."

"She's wearing tights," Eva said. "And I don't think you're scared of water."

"You're so *smutty*, Justin," said Grace, wriggling in her seat a bit. Eva got a sense that Justin was purposefully not looking at his girlfriend now, and Eva wished Luke were there to balance the dynamic. She would have touched his foot, under the table, and smiled at him if he'd been there. "Nobody wants to know about my knickers, darling," Grace said.

"She's wearing stockings," said Justin to Eva, clarifying with a slight smile and adjusting his glasses. Eva looked away from him.

"I faked my orgasm last night," said Grace, finishing her glass. "I've been in a Burger King commercial. I once shaved my head to irritate my mother."

"We didn't have sex last night, but I wouldn't say faking an orgasm while masturbating was beyond her. She's theatrical to the core," said Justin. "Shaving her head is a truth as well, by all accounts she was a unruly little kid who enjoyed pissing off her mum."

"You're not meant to answer, *darling*," said Grace to Justin, while absent-mindedly reaching over and touching

Eva's hand, running a snail trail of warmth over Eva's middle finger. Eva kept her finger quite still, surprised.

She tried not to twitch her finger, and she had a strong desire not to be sitting any longer with these two people as they bristled around her. She would rather have been out in the rain, eating street-vendor mooncake while she walked out of Chinatown back into Soho, or watching the Scorpio Club, thinking about magicians. Grace ran the tip of her finger between two of Eva's knuckles and down the valley between two tendons towards her wrist.

"I wish you wouldn't call me 'darling'," said Justin to his girlfriend, not looking at Grace's hand still on Eva's finger. "You only ever use it sarcastically."

"Let's not argue." Grace smiled at Eva. "Don't you think Eva's pretty? She has such green eyes."

"Sure," said Justin without commitment, not looking at Eva or Grace. He piled a last, desultory mouthful of fried rice into his mouth.

"Do you ever get angry, though?" said Grace to Eva. "You seem like you're a little detached from life. A little apathetic, perhaps?"

"Don't, Grace," said Justin, shaking his head at Grace. "Leave her alone."

"Don't *what*, Justin? Don't ask Eva questions? She seems a bit bottled up. I'd like to unravel her. Emotionally."

"I'd rather not be unravelled right now. It's getting late," Eva said.

"Of course not, honey," said Grace. "I didn't mean to annoy you." Grace's bangles clinked as she reached over and put a conciliatory, apologetic finger on top of Eva's arm, near her wrist. Eva kept her hand motionless on the bleached white tablecloth. When Grace took her hand away, Eva could still feel a slight sting from the contact.

* * *

Outside the restaurant, Chinatown appeared hazy under a needle-mist of rain: gold pagodas winked in the gloom, red-paper dragons dripped. It was the sort of rain that put a film of moisture on your skin even if you have an umbrella up. Eva was relieved to leave Grace and Justin to their bickering, and as she rested her umbrella on her shoulder she thought of the first boy she ever left. His name was Timothy, and it happened in a McDonald's near Victoria Station when they were fifteen.

"You won't find anyone like me again," he'd said.

"I know," Eva had said, confused as to why he thought she'd want to, considering she was sitting there trying to break up with him.

Then, knocking back his chair, he'd leant over to spit into her milkshake. While his saliva disappeared into her drink Eva watched him wind his way out of the McDonald's with his low-trousered teenage lollop. She'd almost wanted to go after him to tell him how strangely amazing she felt seeing him go: the clarity of the moment was far more intense than any intimacy she'd had with him before. She wanted to tell him that she felt much closer to him then, as he became a memory, than she ever had when they were together. It felt nearly ecstatic, a mixture of nervousness and pleasure that sent a long shiver down her spine. It was the excitement of stepping out of a foreign airport into hot air, or waking up inexplicably happy after days of sadness. It was a much more interesting feeling than kissing him or waiting for his phone calls.

Eva's next ending was at seventeen, with a boy called James, outside a bakery in Wales. They'd been going out for a year, had slept with each other, argued, done all the things that grown-ups in relationships do, but she didn't miss him when he wasn't around, and often, when he was around, she would rather have been on her own. They were both eating jam doughnuts and waiting for the 10.50 train back into London when Eva pointed out quite coolly, with her mouth tasting of raspberry jam as she said it, that she didn't think she was going to fall in love with him. It was strange, she thought now, that the first two break-ups of her life had such a strong taste of sugar: childish and immediate. Eva remembered the calm and relief that came over her, even as James's blue eyes widened and he called her "emotionally abortive". It was as if he morphed in front of her, turning back into a stranger while they stood there with sugar-dusted hands next to a main road near the train station. He shrunk slightly and seemed very close to her for half a second – almost on top of her, inside her for a moment, staring at her wide-eyed – but then his eyes narrowed back to a normal shape and he stepped away from her.

Some people, when you see them saying goodbye at the airport, turn into strangers mid-hug, thinking about the next thing, the vodka-tonic they'll have on the plane, the spreadsheet they have to finish by the time they land. Others are still bidding their farewell and glancing back as they pass through the ticket barrier.

Eva could watch people for hours in airports. When she first moved to London she used to catch the Tube to Heathrow after school and drink coffee near the entrance to the departure gates, where travellers parted from their families and proceeded towards security. Eva had missed her parents, although she would never have admitted it, and airports reminded her of them. She felt at home among their bustle and intensity, and breaking up with James made her think of Heathrow's Departures: somewhat theatrical, yet still moving. It was as if she'd been terrified of the gap between the two of them until she just jumped through that gap and then it ceased to matter at all. After James called her "emotionally abortive", he stared at Eva for a long moment, looking hurt. He vanished in front of her long before he jumped into a cab. As he drove off, she quietly ate the rest of her doughnut before getting on the train back to London. Like the previous ending in McDonald's, Eva felt liberated rather than sad. There was just so much potential in goodbye. It was so much more truthful, and as you walked away all the mistakes you had made and the things you had become with that person simply disappeared, leaving you to start again and be whatever you wanted to be.

* * *

Eva picked up post from the mat as she came through the front door of Silver Place from Chinatown, flicking anxiously between bills and bank statements but seeing nothing out of the ordinary. As she walked up the stairs, she opened a Manila envelope with a wedding invitation from a school friend, which she'd have to add to the growing array displayed on the mantelpiece. She might even have to buy some sort of hat, she thought with a shudder.

Luke was bent over the living-room table in an old T-shirt and jeans, piano music on the record player. August's big case involved an East London car wash and mechanics' that was allegedly laundering money for a drug dealer. Luke's notes for the case were spread out around him on the table: statements of facts, Excel spreadsheets full of figures, photographs of his client Andrew Alves, the doughy-faced car-wash manager. Eva and Luke's Scrabble game was out on the coffee table in front of the sofa. She'd put down TUMBLE after the party at Brooks's. They'd moved through DUET, TWIG, SLUG, and she was considering URN against the U of SLUG.

A moth flew in from the hallway, hovering in the fizzy light of the television screen and then getting woozy, twisting in the air, coming towards the sofa. When it was a metre away, Eva lurched forward to clap its ghostly body between the palms of her hands. Luke looked up. Light through the window came in partly white from the street lamps and partly pink from the bar at the Lexington Street end of the alley. Wiping the body on her jeans, she reached over to kiss Luke. He had grey circles under his eyes, his skin bone-white. The broken skin on his lip from Catherine's engagement party had healed into a scar, which Eva kissed it as he turned his face upwards towards her.

"How was your day?" Eva said.

"I met up with Andrew, the money-launderer."

"Nice guy?" Eva said. From the pictures he clearly wasn't.

"No," said Luke. "But I don't think he did it. He just didn't seem particularly business-minded. He wasn't sure what 'equity' meant when I tried to go through some details with him."

"I'm not sure what equity means either," said Eva.

"You're not being accused of perpetrating a multi-million-pound fraud."

"I'm concentrating on moth-breeding this quarter."

"Which it appears you have a real talent for."

"I reckon it's all your cashmere," Eva said.

"Yeah, my fault." He held his hands up for a second in pretend surrender. "I was going to pour boiling water on that colony over there, but thought I'd wait for you."

There was a short pause.

"You didn't fancy Chinese in the end?" Eva got up from the floor.

"I was on my way, but then I didn't feel very well," Luke said. He highlighted a sentence in the brief in front of him.

"Are you OK?" said Eva.

"I'm fine."

"It was fun, sort of." Eva looked carefully at Luke. "The girl, Grace, she's a bit... intense, but interesting."

"She's interesting, or you like her?"

"I like that she's interesting."

"That's such an Eva reason to make friends: *interesting*. Remind me where you met her again?"

"At one of those grim book launches," Eva said. "I think you'd like her, actually."

"Would I?"

"Of course," said Eva. "Or I wouldn't have invited you to come along. You'd think she was interesting, too."

"I sometimes think you don't like people: you just get curious occasionally about character traits you don't understand."

Eva didn't say anything. She went into the kitchen, put the kettle on and came back into the living room with hot water and the dust-buster, placing its mouth on the edge of the growing moth island.

"Just because I don't make many new friends doesn't mean I'm incapable of making reasonable judgements about people," Eva said. She pressed down on the dust-buster as a buzz of loud suction dragged the larvae away from the carpet along with a lot of woven wool. When she was done, the carpet looked bald. She poured boiling water just to be sure, then sat down there on the floor, on the opposite side of the room to where Luke was working, with her back to the wall and her elbows on her knees.

"I just don't think 'interesting' is a good reason to make friends," said Luke. "Are you going to see her again?"

"Probably not, no. What's wrong with you tonight?"

"Nothing, I just don't feel very well."

"Luke? What's wrong?"

"I had a *small* seizure earlier – just a small one, so don't panic – when I got home from work." He illustrated how small the seizure was by showing an inch between his thumb and forefinger. "I guess I haven't been sleeping very well. Work's been hectic – this case is getting to me, maybe." Luke was staring straight forward at his papers, not at Eva.

"Why didn't you tell me you felt ill?" said Eva quietly, as anger and worry tensed the muscles of her face so her eyes narrowed and her tongue pressed at the roof of her mouth.

"I just did tell you," said Luke, still not looking at her.

* * *

Eva only discovered he was epileptic by accident, more than a year into their relationship: another example of Luke's reticence about personal information. He'd never once mentioned that he had this condition, so when he passed out in her kitchen on a Saturday morning, it came as a bit of a shock. He'd stayed the night, and she was just getting out of the shower when she heard a plate break in the other room. The sound that followed was more of a thud. Luke was clumsy and often broke stuff, so the plate-smashing wasn't a surprising noise. He was also very tidy, though, so he usually made a fuss and banged around afterwards, anxious to clean up.

"Luke?" Eva said, through the wall separating bathroom and kitchen. Luke didn't answer, and Eva opened the bathroom door in her ragged grey towel, padding the two steps through the hallway and leaving wet footprints on the bathroom tiles and the carpet. She peeked through the door and saw Luke lying on the kitchen floor with his back to her, wearing a pair of blue plaid pyjama bottoms, the plate smashed next to his outstretched hand. Luke's neck was arched backwards, and as Eva took a step forward she saw foam and vomit around his clenched-up mouth. Blue veins bulged from his neck, and his taut spine was rocking his head back and forth. Eva kneeled down on the floor next to him, grabbing her phone from where it sat on the counter, among Tesco bags and coffee cups, and dialled 999. *1D Silver Place. Eyes open. Mouth foaming, body swaying, tense muscles. Can't seem to see me.*

Eva's stomach tightened, and her eyesight became very clear. Everything became hot. At first she thought he was having a stroke. It didn't seem so long ago that she'd walked into the living room of Silver Place and found her grand-mother unable to control the muscles of her face and arms – three weeks later her grandmother was dead. As Eva spoke to the ambulance operator, Luke moaned and a damp patch spread from his crotch over his pyjama trousers and onto the floor. A gurgling sound came right from the back of his throat, and every muscle in his body appeared to have turned to stone – even his bare feet and the knuckles on his hands had hardened into sculptures. Eva kept repeating his name in a daze, and he just kept staring straight ahead at the dust under the kitchen cabinets. Eva wasn't so sure it was a stroke. Her second thought was that he'd taken something that wasn't right. Newspaper headlines flashed through her head: "CONTAMINATED ECSTASY KILLS BARRISTER".

She remembered watching her friend Amy after she'd taken a line of what she believed was cocaine but turned out to be ketamine. She had ended up spending the rest of the evening dribbling on her shoes. But it was eleven on a Saturday morn-ing, so that couldn't be right – could it? Luke hadn't got back from work until one in the morning the previous night, and he'd sat down to watch the end of a movie with Eva. He'd smelt of work sweat and coffee, not alcohol.

71

"Luke," Eva kept saying while he twitched on the kitchen floor. "It's going to be all right, Luke." But for minutes he didn't respond at all. His bloodshot eyes just grew wider, and Eva could count the ripples of the muscles around his spine. Then the shaking calmed down and eventually stopped. Luke looked confused and blinked around him, then gazed with a blank expression at Eva.

"Luke?" Eva said. He looked scared. "It's OK, Luke, everything is going to be OK."

"Oh fuck," he said eventually.

"The ambulance telephone operator thinks you might have had a seizure."

"The ambulance? You called the ambulance?"

"It's on its way."

"Oh fuck," he said, trying to raise himself.

"Don't," Eva said, but he was already sitting up, so she helped him lean against the kitchen cabinets with his bare feet on the tiles. He noticed the wet patch on his trousers and wiped vomit and saliva from his mouth with the back of his hand. The room smelt of illness. Eva got him a glass of water and crouched down next to him, but Luke held the glass limply in his hands and didn't drink anything. He closed his eyes and then opened them again, white-faced. She took the glass from him and put it on the floor so he didn't drop it.

"No," he said, putting his head in his hands. "Fuck."

"It's going to be OK, Luke, the ambulance will be here in a minute."

"I don't need an ambulance," he said. "It's over now."

"You need an ambulance."

"It's epilepsy," he said. "Did I hit my head or anything?"

"I don't know. I heard a plate being smashed. I was in the shower. You've been out for a while." Eva paused, looking at her phone and noticing that she had only called the ambulance nine minutes ago. "You have epilepsy?" she said.

"Yeah, since I was a kid."

"So this has happened before?"

"Yeah," he said. Then the doorbell rang and Eva realized that her hair was sopping wet and she wasn't wearing any clothes. Her towel was somewhere in the doorway: she must have dropped it when she saw him on the floor. The phone also started to ring. She got up and answered it as she grabbed the towel on her way out of the kitchen.

Eva buzzed the paramedic into the building and directed him to the fourth floor. He wore a blue jump suit with a red plastic satchel.

"He just came out of it, and he says he has epilepsy," Eva mumbled to the man without saying hello, pointing to the kitchen. "I don't know. He says he's fine. Maybe he hit his head."

"Let's have a look, shall we?" said the paramedic.

* * *

Luke didn't appear to have any sort of concussion, so he just needed to take it easy for a while and call the hospital if he felt unwell at any point in the next few days. Luke showered while Eva put his pyjama trousers in the wash, and then they both crawled back to bed in silence and slept for another four hours. Eva woke up first, her back to the wall and her nose nearly touching Luke's shoulder, unusually close to him. She opened her eyes and looked at him.

First she had an overwhelming sense of relief, of warmth, on seeing him, then she felt a sudden, incontrollable anger, as if she'd just remembered that he'd slept with another woman. Often Eva didn't react to things she ought to react to, she had a habit of burying her emotions, but not this time.

She reared up from the bed and reached over to a glass of water on the bedside table. She drank and looked down at Luke. She knew he was only half asleep because of the way he was breathing, his mind climbing out of slumber, and soon enough he yawned with his eyes clamped shut, mouth agape like a bear, and a moment later he'd sat up and Eva handed him the glass.

"How you feeling?" Eva said.

"Fine. How long did we sleep for?"

"Hours. You scared me."

"I'm sorry."

Luke fiddled with the glass, not looking Eva in the eye.

"You didn't ever think to mention that you had epilepsy?" Eva asked. "Is there anything else I should know?" Eva continued, despite herself. "Genetic diseases? Have you had open-heart surgery in the last ten years? Do you have all your organs?"

"That's harsh, Eva," Luke said. He still looked washed out, and Eva tried to bite back on her anger, but her whole body was still full of adrenalin.

"You could have told me."

"You're acting like I lied on my insurance form. Is it void now?"

"I just think you might have mentioned it before, so that when I walked in on my boyfriend squirming on the floor and foaming at the mouth I didn't nearly have a heart attack."

"So this is about you, then, is it?" he said, putting the glass down on the bedside table and sitting farther up in bed. "I like how you turned that one around."

"It's about *us*, though, isn't it? You, me, bodies, kitchen floors, the potential future where we maybe share a kitchen floor and where you don't suddenly reveal chronic health problems to me on a Saturday morning."

"Are you saying you don't want a future with someone who pees on your kitchen floor? Cos I could try and only have fits in the bathroom, if that works better for you. To be honest, you should be thanking me for not doing it on the carpet."

"No, I'm not trying to protect my soft furnishings," Eva said. They were both sitting up in bed now, as far away from each other as the bed would allow.

"You are genuinely acting like I've broken some sort of contract," Luke said, turning his shoulders towards her.

"I'm saying you're a fuckwit for not telling me, that's all," snapped Eva, dragging her legs farther up against her body, her fingers unwinding the hem of her pillow.

"A fuckwit?" he said, raising his eyebrows.

"Yes," said Eva.

Luke got out of bed and started to get dressed. He pulled on a pair of trousers. "I didn't tell you cos I knew you'd get *stressed* – like you are now."

"I'm stressed because I was scared."

"You don't need to be. I'm fine." He fumbled with the button of his trousers, then looked a bit dizzy and sat down on the office chair by the closed curtains. Eva swung her legs out of bed. "I just don't need you to feel sorry for me," he said. "I've been dealing with this my whole life."

"I don't feel sorry for you. I think you're a cunt," Eva said.

Luke laughed. "Thanks," he said. "That's better than a fuckwit, right?"

"I do, though. It's not fair. I love you. That was the most horrible thing I've ever seen."

He looked at his hands and his feet, then back at Eva.

"I love you too," he said, and they both realized that they hadn't said those words before. "I'm sorry. I should have told you about it," he continued, quickly, leaving the words "I love you" lingering. He sat back on the chair and put his legs up on the desk. She didn't really understand why he hadn't told her – a boy thing, not wanting to show weakness – but it still didn't make sense.

"I'm allergic to penicillin. And potpourri," Eva said in a conciliatory tone, thinking about the words "I love you" as much as the epilepsy now.

"Potpourri?" he said, still sitting on the office chair.

"Only when mixed with hot water in an effort to make perfume – which I did when I was eleven, and somehow my tongue swelled to double the size and I couldn't breathe."

"Right," he said. "Good to know. I'd like to keep your tongue the size it is now."

"And penicillin. That's more important. No penicillin."

"Shouldn't you wear a bracelet or something?"

"Shouldn't you?"

They paused again. Eva scratched her knee.

"Penicillin. Fourteen points," said Luke.

"Worried. Eleven points," said Eva.

"OK, so after the dog incident at Dad's farm, I started getting seizures, which trace back to the head trauma. It was a big deal, the dog really tore me apart. The seizures were worse when I was younger. I've only had four in the last ten years, which is actually pretty good considering I used to have them all the time."

"That's *good*? It looked like the Terminator's death scene."

"Thanks Eva," said Luke. "They usually happen when I'm drunk, or over-tired, or when I'm stressed."

"But you're *always* over-tired," Eva said. Luke looked darkly at her, and she realized this note of panic in her voice was probably the reason why he hadn't told her. He enjoyed staying up late, working too hard, drinking espresso. "Do you take medication?"

"Little white pills, every day."

"I've never noticed."

"It's not like I make a big scene about it, they're just in my bathroom in Hackney."

"Do you always take them?"

"Don't start."

Eva was quiet for a second. "I bought croissants. You want breakfast? I'm angry with you, but I'll make you breakfast anyway."

"Pity food?"

"Yup."

"Can I have a pity fuck after?"

"Probably not."

"OK," he said. "I'll settle for breakfast."

Later, they sat opposite each other at the table in the living room, eating croissants and scrambled eggs, drinking cups of sugary tea. They were silent for a while, and Eva couldn't stop smiling at Luke. She had this strange feeling in her stomach, and constantly had to stop herself from reaching over and touching him.

"Did you know that Timothy McVeigh – the Oklahoma-bombing guy – had two pints of mint-chocolate-chip ice cream for his last meal?" Luke said.

"Mint chocolate chip? He could have anything, and he had mint chocolate chip? Madness," Eva said, but really she was thinking: *Shit, I think I love him. I think I've fallen in love with him – just that minute, just a minute ago.*

"Ronnie Lee Gardner had apple pie and vanilla ice cream. That was in the paper a few weeks ago, wasn't it?" said Luke.

"I don't remember," said Eva. She had loved people before, but in the same way as when you lose your temper and then feel burnt out. She had loved – but not like now.

"This would be a good last meal," said Luke, eating a bit of croissant.

"If you're ever convicted of murder," said Eva, "I'll bring white truffles, fillet mignon and some overpriced red wine."

"I think if I'm ever convicted of murder I'll have someone else chose my wine," said Luke.

"Vote of confidence," said Eva.

"*Overpriced* isn't what you're meant to look for in a vintage, though."

"If you were about to get electrocuted I'd do some research."

"Well, then if you get convicted of murder I'll bring you a toasted cheese sandwich with an excessive amount of ketchup, and some crappy iced coffee."

* * *

On the Tuesday following dinner with Grace and Justin in Chinatown, Eva spent the morning in a café on Charlotte Street with the author of a novel entitled *Incubus Unleashed*, a softly spoken biology teacher in a boys' day school who enjoyed long walks on the beach with her border collies and writing explicit sex scenes about Victorian women transformed by the carnal desires of ghosts. Her approach to grammar was particularly abstract, and *Incubus Unleashed* had been a nightmare to edit. Eva was depressed when she heard that book number two was already finished. "Use italics sparingly for emphasis; the apostrophe is used to indicate possession," the voice of *The Oxford Style Guide* spoke in Eva's head while she looked over the first pages of the manuscript, full of "housewive's *moaning* on kitchen tables, mouths *salivating* and bodies *pulsating* like white hot-metal".

While Eva flicked through the pages, she listened to tales of the author's non-existent love life. "My last boyfriend wasn't awful in any *particular* way, you see," the author said, adding sugar cubes to her cup of tea. "He bought me flowers sometimes. It was the doom though," she said. "That was the problem". (Doomfully, Eva thought: eighteen points.) "I felt this sense of doom descend on me whenever I looked at him. I knew he wasn't the right one, but I'm getting so impatient."

Eva peeked at her watch (one p.m.) and then up at some teenagers arguing on a bench outside the café. The girl had her hand clenched and her finger pointing repeatedly at the boy's face. He kept putting his hands around the girl's finger and pushing it down, but her fingers pinged right back up. A moment later there was a knock on the café window in front of Eva's face, and she re-focused her eyes from the teenagers across the road to the unexpected sight of Grace an inch from the window: her big smile a little lopsided and her eyebrows raised. She was wearing a dark skirt suit with a large-collared white shirt. She carried an umbrella in one hand and her coat hung unbelted over her shoulders. Although Eva never admitted this to anyone afterwards, she was flattered by Grace's insistence: this animal-eyed, incandescent creature asking to spend time with her.

"I'll just be a moment," Eva said to the author.

"Oh, I should be off." The woman pushed her chair back. "Can't wait to hear what you think about *The Debutante's Craving*."

"Look forward to reading it," Eva said.

Outside the café Eva gave Grace a quick kiss on the cheek. Grace said that she was passing Echo Books on the way back from a client's office and had decided to see if Eva wanted to have lunch. Someone at the office had answered the door and directed Grace to the café.

"I've never seen anyone look so bored as you did in there," Grace said.

"Erotica authors are an exciting bunch."

Without thinking twice, Eva walked off with Grace, talking of possible lunch destinations: sushi versus burritos, the merits of soups over sandwiches. They passed Italian delis, Spanish restaurants and greasy-spoon cafés while Grace lit one cigarette after another. Eva smiled at the sight of Grace's long neck dipping to light up at street corners.

"Do you have to be back at work?" said Grace.

"Afraid so."

"Do you have an hour? I'll take you to get the best ice-cream sundae. I swear. The sundaes there always cheer me up."

Eva followed Grace through Soho towards Piccadilly Circus, then between two white, shoulder-high lion sculptures into a casino lobby illuminated by the flickering squares of slot machines. "Rainbow Riches!" a machine flashed. "Number Runner!" "Gold Digger!" "Lucky Dip!" Grace waved at a pony-tailed bouncer leaning on a vast wall-sized mirror near the door and a little man in a sweaty blue shirt with a red nametag who stood behind a desk computer. "Go right ahead," said the little man, shooing them past. The tinny sound of coins falling rained in the air even though no one seemed to be playing the machines.

The lift had an "Out of Order" sign taped onto it, so Eva followed Grace up three flights of stairs past a closed coat-check kiosk and into the syrupy lamplight of a small top-floor casino. The carpet was red and yellow, while the low ceiling was gold, the hanging lamps almost scraping the heads of taller gamblers. It was curiously full for a Tuesday afternoon, with croupiers dealing cards to tables packed with groups of young Asian men drinking beer, tourists wearing "Ripley's Believe It or Not" T-shirts and small Chinese women clutching their handbags or counting their chips. Tables of baccarat, blackjack, roulette and Texas-hold -'em poker floated like boats in the middle of the floor, while slot machines circled the edges and a small restaurant was cut off from the floor by a series of fake potted plants wound with fairy lights. The casino light bounced off Grace's skin and tight bun of hair, making her appear sculptural.

"I come here when I'm sad, sometimes," she said, winding around into the restaurant area and standing at the wood-veneer bar to pick up a laminated menu without looking at it. "Maybe it's because everyone else is sadder?"

"Free *Schadenfreude* with every ice cream," said Eva. Around them a Slavic girl played with her earrings, a haunted-looking older man stacked his chips, an obese woman wearing too much eyeliner spoke on her mobile phone.

"It's the best people-watching in London," Grace said. She caught the eye of the waiter behind the bar. "Two special sundaes, please, with extra chocolate sauce."

Eva followed Grace over to a table between two fake potted plants, so they could look through the plastic leaves at a roulette table. Eva had lived in Soho for twelve years and still turned corners into shape-shifting alleys she didn't remember existing, doors she'd never noticed that appeared to lead into bars she'd never seen before. The same was true with this casino, which she'd never noticed before, although she must have passed it a hundred times. Across the table from Eva, Grace took a strip of foil pill blisters from her bag and popped one out into her hand.

"Want one?" Grace said.

"What are they?" Eva squinted down at the packet in Grace's long fingers.

"Just Dexedrine, for when you're feeling a bit scattered. I had a horrible morning. Dropped coffee on my boss's computer, argued with Justin."

"I'm OK," said Eva.

Grace swallowed the pill without water. They both turned their heads to watch the haunted middle-aged man betting chips on red. He pushed them over with the resigned expression of someone down on his luck and took another sip of his drink.

"My aunt used to say that marriage is just roulette," Grace said as the wheel began to spin. "You marry the guy you're with when you start to become aware of babies. When that happens, the ball stops, and wherever you are is where you stay."

"Is your roulette ball stopping on Justin?" said Eva as Grace took her thick hair out of its tightly wound bun, so it sprung up around her face.

"I doubt it," Grace said. "I love him, but I don't really understand him. He's obsessed by things that aren't real – old stuff, museums, star constellations." Her tone was solemn. "Plus a few weeks ago I found a flirty email on his printer from a work colleague. It wasn't even well written."

"Dumb of him to leave it around," Eva said.

"Duplicitous *and* stupid," Grace said. "Lethal combination."

"Do you think it matters that you don't entirely understand him?"

"I don't entirely understand myself either, I suppose," said Grace. In the corner of the room someone won, and a small ripple of pleasure swept round the table. It lasted a second, and then all the heads bowed again to continue. Soon the ice-cream sundaes turned up in retro-frosted glasses with long silver spoons.

"Try it," said Grace. "Get all the layers in one go."

Eva's spoonful tasted sweet and chemical, the chocolate sauce melting with vanilla ice cream and sprinkles on her tongue, while the sounds of pinging coin games and mumbled conversation filled up around her in the windowless room. It tasted of days out at fairgrounds or treats at birthday parties.

"Are your parents still together?" Grace asked.

"Technically," said Eva. "They live in Singapore and try not to speak to each other."

"Wild," said Grace.

"No, my mother has made an Essex out of Singapore and Dad's hardly ever there. He works for an airline and travels a lot. Are yours together?"

"Catholic, so no getting away from each other. We get on OK I guess, although of course they're disappointed in me. Familial guilt, Catholic guilt, it all adds up. I feel guilty about the pleasure I'm getting from this ice-cream sundae and I'm not even done." Grace licked the back of her spoon, leaving skids of chocolate on her lip that she wiped on the back of a finger. At the roulette wheel outside the restaurant area, a man put his hand over his mouth, and his eyes widened until they threatened to explode from his face. "You look like an only child to me. Self-contained," said Grace.

"You think I don't share my crayons?"

"Do you share them with your boyfriend?"

"Some of them, I guess."

"Did you ever want a sister or brother? Were you lonely? I came from a big family – three siblings, lots of hangers-on, foster kids and what not, always a crowd in the kitchen."

"I don't think I ever wanted to share my crayons," Eva said.

"It's never a good idea to share all of them," Grace nodded, as if this was a well-known fact. "Would your boyfriend ever cheat on you, do you think? Have you ever suspected it?"

"I don't think he would," said Eva, a little perplexed by the question.

"I get crazy jealous, it's really vicious. It's a horrible feeling." Grace rested her face on her hand. She looked down at the table then back up, through her long eyelashes at Eva. "Recently I've had this habit of only dating beautiful men," she said, "which is really quite counter-productive. Ugly people work hard. They're better lovers."

"You sound like a plantation owner," said Eva.

"And of course the better-looking they are, the more likely they are to cheat."

"So you think Justin is cheating on you?" A clattering sound of falling coins filled the air, but Eva didn't turn around.

"I don't really know. I think he's going to leave me, though. He wants to meet tonight, actually. I think we're about to have the 'conversation'." Eva realized that an unexpected, theatrical tear had formed in the corner of Grace's eye. It swelled, and she wiped it away before it tumbled. "I'm sorry," she said. "God, I'm ridiculous, aren't I? I drag you for ice-cream sundaes and then I cry."

"I'm sorry things are tough."

"I bet you're happy with your boyfriend," said Grace. "I bet he loves you. I don't want to be on my own again. I'm not self-sufficient like you."

The girls fell silent again.

"I found some teenage diaries a while back with a list of requirements in a future boyfriend," said Eva to break the silence, "and among 'nice smile' and 'sense of humour' was the wish to find a boy who knew without any explanation that meeting 'at Waterloo Station' meant underneath the big clock and 'at Selfridges' meant the stationery section, and who knew that if we both went to the bathroom in the cinema he should wait outside the Ladies rather than wandering off and leaving me outside the men's toilet wondering if he'd fallen in. I think, at the romantic age of fifteen, what I wanted from a lover was *uncomplicated travelling*."

Grace laughed and put her hand over her mouth. "It's all about where you'll meet them when the Apocalypse comes."

"I should probably get back to work," said Eva.

"I have the rest of the day off, so I might get some noodle soup and play a few rounds of blackjack. You sure you don't want to stay? I'm really good at blackjack."

Eva hesitated. The slot machines blinked, and mirrored walls gave an impression of infinite space. Without windows it didn't feel like afternoon or any other time. The whole room could have been a spaceship that never had to land back on earth: its illuminated gold-ceilinged pod would continue to speed forward without a destination.

"One game of blackjack," Eva said, just to make Grace smile.

* * *

Back at work two hours later, Eva flipped a plastic chip in her hand. Grace had lost fifty pounds and was still betting when Eva extricated herself from the casino. Eva, ever careful, had broken even and then stopped. She spent the last half-hour watching Grace tap the turf of the table and glare with reverential curiosity at the cards in front of her. Every so often Grace had smiled at Eva. It was an insincere smile, Eva thought, but conspiratorial.

Eva could feel her heart beating a little too fast, so to calm herself down she summoned up a mental image of Sophia, the bony-faced magician's assistant from her grandma's story, sitting just beyond the curtains across the road in the Scorpio, perhaps cross-legged on the floor with a bunny rabbit in her lap or asleep with her thin face on her knees in the corner of a room full of doves and flowers. Every so often, perhaps, a daisy or a rose or a gold coin or a playing card would appear around her. Sometimes a whole bunch of blooming red roses would appear at her bare feet, or a snake or a man's Rolex or a wedding ring. Or an albino rat, or a flock of butterflies. Doves would shudder into the air – white wings solidifying in a blink – and start flying at the windows. Sometimes even another girl would materialize, shaken by the process of disappearance and reappearance, curling her legs, lifting her neck, opening her eyes hesitantly in this new half-world. They'd come from Las Vegas, from Morocco, from Brighton, and open their eyes in Fitzrovia. Sophia would have to explain the situation as others had explained it to her: that they were stuck in limbo, forgotten by their lovers or keepers.

Eva felt the hairs on the back of her neck standing. She imagined that inside the Scorpio Club, the magician's assistant spent all her time thinking about her lover, her magician. Embalmed in magic and surrounded by roses, Sophia thought about her lover so hard that her mind hurt and her palms sweated and the curve where her eyeballs slotted into their sockets burned. the Scorpio Club smelt of bird shit and feathers and red roses. Doves flew at the walls and snakes slithered at her toes, but Sophia hardly noticed them. She missed him and felt the absence like a stomach ache.

* * *

When Eva got back from work that day, she listened to a message on her mobile from Luke: he would be working late because he had a big court date with the money-laundering case scheduled for the following morning. Tired from her odd lunch with Grace, Eva watched Regina in close up, grossly intimate on Luke's flat-screen television. Three weeks after the eagle's dramatic escape from London Zoo, she was still "at large" in London, huddled in trees or riding currents of air over Regent's Park. As she flew off screen, in Silver Place a moth seemed to take over where Regina left off and launched from behind the television towards the ceiling. Eva had put moth traps all around the flat and she could swear the smell in there was no longer just mothballs and damp, but something weirder: persistence and sweetness. As the camera zoomed in on Regina, her eagle face glanced left and then right with a flick of her vicious hooked beak, twitching slightly and shaking her feathers to smooth them, then breaking into an almighty yawn. She appeared both stoic and dignified on the television. *"Pairs mate for life in the wild, that's true, using just one nest site year after year. Wonderful aerial courtship displays are performed,"* a zookeeper explained on the TV while footage appeared of Regina's wings arching, not flapping but rolling muscles under her feathers, then skimming so close to the keeper that it was almost an attack. With a sharp flap – revelling in her freedom – she launched off the earth and into the sky.

Eva thumbed a couple of her grandmother's magic books from the shelves while she watched Regina: she flicked through *Escape! The Life of Great Illusionists* and *Miracle Makers and Their Methods*. Then she opened up *Magical Rope Ties and Escapes*, which had black-and-white drawings and step-by-step instructions to all sorts of tricks, such as "The Revenge Tie" and "The Tom Fool Knot". Eva shivered and took the book next door to read in the bath.

She sat in the blueness of the tub without moving or washing herself or reading her grandmother's book, instead looking absently at her body while the television presenter chirped on about a group of protesters who were campaigning to get Regina's mate, Goldie, released from the zoo. Then the presenter spoke about the rain and wars in Africa, and a bus bomb in Turkey. A moth flew at one of the traps next to the bath and caught its wing on the yellow glue, struggling for a while and then falling limp. Other moths, presumably the females being ignored for their strong chemical rivals, pockmarked the bathroom walls or lay wetly dead in the corners of the bathtub. It would be good to just lie in the bath for hours or, better yet, be asleep for as long as possible. Eva hadn't realized how little Luke liked sleep before he moved in. Even though they'd been seeing each other every few days for two years, going on holidays together, thinking of themselves as co-existent and connected, they hadn't really understood each other's basic patterns until the burst-pipe accident had forced him to Eva's door. No wonder he had seizures, Eva thought. She'd probably have seizures, too, if she slept at little as Luke did.

"You can sleep when you're dead," Luke would say, now they lived together and Eva was frequently napping.

"But you won't enjoy it then," Eva would reply. Luke didn't understand. Eva loved climbing into bed, and the luxury of slowly sinking into non-existence. She enjoyed the low-lying fuzz between wakefulness and sleep where thoughts took on new forms and forgotten ideas rose through the bog in a way she could only half-control. She enjoyed dreaming, but most of all she liked the thoughtful pre-sleep layer of half-dreaming. By contrast Luke liked staying up with glassy eyes locked on his computer screen or the television until his fingers shook from caffeine and exhaustion. He only came to bed when he was a stage beyond tired – the logic being, perhaps, that he didn't like being half-hearted about things: he would like to be either asleep or awake, not in some world in between. Or perhaps he just didn't enjoy sleeping. When he was awake, he never stopped moving – and he wasn't that much better when asleep. Awake, he paced, typed, cleaned, worked. Asleep he tossed, turned, mumbled, dreamed. In both states there was a sense of expendable energy pouring off him, being constantly generated and shrugged off. He was a very deep sleeper, but sometimes he'd wake up all of a sudden, his body stiffening and his big body sitting upright, in the early hours of the morning. Once or twice she'd thought he was having a seizure, but it was just bad dreams. If Eva reached out to touch him he was often slick with sweat, but she expected (with a sense of guilt) to be sleeping through his nightmares most of the time. Every so often she'd wake up to an empty bed and hear Luke in the kitchen at three a.m. or see him moving around in the room, even though she hadn't really woken up enough to gauge how scary his dream had been. He was not a man you would expect to be plagued with night terrors – he was so solid-looking, so firm in his views, he held his umbrella so straight above his head, yet his nightmares were terrible.

Because Eva went to sleep before he did and he woke up before she did, that summer when Luke moved in they developed a peculiar habit of having sex in the middle of the night, almost unconscious, quiet in the darkness, and not mentioning it the next day. He never dared wake Eva when he climbed into bed late at night, but hours later, through the layers of sleep, she was happy to have a hand reach over to her skin, and she'd react, half-asleep, turning or lifting or doing whatever was required to end up in some position where they'd slot together at last. It probably didn't bode well that most of the sex, that summer, was semi-unconscious.

* * *

Eva woke up to the doorbell ringing. Luke was deeply asleep and snoring next to her. Eva remembered watching Regina on the television and lying in bed thinking about eagles and moths, but she didn't remember hearing Luke come home, so she must have been slumbering since early evening. The doorbell rang again – twice in quick succession – and she pulled the cool outside hem of her duvet through between her fingers. Luke stirred as she eased herself off the bed, toes wriggling awake on the carpet. She shivered in a pair of shorts and one of Luke's old T-shirts, treading over to the intercom.

"Hello?"

"I've drunk too much," came a voice through the mouth-piece. Eva hesitated, baffled. She rubbed her eyes.

"Sorry?" Eva said, waking up a little. Through the living-room door she could see Luke's papers and Post-it notes laid out with precision on the table, so he must have kept working even after he got home.

"Can I come up?" said the voice. "I can't find a cab any-where, and it's raining. Justin and I had a huge argument."

"It's four in the morning," said Eva. She couldn't re-member telling Grace her address, but then it had been a distracting afternoon.

"Just for five minutes."

"My boyfriend's asleep, so you have to be quiet," Eva said through the intercom. She pressed "unlock" and heard Grace push through the front door of the building into the communal stairwell, four floors below her flat.

Behind Eva, a floorboard creaked and Luke appeared from the bedroom wearing tracksuit bottoms. "Who is it?" he said sleepily from the doorway. "It's late."

"Sorry," said Eva. "Go back to bed, I'll be there in ten minutes."

"Who is it, though?"

"It's the girl I had dinner with the other day," Eva said as she made her way down the white stairs of the flat. "She can't find a cab."

"The girl you had dinner with?" said Luke. The stairs' handrail curved to the left at the top, creating a balcony from where Luke could look down on the tiny entrance hall.

"Friday last week." Eva opened the door to wait for the unsteady sounds of heels on carpet. She flicked the stairway light for Grace. "The night you had a seizure?" Eva said, tipping her head up to look at Luke.

"I thought you weren't going to see her again?"

Eva shrugged.

"I don't want her here," said Luke. "Tell her to leave."

"She's coming up – she can't get a cab." Grace's footsteps padded on the landing one floor below. "She'll be gone in ten minutes – I promise we won't keep you up. Just go back to bed and ignore us."

"Tell her to go home," said Luke.

"Why?" said Eva. "She's drunk. I'll just call her a cab."

"She's not your friend. Get her to go home."

93

But Grace had already appeared on the fourth-floor staircase and Eva was smiling at her. She was dressed like someone who'd survived from The Titanic, wearing a black sequin dress with wrists covered in coloured bangles.

"Hi," Eva said to Grace, whose hair was pinned up as it had been in Chinatown, although the bun had slipped down her neck. Pins hung from stray strands of wet hair, and she'd spilt red wine on her bare legs and beige shoes. Her make-up was all smudged.

"I'm so sorry to wake you up," Grace slurred, making it to the top of the red-carpeted staircase and pausing under a dusty light bulb on the landing outside Eva's front door. "I know we hardly know each other really, but I just thought because we hung out..." She trailed off.

"What happened?" said Eva, aware that Luke was listening above.

"I met up with Justin, and I was totally right. He ended it, and then I went to a party, but I got..." Grace paused.

"Drunk?" Eva suggested, feeling sorry for Grace's rained-on, bedraggled face.

"Drunk," Grace confirmed. "I'm sorry to turn up here like this. I know it's late."

"Don't worry about it." Eva stepped backwards into the flat. She turned to allow Grace into the first-floor hallway. Luke wasn't there any more. Grace followed Eva up into the corridor. Luke was outside the living-room door now, leaning on its frame with his BlackBerry in his hand.

"I'm going to call her a cab," said Luke, without introducing himself to Grace or waiting for an introduction.

He hardly even looked at her, just turned his back to them, moving into the living room.

"Sorry about him," said Eva, a bit confused, and defended his rudeness to her guest. "He has a big court case tomorrow." With a tired smile she motioned for Grace to follow her into the kitchen. She put the kettle on, while Grace bent down to slip off her stilettos. Her nose was dripping, and she sniffed as she kicked her shoes across the kitchen, then stretched out her toes and picked up one of the empty mugs Eva had ready for tea.

"The cab will be here in five," Luke said from the other room, and Grace's mug dropped immediately from her hands to the floor, smashing into pieces around her bare feet. Both girls jumped. Luke put his head around the kitchen door.

"Oh fuck," Grace said, but she was smiling. Luke said nothing.

"Don't worry," said Eva.

"Sorry, honey," Grace said.

"Mind your toes," said Eva, reaching under the sink for a dustpan and brush to clean up around Grace's feet. Grace had fluff between her toes, perhaps from black tights she'd discarded for some reason earlier in the evening. Eva could smell her friend – feet recently released from nylon, alcohol, warm skin. Grace wiggled her unpainted toes and stood very still while Eva cleared up around her.

"Sorry," Grace said again.

"It was ugly," said Eva. "Glad to be rid of it."

The kettle fumed and Eva stood up. She got out another mug, poured them both a cup of tea and added milk. Grace ran her fingers through her hair. She sniffed and wiped her running nose with the back of her hand, then reached for the mug.

"Her cab's here," said Luke, appearing again in the kitchen doorway, holding his BlackBerry. A moment later, the bell rang. "I think your friend should go."

"But she can hardly stand up," said Eva. "Let her drink her tea and I'll call her a cab in a few minutes, when she's sobered up. Tell the cab to go away."

"Yeah, Luke," said Grace, shooting a slurred smile in his direction. "We'll be as quiet as mice," she whispered at him. "Scout's honour."

"I'm sorry, but I have a big day in court tomorrow," said Luke. "I'd rather she went home."

"I promise I won't make a scene, if you let me stay," said Grace, her lower lip protruding as if in a sulk. "You heard your girlfriend, I'm too drunk to go home. If you send me away I'll just sit on your doorstep till the morning."

Luke hesitated, and then turned sharply away from the kitchen. He didn't go back into the bedroom, but into the sitting room. Grace, wide-eyed, broke into a light giggle.

Eva went into the bathroom to fetch her guest some toilet paper for her running nose, which she kept wiping with her hand. Grace followed her, crouched over the toilet and peed while Eva turned away, unsure where to look. The last time anyone had done that in front of her was in pre-school.

"Do you think Luke would go mad if I had a bath?" said Grace, still peeing. "It's always the best cure when you're fucked."

Eva looked over her shoulder towards the living room, then back at Grace as she pulled her knickers up. "Just ignore him," said Eva. She reached over to turn on the bath taps and then she went out to find a clean towel. When she came back into the bathroom, Grace was easing her bangles off her wrists one by one and piling them in the sink.

"Will you stay with me a second?" Grace stepped into the half-full bathtub while the water was still running, with her clothes still on. Already ankle-deep in the bath water, she dragged her dress up over her body and sat down in the bath. The bathroom lights were off, and in the half-darkness, with only the glow from the street lamp outside the window to illuminate her, Grace appeared as slick as an eel in the blue water. Her ribs were pronounced under tanned skin and her lips were dry.

"Do you mind just sitting with me?" Grace whispered. "I like you. You make me feel calm. I'll just be a minute. I'll be sober soon." The water ran over Grace's legs, and Eva sat on the closed toilet seat, thinking about the magician's assistant in limbo, surrounded by snakes and doves. She had a sense of synergy, of unexpected or unwelcome intimacy.

"So what happened?" Eva said, switching on the mirror light. Grace's pupils were fat to bursting, with only a thin layer of brown iris around the black centre.

"Just what I thought. He was fed up. It's not you, it's me – except really it's you." Grace looked away, at her hands in the bath water, then around the room. "You're so funny, you have a *London Review of Books* on the bath shelf. I can just imagine you reading it in the bath," Grace whispered. Above the bath, opposite the tap, were three shelves full of glutinous bath products and old make-up. A crinkled *LRB* had been up there for ages, folded at the back. "You guys are messy," Grace said, dislodging the wrinkled newspaper from its home.

"I'm messy," said Eva. "And dragging Luke down with me."

Grace flipped from page to page, and stopped at the classifieds. "*New Yorker (smart, beautiful, funny),*" she read, "*seeks man (smart, handsome, funny) who also lives in New York and reads the LRB to do all the usual things people do when they fall in love in the Big Apple. Woman, 45.*" Grace paused. "*Active, attractive lady (32),*" she continued "*curvy, broad-minded, very cultured and refined, seeks attentive benefactors for the pursuit and realization of mutually interesting projects.*"

"Fat girl seeks cash," Eva said.

"This is going to be me," Grace whispered. "*I celebrated my fortieth birthday last week by cataloguing my collection of bird feeders. Next year I'm hoping for alternative activities. And a cake. Join my invite mailing list at box no. 6831. Man, 65*"

"Sex *and* cake is just greedy," said Eva.

"*If I could be anywhere in time right now, it would be 17th December 1972. I have my reasons. Man, 57. Box no. 1553.*"

"Where would you be?" asked Eva.

"I don't know," said Grace, letting the *LRB* drop by the side of the bath. "I can't get over how miserable I feel all the time. I'm OK when people are around, mostly, but when I'm alone I just feel so *sad* – so guilty. If I could be at any point in time, I'd still be a child. Young. Ten years old. That's when I was happy. We were all happy then."

"Why do you feel guilty?"

Grace shrugged. In the pale light, with the blue tiles and blue bubbly water, her skin looked translucent. Eva had a sense that Grace was inflatable – the bath, and the water, all Eva's shower products and sponges – it could all deflate with a pin. Grace could deflate, too, if you stuck a pin in her mouth above the green water.

"Did you play netball?" Grace whispered to Eva after a pause. "At school?"

"I was a goalkeeper."

"Course you were, honey. I was centre."

"Course you were."

"Reading the *London Review of Books* in the bath and defining our characters by school netball positions." Grace smiled and dunked her head under the bath water, the shiny contours of her body rising above the water surface and then sinking again as her face re-emerged and she yawned. She tucked a strand of wet blond hair behind her ear and said:

"What are the yellow things?"

"Moth traps," said Eva.

"*Of course*," smiled Grace, arching her eyebrows. "Can Luke hear what we're saying from the other room?" she added.

"Nah, we've been quiet," said Eva. "Don't worry. Anyway he's probably working in there. He has the concentration of a Buddha."

"Yeah," said Grace, then paused. "I guess I should get a cab now."

"You're welcome to sleep in the spare room if you like," Eva said, hoping Grace wouldn't accept, but pitying her enough to ask.

"I'm really sorry," said Grace. "I'm sorry for everything."

"It's not a big deal at all," said Eva, and she meant it. Grace's lips were vaporous, almost the same colour as her perfectly straight, oversized teeth. She appeared as a ghost version of herself, a sketch without the colour filled in yet.

"You've been really nice."

"No problem."

"The water's all cold now," said Grace. "Is there anything worse than cold bath water?" She looked up at Eva with unblinking eyes. Light was beginning to stream though the window, and Eva could see the speckled growth of hair between Grace's legs, the dark moon-surface skin of her nipples and the dry skin on her neck.

"Will you call me a cab?" said Grace. "I'll get out of the bath."

"Sure."

Eva went to the bedroom, picked her phone from the side table and sat down on the bed, listening to the bath water gurgle down the antique plumbing of the building. Eva was about to call a minicab number when she heard the bathroom door open outside in the hall. She got up off the bed as her friend said something out in the hallway. She stepped towards the door, about to ask her to come into the bedroom, but when she looked into the hallway Luke had come out of the living room and was opposite Grace, who stood with her back to Eva.

Grace had just said something to Luke – whispered it – and in response he put his hand roughly on her upper arm. The spine-tracing zip of her dress hung open in a floppy Y, not done up yet. The curve of her backside was only just covered by the glinting material of her skirt, riding up or not yanked down properly.

Eva couldn't see Grace's expression, just Luke's frozen lips and sunken eyebrows glaring down at her friend as his hand gripped the bare pinkish skin of her arm.

"Get your hand off me," Grace said. As he let go, her long wet legs stumbled backwards a couple of steps in Eva's direction. She then steadied herself.

"Luke," Eva said, walking towards them. Grace didn't take her eyes off Luke's: she picked up her shoes, pulled the belt of her raincoat around her waist and hurried down the steps. She didn't say goodbye, just ran out of the flat as quickly as possible, while Eva stood at the top. The door to the flat slammed first, then the front door. Silence descended, a sudden suction of energy, and all Eva could hear were the last creaks of bath water falling through the pipes.

Before saying anything, Eva went to the living-room window and peered out at Grace as she walked off un-balanced, first barefoot, and then slipping her shoes on against a lamp-post. It was drizzling outside, a scum of liquid blurring the early-morning light. Bath water steam and rainwater had loosened Grace's straight hair into frizz around her eyes, so that she looked like some tropical animal. She reminded Eva of a flamingo, balanced there for a moment on one leg — and Eva realized that she'd had this same thought before. Her breath made a cloud on the glass of the living-room window, which expanded and contracted.

"She's an old friend from Devon," Luke said behind her.

"Why didn't you tell me as soon as she came in?" she said quietly, watching Grace disappear off into Soho.

"Her parents ran the farm nearest my dad's farm in Devon, so we were friends – sort of – growing up. We bumped into each other for the first time in years at Catherine's engagement, and since then she keeps trying to get in contact."

"She was the girl you were talking to outside the pub, in the red jacket?"

"Yeah, yeah. You saw me talking to her?"

"Yes."

"Why didn't you say anything?"

"I thought if it was important you'd mention it."

"It wasn't important. She's an old friend, not someone I get on with too well or particularly wanted to be talking to."

"You're not surprised that she and I have been spending time together?"

"That night you had dinner with her. I came to the restaurant and saw you through the window. That's why I didn't come in. She wanted me to walk in and be shocked, so I didn't give her the satisfaction."

"You didn't mention that either."

"I did to her. I told her to back off," said Luke, opening up his palms and gesturing around the flat as if Grace were still there, invisible in the room. "She was always a nightmare. Nightmare kid, nightmare teenager."

"She was with you the first time you came to look at this place," said Eva. "Her hair was black then, not blond."

"I'd forgotten that." Luke shrugged. "We kept in touch for a while. On and off. Our fathers are friends."

"You said she was your sister that night."

"She's not my sister," said Luke, then forced himself to smile. "I said that to make clear she wasn't a girlfriend. So you'd come out to dinner with me."

"Why didn't you tell me you knew her as soon as she came up the stairs?"

"Because of all *this*," Luke said with an exasperated tone. "Making friends with you and turning up here. She's a drama queen, she thinks the world spins around her. She just wants to make a scene. I didn't want to give her the opportunity."

"That didn't work out too well," said Eva. She touched the window pane behind her with her knuckles, and it was cold. The sky above Soho was beginning to glow pink behind them. Cars were buzzing in the distance, a police car's siren faded. "What was she saying to you before you grabbed her arm?"

"She said you were lovely." Luke scratched his chin.

"Lovely?"

"Yes." In the dark of the flat the moths were ramming against the window, trying to get to the light of the street lamps and the neon of The Pink Angel.

Eva turned to face the window. On the cobbled street below, a tabby cat roused and yawned in a doorway, her paws outstretched as if readying herself to attack the raindrops.

* * *

Neither Eva nor Luke fell asleep again that night, but they lay side by side listening to each other breathe while rain fell on the roof. There is something particularly repulsive about mutual insomnia, when you're not awake enough to talk to the person you are in bed with, or calm enough to dream. You just lie there trying not to wriggle, guessing what the other person is worrying about. Her eyes firmly closed, Eva imagined Sophia, the bony-faced magician's assistant taking a bath in the parallel universe opposite Echo Books: an unreal expression on her damp face as steam blurred her features. In Eva's imagination, Sophia slipped her arid fingers under the water, surrounded by bunches of roses that appeared with strong arched petals trapping summer smells, but soon turned into potpourri on their stalks. Sophia's fingers had always been worryingly adept at sleights of hand. As a child they'd itched to tease cufflinks out of shirt cuffs or pinch any wallet with the flick of her wrist and the aid of a distracting smile. As if this wasn't enough talent for one girl, Sophia had an origami body that could fold itself into the smallest of spaces to hide. Even her parents agreed that there was something unnerving about the conspiratorial way she smiled to herself as she walked down the street, or made desert flowers disappear with a blink of her big eyes. The only person who ever understood Sophia, growing up, was a boy who came through her village with the circus one summer: Dante taught her to make a dove appear out of thin air, to turn the dove into a rabbit, and to make the rabbit disappear.

In the bathtub of the Scorpio Club's parallel universe, remembering her lover and their first summer together, magic-eyed Sophia started to cry. She lowered her head under the bath water to try and stop herself, but huge, inelegant teardrops crawled down her face and got stuck in the edges of her mouth before plopping into the bath.

Nearby, the rabbit, oblivious, licked her little black paws on the window ledge.

The story of Sophia and Dante didn't help Eva to fall asleep. Eva kept listening to Luke's breathing, wondering what he was thinking about, and she couldn't stop the flood of Sophia's imaginary tears from making puddles in her mind. Telling herself stories when she couldn't sleep was a habit Eva picked up when she was twelve years old in Bali, during a winter when her father wasn't around much and her mother spent all her time biting her fingers till they bled, staring into space as if looking for something in another world. In Soho her grandma would have told Eva stories, but Eva's mother wasn't into that sort of thing. Her bedroom was next to her mother's in Bali, and at night she could hear her shuffling and crying, so instead of sleeping Eva started getting books out of the library to read through the night, or making up her own stories. Later she discovered her mother had had a miscarriage that winter, but at the time Eva didn't know what was going on. Perhaps if Eva had had a brother or sister, things would have been different. As Grace had pointed out, she never had to learn to share her crayons. Human interaction wasn't always one of her skills.

That winter in Bali was so humid that even at night, with a fan on, the pages of Eva's library books were moist when she turned them. She read *Vanity Fair*: "Come, children, let us shut up the box and the puppets, for our play is played out". And she read *The Wings of the Dove:* "We shall never be again as we were!"

"And how do people perform that ceremony of parting, Jane?" Mr Rochester says to Jane Eyre. "Teach me – I'm not quite up to it." "They say farewell, or any other form they prefer," replies Jane. "Then, say it." "Farewell, Mr Rochester, for the present," says Jane.

And *Gone with the Wind*: "I was never one to patiently pick up broken fragments and glue them together and tell myself that the mended whole was as good as new," Rhett says to Scarlet. "What is broken is broken."

That sleepless winter Eva read *To Kill a Mockingbird* and *The Bell Jar* and *Lolita*: "One last word," Humbert-Humbert says desperately when he finds Lolita all bloated and barefoot near the end. "Are you quite quite quite sure that – well, not tomorrow, of course, and not after tomorrow, but – well – someday, you will not come to live with me?"

"No," Lolita says, smiling. "No."

* * *

The third boy Eva had ever left was probably the first one she had loved. Aden was a perpetual academic ten years her senior. She'd broken up with him on the steps of St Paul's Cathedral. She'd been with him for six months – a personal record at the time – and leaving him was the closest Eva had ever got to the endings of the novels she read in Bali and some of the parting scenes in the romances she later worked on as an editor. In the novels she edited there was always some passionate goodbye around two thirds through the book. Chambermaids did it before being sent to nunneries to have the bastard babies of princes, werewolves did it in alleys with vampires they were forbidden to love, Greek gods did it with mortals and tycoons did it with secretaries during snowstorms outside opera houses. Tears *raged*, the threat of absence *burned*, fingers *dug desperately* into flesh, refusing to let go. Eva did it with Aden while smoking Lucky Strike cigarettes on the steps of St Paul's, and she touched him like a blind girl memorizing a poem. She counted the freckles on his hand and loved him more than she could imagine ever loving another person. She couldn't remember much about the first time they kissed or made love, but she did recall every minute detail of the last moment, from the rip in his trousers at the knee to the smoky smell of his skin as she held him. She remembered how he stared off to the side when she said she wasn't happy any more.

"I can't make you happy," he repeated, more to himself than to her, while still staring at the steps of the church rather than at her. "But is there anyone else?"

"No," Eva said. She broke up with him because he was at a different stage of life to her, wanting a more solid world, while she was only just discovering the world she might want. He was jealous, their wires constantly crossing and uncrossing and causing trouble. However, after she left him she didn't remember any of that. They wrote more emails to each other in the two weeks after the end than the six previous months. The slow tear of their lives breaking free of each other, the unravelling of it, was undoubtedly pleasurable: it made her skin tingle. She had felt giddy and gleeful once he was gone, as if she could fly. The tighter the grip, the more relief the escape was, perhaps.

* * *

The morning after Grace's appearance at Silver Place, the rain let up for a few hours and Eva walked to work without an umbrella. Soho was always washed out and somehow a little baffled at each new dawn. Office workers had their coat collars pulled up against the hints of last night, still there if you look – a shoe, a smashed beer bottle, a club flyer in the gutter. On the front cover of *Metro* was a photograph of Regina's knife-like feathers spread out as she attacked an oblivious white duck. Eva tore the page out from the newspaper, stuffing it in the pocket of her jacket where the other article about Regina was still folded among tissues and pennies and a five-pound chip from The Golden Gate Casino.

Outside Echo Books, three road-workers were digging up the pavement with a huge drill and the air was full of concrete dust. In the office entrance hall a loose piece of carpet was held down by a five-hundred-page brick of a novel called *The Paradise Motel*, and a pile of envelopes containing a book called *Champagne Surrender* were waiting to go out for review. Eva mumbled good morning to her boss, who was hidden in her lair to the left of the stairway. She came from an era before "Health and Safety", so she still chain-smoked in her office, a haze of grey around the edges of her door. The office next to the boss was the marketing manager's tidy room that smelt of rose-scented candles to mask the book dust and cigarette smoke. The marketing manager was talking on the phone about a romantic-novel festival in Cornwall where half of Echo's authors were going to be speaking soon. Events included "The History of Werewolves in Western Literature" and "How to Build a Man in Five Easy Steps".

Her office door was wedged open with yet more novels: *Recipes for a Broken Heart, Only Fools Fall in Love, The Scent of Hatred*. The corkboard in front of her desk was covered in dark-eyed men and rosy-cheeked women looking seductively over their shoulders with pouting mouths. Eva didn't really know how the covers came into being. They had two designers in Jersey who churned them out, presumably buying the photographs from some picture library on the net and then Photoshopping different backgrounds, although Eva liked to think of the designers taking the photos themselves, perhaps in some sort of kinky basement studio full of ball gowns, cat suits, vampire teeth and backdrops involving beaches, burning fireplaces, the sea and red silk-covered four-poster beds. Four huge boxes of first proofs were waiting for the recycling bin, but they'd been there for so long now that they were almost part of the furniture. Eva stepped over the boxes, twisted one of three wheelie chairs where she kept yet more papers and sat down in front of a book she'd just started editing, called *The Pirate's Mistress*. It looked uninviting that morning with its tiny type flanked by clusters of red squiggles along the margins. "Serenity coyly wiped her sweating hand on the thin material of her nightdress, which hung over the contours of her luscious thighs and undulated flirtatiously in the moonlight." Eva picked up her red pen to change Serenity's "gleaming violet eyes" to "gleaming azure eyes" to ensure that they matched the colour of the character's eyes in the rest of the text, but was interrupted by the drill beginning again under her window. She yawned and put her head in her hands with her elbows on either side of the manuscript. "Serenity could feel goose bumps rise on her alabaster neck." An old coffee cup was growing mould next to Eva's computer. She ought to go downstairs and clean it. "Tremors shuddered through Serenity's body, and her gaze lingered at the doorway of her bedchamber."

Eva took her head out of her hands and glanced out of the window at the Scorpio Club, with its shadowy rows of windows. She thought of Grace's pronounced ribs in the bath, her dilated eyes and chapped lips. She thought of Luke perhaps touching the skin stretched over her ladder of bones, feeling them one by one, maybe kissing Grace's large mouth, her slight body, the curve of her neck as she leant up to whisper something in his ear. In the early light of that morning, while Luke dressed in his grey suit and skinny tie, neither of them had mentioned Grace. He had kissed Eva's forehead, tied his shoelaces and eaten toast as he spoke to his secretary about a change of courtrooms. Then, after picking up his trolley bag with his barrister costume, had gone off to work, leaving Eva to shower in the bath that still probably had bits of Grace in it, her skin and smell.

"Serenity hungered for her lover. As she climbed shakily to her feet, tears stung bitterly in her eyes, and she itched for this beguiling moment of connection..."

In the half-dreams as she lay awake earlier that morning, Eva had left the magician's assistant lying sobbing in the imaginary bath of the Scorpio Club. If Sophia had kept crying like that for the past few hours, then perhaps the bath water would be overflowing by now, bubbles of soap and dissolved soft skin flowing over the edge of the tub, spreading far out into the hallway as blissed-out snakes slunk from behind curtains or cupboard doors to roll in the wetness and a few doleful rabbits padded around with soggy paws to see what was going on. White doves flew in circles above the flood. Bunches of roses lifted from the floor and bobbed on the liquid.

"Stop crying! Stop crying!" voices shouted, but Sophia was sobbing so hard that she couldn't have stopped if she wanted to. While the magician's assistant cried in the bath of the Scorpio, nobody in the other dimensions of reality – the office workers and builders and editors and shop assistants and tourists on Goodge Street – noticed that the club seemed to be sweating. The bouncer outside the front door continued to chain-smoke on his stool, not hearing the hubbub inside the building or realizing that he was ashing in a half-inch trickle of soapy liquid sliding over the pavement, with the occasional playing card slipping by his feet towards the gutter in the road. It was only when he stubbed out his cigarette that he noticed an ace of spades had skimmed out under the front door, followed by a few already half-dead rose petals curled at the edges.

The bouncer frowned even more than usual as he thought he heard a noise inside the club – a wail, or a scream? He reached for the front door's handle, opening it just slightly to peak through, but in the process releasing a calf-high tide of liquid carrying with it a wet white rabbit.

The bunny landed a few yards to the right, outside a hairdresser's, and lolloping ungracefully, shocked by daylight and dampness, turned her squat little head left and then right with a dim-witted expression on her furry face, as if trying to decide whether it would be better to escape towards Tottenham Court Road or Charlotte Street. Before the rabbit made her decision, the bouncer scooped her up in his arms. Pinned to his chest, she felt his sigh of relief, but did not share it.

The phone rang in Eva's office, interrupting her thoughts of flood and magic. An author wanted to talk about her word count, and Eva answered vaguely, interjecting a "yes" or a "no" when it was needed. While the author chatted on, Eva summoned a mental image of Grace across the room in Brooks's Club three weeks ago – how her lips had been painted the exact same colour as the flowers on her long-sleeved dress and how she'd been fidgeting from foot to foot, constantly tucking her hair behind her ears. Grace had been talking to the author next to a table covered with piles of his book, whose title Eva struggled to remember. *Foreign Bodies*? *Affairs*? *Lives*? Eva keyed "Foreign Bodies" into Amazon and found a book of medical short stories and a non-fiction history of American foreign policy. She changed the word "Bodies" to "Affairs", and the cover of the journalist's collection of columns came up. Grace had said she was doing the publicity for the book, and sure enough, when Eva went to the publisher's website, at the bottom of the webpage it said: "Press enquiries: Grace.Taylor@Spidermedia.co.uk". Spider Media appeared to be a public-relations agency who worked mostly with arts and publishing clients.

It was eleven o'clock already, and Eva had only read two pages of *The Pirate's Mistress*. Across the bridge in Southwark, Luke would have been in session for an hour and a half. Court started at nine thirty each morning and two most afternoons. Eva tried to visualize Luke's face topped with his scrappy horsehair wig, those ringlets hooped around his frown-wrinkled forehead. He looked more ridiculous than most in his wig on account of his spiky black hair, which put up a constant fight against the foreign white stuff on his head. Eva shoved *The Pirate's Mistress* into her bag and told her boss she was going to work from home because of the noise from the pavement. Echo was so hectic that nobody usually minded the hours she worked, as long as the books didn't have any typos and were delivered on time.

Eva headed up Portland Place into Regent's Park in the drizzling rain, and she thought of Luke calling Regina a "flirt" for swooping as she had done three weeks ago when they'd walked, hung over, through the park. Then four days later: "I really have to get back to this stupid party. I'm waiting for someone," Eva had listened to Grace say inside the toilet cubicle at Brooks's. The thought of Grace waiting for her to arrive at the party, of specifically inviting her, made Eva feel queasy.

Midday on a Wednesday, the park was empty except for the occasional mother with a baby and elderly couples walking their dogs. Eva turned left off York Bridge towards the back of the lake, a sagging grey sky hanging overhead. Mallards with peacock-blue helmets crouched in the grass and knobbly-kneed herons paddled in shallow water near the shore. As she followed the riverbed up past Winfield House, a few lonely blue rowing boats came into view with heads and shoulders peeking up over the sides, wearing rainproof coats under umbrellas. A flock of seagulls rose up abruptly and ruffled the water, making for a nearby island. One of the birds scrolled down for a landing on the football pitch. With its black-tipped wings and outstretched tapered nose, the gull resembled a small aeroplane.

Once or twice a year, Eva met her father at the Renaissance Hotel near Heathrow for dinner in the restaurant overlooking a runway where Shanghai Airlines landed and took off. She'd nurse a drink and watch the gaggles of white jets congregating on the tarmac or queuing for their turn to lift off into the clouds. Her father didn't fly planes any more, but he was part of the management team, so he still travelled a lot. Dinner with him was usually strained. He shifted in his seat, demanding more salt or different condiments or more ice in his whisky, or less, and rarely asked anything other than rudimentary questions about his daughter's life in London. He was a fidgeter: he lit cigarettes he didn't finish smoking, tapped his foot against the floor. If he did ask about something, he'd interrupt with a comment or another question halfway through the answer. Business travellers laughed around them, big groups shared bottles of wine, while Eva and her father watched aeroplanes landing or taking off and he told her things she didn't want to know about engines and fluid mechanics.

When Eva's mother came to London, which happened from time to time, dinner was even stranger, because her mother would stare at her husband while he shifted and wriggled and looked at the planes. After years of saying goodbye to her husband, when he was in her sight she watched him as if he might just disappear if she was careless enough to blink. Every time Eva saw her mother, she seemed smaller, a human forged out of some insubstantial matter that was drifting away. Eva assumed that her mother had been on antidepressants ever since that winter in Bali, when she stayed in bed without sleeping for a month. She spoke so quietly, almost in a tone of reproach, as if each sound was crossing a void to reach its destination. Her movements were slow, too, as were her thoughts. She walked as if she had no spine, as if she needed someone to hold her up at every step.

In Regent's Park another flock of seagulls lifted up into the sky. As Eva turned the corner onto the bridge over the lake, Eva spotted a crowd of people in the dip behind a wall of trees. "REGINA FLY AWAY!" said a sign held aloft by a woman with dreadlocks. Did this woman expect the bird to heed advice crayoned in capital letters onto a piece of cardboard box? Surrounding the neck of the bridge were four empty football pitches, and among the trees to the left of the path several hundred people stood with binoculars and cameras.

"Where is she?" Eva asked a small boy with a pudding-bowl haircut standing at his father's heels and squinting into the sky.

"We saw her an hour ago," said the boy. "Don't know where she's gone now. Maybe she's flying home."

"Home to the zoo or home to Canada? Isn't she from Canada?" said Eva, looking up and thinking about watching fireworks with Luke up on Primrose Hill the first year they were together.

"If I was her I'd go to the beach," said the kid. "I really like the beach."

"That's a good idea," said Eva.

"An hour ago they put a bunny down, and the bird didn't come near, because it ate a dog this morning. That's right, *a dog*," the boy said, and grinned to reveal a missing tooth.

"How big?"

"A little dog," the boy said. "But there was blood. That's what someone said."

A camera flashed in the crowd and a hundred chins jolted towards the sky, but there was nothing up there apart from crows, clouds and falling leaves. "Anyone would think she was a miracle. She's just a bird," noted someone in the crowd. A man with a flat cap appeared to be making notes, a tourist in a poncho was thoughtfully eating a sandwich, and in a gap in the crowds Eva noticed that some sort of Japanese news programme was filming.

"Don't you think they should let her go?" the boy with the missing tooth said to his father.

"She won't be captured unless she wants to be," his father replied.

Eva continued plodding on past the Regent's Park Hub, that UFO-shaped café in the middle of the lawns. She kept treading in puddles. She tried to think of the exit scene that followed breaking up with Aden on the steps of St Paul's Cathedral. As rain drizzled down on her neck, she remembered Sam, whom she split up with outside the UCL student library when she was twenty-one. She didn't love Sam. For three or four months the two of them just drank too much together and danced at cheap R&B nights around London. When she went to a party with Sam, she enjoyed herself and didn't constantly wish to go home and

116

take off her shoes – but that was about all she got from the relationship.

Drinking sticky vodka shots and getting hysterical giggles at bus stops came nowhere near the intensity of loving Aden, but Sam enabled her to blow off steam. Loving Aden was a restrained feeling, which aborted before becoming too strong. When Aden had stayed in her student rooms at UCL, she always slept on the tiny single bed while he lay on the floor, but with Sam she'd stumbled into unconsciousness easily, curled in the space left by his big, usually drunk body. Sam coaxed her out at night, to parties where they weren't invited or to clubs she didn't know existed. With Aden she always wanted to achieve something every day – go to a gallery or the cinema or out to dinner – but with Sam she was more than happy to spend all day in bed eating peanut butter with their fingers out of the jar. Letting down her guard with Sam didn't lead anywhere near love, but it was a liberating experience, it gave her a sense of free fall.

She broke up with him because of a hundred little things, not one big problem. There was no cheating or fighting, just a trail of miscommunication: him ringing her doorbell at three a.m. the night before she had an exam, a lamp he broke and never fixed, the way he talked through movies, the way she wouldn't sit through a football game with him and how he ate all her housemates' food whenever he came over and then everyone got angry with her. One day he came to pick her up from the library to take her out to dinner, and he was clearly on some chemical concoction. Eva didn't ask what he'd taken, and didn't mind that he liked the odd pill or line, she just had no desire to sit through the night while he grinned and talked gibberish at her. He stood on a street corner outside UCL library with a puzzled look on his face while she told him she thought they should go their separate ways. He didn't seem to mind much – not that evening while dopamine was bubbling in his mind, not the next day. She didn't miss him, even for a moment.

Despite being at times a little baffled by Luke, when he wasn't there she wished he was. Unlike saying goodbye to Sam and the others, Eva never succeeded in her attempts to leave Luke. The first time Eva left him was a rather un-emotional, but altogether ineffective exit. It happened at a bed & breakfast called The Cleopatra after a wedding in Brighton just two months into their relationship. They'd sat together at the pews as the bride tottered down the aisle in a backless white dress with a lace trail. Eva must have been to weddings before, as a child, but this was her first as an adult, and the first one she'd been to with a boyfriend. There were lots of little bridesmaids with blue ribbons in their hair, and the groom was wearing a blue flower in his jacket, to match the colour scheme. Afterwards they ate smoked salmon and lamb and chocolate mousse in a town hall where the tables appeared dwarfed by giant centrepieces made of delphiniums and palm leaves.

"Lovely wedding," said Luke once they were lying on their B&B bed later, eating goodie-bag Love Hearts from a pink organza bag. Eva glanced sideways at him and placed the word "CUDDLE ME" onto her tongue, while Luke didn't look at the words he was eating. Eva ate "YOU'RE SWEET" and let it dissolve. She had assumed they would make fun of the wedding together, once they were alone. Perhaps, Eva had imagined, she would stand in her underwear and pretend to be the groom dancing sheepishly to Ella Fitzgerald's 'I've Got a Crush on You' while Luke hummed, and they'd laugh about the heart-design topiary place-card holders and the receding hairlines of the wedding singers. Eva and Luke were both champagne-drunk and only half dressed already, with equal parts moonlight and car-park light streaming over them from the window. The Cleopatra was twenty minutes from the centre of Brighton, with a window looking out on tarmac. It was decorated with quilted floral bedspreads that clashed with the wallpaper, and it smelt of salty wet dust. Two porcelain dolls in faded lace dresses sat on the wardrobe with their legs splayed open.

"I like weddings," Luke said, eating a Love Heart, "it's such a quaint thing to do, to promise yourself to someone for eternity."

"Unconditionally," Eva added. "It's a bit Old Testament."

"Old Testament?" said Luke.

"Dramatic. Unlikely. Ominous," Eva said. Two months into the relationship, Eva wasn't sure what she felt about Luke. They were still very much at the stage of semi-strangers trying to find out about each other. He was alarmingly good at reading her, not letting her say "I'm fine" when she wasn't, making her laugh when she was sad. But she wasn't sure she wanted to be exposed in front of this lawyer with deep-set grey eyes. She was drawn to and worried by his contradictions, which she spent too much time thinking about. He was territorial and jealous about other men she spent time with, yet he didn't smother her with texts and phone calls. He could be sweet, but once or twice in the last month he'd put his hand over her mouth while they were having sex. Not for long, but it was still strange and unexpected. He had this poker face, as if emotions didn't pass through him, but he woke up in the night after a bad dream. He always got what he wanted, whether it was a case at work or a restaurant booking. She didn't think compromise would suit him. Yet he was kind. It was very confusing.

"Aren't you a romantic one?" said Luke, reaching over the bed to rest his hand on her thigh. "Lucky me. Does this mean I won't see you in white any time?"

"*Unconditionally* to honour, respect and cherish *till death us do part,*" said Eva quickly, sitting up in bed. "There are always conditions, you know? Life is full of conditions. What if he becomes hooked on celebrity porn and she starts eating an entire chocolate cake for breakfast every day?"

"I think you just have to deal with it. Till death and all that," said Luke, which made Eva shudder. *Till death.* Why would anyone want to stand in front of friends and family and agree that they would one day die together? Stand there and face up to how you will, one day, no longer exist. Luke and Eva were both lying on the bed with their heads on the pillows and their hands touching between their bodies, moving every so often to pick up a Love Heart. He looked over at her more than she glanced sideways at him.

"But say she walks into the bedroom to see him crouched over Lindsay Lohan giving head on his computer screen or he walks into the kitchen to see icing drooling down her nightgown and crumbs in her hair – and in that exact moment, just in that exact moment, whatever they've told God at their wedding service, there will be conditions to their respectfulness and honouring."

"I don't mind if you eat chocolate cake for breakfast," said Luke.

"Or go smaller. They're at dinner, and while he's ordering he's staring straight at the waitress's breasts. It's not a big moment, it's not going to ruin their marriage at all, but *in that moment* she will not respect, cherish or honour him. The next moment might be fine, but there are conditions, and she will not respect him for ever."

"They can try."

"I just mean there will be moments of unlove," Eva said, tipsy and too insistent, wanting him to understand. "It won't suddenly be this constant, solid, absolute, unconditional thing because they got married, will it? Nobody can promise that – it doesn't make sense."

"It's hopeful," said Luke, quieter. "That's all."

"So people know they're lying?" She thought of her parents, who didn't seem ever to have anything to say to each other and yet appeared irrationally bound never to quite leave each other. Her father always came back.

"It's not a lie, I don't think. Perhaps it's an aspiration," he said.

"Oh," said Eva. She paused, knowing she shouldn't continue. "But it's like a cult, like you're not really meant to think about it too much or express any dissent, or you're immediately some sort of heretic. Just like you're not allowed to say you don't like dogs."

121

Luke laughed. Then he looked away. The two porcelain dolls on the dresser appeared to be surveying Luke and Eva with querulous blue eyes.

"That's good to know," he said.

"That I don't like dogs?" She stiffened on the bed.

"That's a whole other issue, but I don't see why marriage is so grim. They've promised something grand and hopeful, and all you can think about is how they're going to slip up and fuck up along the way."

"A romantic criminal barrister," Eva said and put a white "SWEET KISS" heart into her mouth, tasting a faint tang of Fairy liquid. She rubbed her eyes and shivered.

"A romance-novel editor who doesn't believe in marriage," he said. "It's not as if I'm asking you to marry me. Don't look so tense."

"Of course not. Just forget it. Let's talk about something else."

"Are we having our first fight?" said Luke. He raised his big eyebrows at her.

"Eat your Love Hearts and be quiet," said Eva, joking, but she felt suddenly restless as she got up off the bed and stepped into the tiny bathroom, just big enough for a toilet, a miniature shower and a plate of complimentary soaps from other hotels: Holiday Inn, Travelodge, Best Western. It wasn't just the conversation about weddings that she found jumpy, but the uneasily compelling energy of the boy she was lying on the bed with. It was as if he filled up the room, and she could feel him thinking about her as if his thoughts were heat. She turned on the shower and stood in the lopsided trickle of water while Luke crashed around in the bedroom hanging up his morning suit. Eva realized that she very much didn't want to sleep in the same bed as him that night. The desire not to be near him just then was strong and childish, like missing the smell of your mother's perfume at sleepovers. She wanted to be outside in the salty air, not trapped inside thick floral wallpaper and damp ceilings with this stranger who was always casting searching glances at her, wanting to know her. She dried her body with a towel the size of a dishcloth – carefully between her toes, behind her ears, the back of her neck, biding her time. She pulled her knickers and bra back on before pushing open the bathroom door and beginning to get dressed in jeans and a jumper while he watched from the bed.

"Where are you going?" said Luke as she turned her back on him to bend and pick up her socks and T-shirt from the floor next to the chair where she'd discarded them before the wedding earlier that evening.

"I'm going to buy cigarettes."

"At one in the morning?"

"There's a twenty-four-hour Tesco a few blocks up." She didn't look at him.

"Are you angry because I said marriages are hopeful rather than insincere?"

"Course not," snapped Eva. She didn't want his presence so close to her skin. She could feel "them" like an animal wriggling in the room, a completely separate entity from her-without-him and him-without-her. It was potentially engulfing. She didn't want to be a part of that separate thing.

"What just happened?" said Luke, without a trace of emotion on his face. "You were fine a minute ago." His grey eyes didn't blink, his mouth hardly moved. It was quite remarkable how little emotion his face revealed. It was partly the scars on his face that gave the impression that his features were stiller than other faces. His face didn't have the range that others had: it was stiffer. Eva felt a bit sick.

"I *am* fine," she said. "I just want a cigarette."

"You're not fine," Luke told her as he stood in the doorway. She stepped out of the bedroom into a carpeted lobby with more porcelain dolls lined up in cabinets along one wall. They threw jagged shadows out of their glass windows: arms, pigtails, pointy shoes.

"I'll be ten minutes," she said, leaving him in the doorway, and he turned away before she closed The Cleopatra's front door. She was relieved to be away from him. The salty air tasted lovely outside. The cigarettes she found and smoked while sitting on a brick wall tasted even better. She stared up at the stars for a while and broke up with him when she came back from her twenty-minute, four-cigarette walk.

In the doll-lined lobby she stood at the doorway of their room for a minute, and he looked up from his BlackBerry, which he was playing with in bed. Neither of them spoke. Then she sat on the end of the bed with her back to him, her body twisted half towards him at first and then leaning down with her elbows on her knees so she didn't have to face him. She said that she wasn't ready for a relationship, and she was sorry to have let him believe she was. He was sitting up in bed and she stared straight ahead at a crease in the wallpaper, which wasn't like her. She usually ended a relationship head-on, believing that ends were as important as beginnings, if not more so, and ought to be remembered.

She imagined that his eyes didn't flicker and his face remained impassive throughout.

"Seriously?" he said. "You're breaking up with me because of that conversation?"

"Not because of that conversation."

"But you think this is the end?"

"Yes."

"No."

"It's not really your decision," said Eva. They hadn't been going out long enough for high passion. No promises were being broken here. Eva sensed a weight lifting off her as she spoke, the animal of "them" dissolving. She slept deeply in bed next to him that night.

Still not showing any emotion, Luke went to a brunch with the ushers and groomsman the next day, while Eva took the train back to London on her own, watching fields and sheep and towns flash by the window. Eva thought of Audrey Hepburn's tearful goodbye to her lover at the end of *Love in the Afternoon*: "*It always happens to me in railway stations*," she says, wiping away her tears, "*I'm susceptible.*" Eva closed her eyes and focused on the moment Thelma and Louise decide to drive off the cliff: "*Ok then, let's not get caught, let's keep going!*" smiles Geena Davis, cops behind her and nothing but an empty space in front. It made Eva's blood tingle and her pulse thump just thinking about it. Or Butch Cassidy and the Sundance Kid who continue to talk like normal, a different goodbye style but equally poignant, both of them knowing full well they're parting ways for good. Maybe Eva's favourite goodbye, though, was Dr Zhivago's little wave as he puts Lara on her sled in the David Lea film, and then the panicked way he runs up to the top-floor window in order to stretch the ending, desperate to watch her until the exact moment she vanishes over the horizon. "Farewell," Pasternak writes in the novel, "my great one, my own, farewell, my pride, farewell, my swift, deep, dear river, how I loved your daylong splashing, how I loved to plunge into your cold waves…"

The odd thing was, as fields and trees fled past, away from Brighton and from Luke, Eva didn't feel nearly as relieved as she thought she would. Perhaps she did it *wrong* this time, she thought. She wished she could go back and do it *right,* look him in the eye.

Perhaps it was the desire for another chance to leave him that prompted her, when he turned up at Silver Place two weeks later with a bottle of whisky and a deluxe Scrabble set, to allow the evening to end with him placing "SASSY" and "RUFFLE" and "BOSOM" and "SURGE" and "DELI-CIOUS" in cold Scrabble tiles on her stomach, better than love hearts, yet with a nice symmetry. He said that he never had any intention of letting her leave. "I won't always turn up with gifts when you leave me though. Don't do it again," he joked without smiling. Perhaps she felt cheated out of a proper break-up, but she had to admit that there was something about Luke that made her want him near him.

* * *

Eva stood on the Outer Circle of Regent's Park planning to wind herself back towards Soho. She turned right to go a different route than she came. Her feet were damp, so she figured she'd walk all the way around the Outer Circle instead of cutting through the park again. In the back of her mind she had an idea of heading to Mornington Crescent, and then south of the river by Tube to Southwark to see Luke in his ridiculous horsehair wig. Admittedly Luke had banned her, along with anyone else he knew, from watching him in court, because he thought it put him off, but if she timed it for two p.m. she could get in without him seeing her and then surprise him on his way out. Luke had taken her on a tour of Inner London crown court in Newington a long time ago, and she'd been shocked by how untheatrical the court rooms were – more like school rooms than the mahogany-lined halls you saw on TV. If Southwark was similar to Newington, then the viewing gallery would be tucked away either behind the dock, where the defendant sits with a police officer, or to the side near the door, to cause minimal disruption. Eva could slip in and watch unseen.

Along the Outer Circle of Regent's Park there were joggers, cyclists and sugar-hyped families clutching penguin-shaped balloons. Eva stopped at the entrance to London Zoo, under the mural of giraffes and zebras. Inside the gate, a man was taking photographs of people in the queue. Eva blinked and saw a blonde standing between an old man and a woman with a pram just in front of the ticket kiosks. The blonde had her face turned away and was looking for something in her handbag. She wore a pleated black skirt and a Burberry-style mac with her collar up over her neck. Eva stepped into the zoo towards her, and when the blonde turned her head slightly she revealed herself to be a middle-aged woman with too much make-up and a bump in her nose. Not beautiful Grace, of course, with her extravagantly big eyes. It was still a bit before one o'clock in the afternoon, though, so Eva stayed in the queue, biding her time, and entered through the barriers into a rain-slick place scattered with jellyfish-like tourists in yellow plastic ponchos. She pushed through the turnstiles towards the round stone doorway of the aquarium, where a teenager in a hoodie was texting on her phone. If the teenager were a zoo animal, she would have been a hyena, stoop-shouldered and drowsy. The aquarium gurgled, interrupted by the occasional kid's shout: "Nemo! Mum, I found Nemo!" A wooden ice-cream truck just outside the aquarium was locked up, and a picnic table had a meniscus of rainwater wobbling on top with leaves and dirt. Quite a few of the figurine clay and porcelain monkeys on the staircase window sill of Silver Place were from the London Zoo gift shop, but Eva hadn't been to the zoo for ages.

She turned right at the aquarium doors towards the tunnel, following signs to "Africa", and "Birds of Prey". She passed under the concrete underpass, painted with gaudy faux-cave paintings of elephants. A woman and her daughter, both with the same button noses, were waiting quietly under the tunnel for the rain to stop and discussing whether they should visit the Pelicans first, or the tigers. "Pelicans are silly," said the little girl thoughtfully. The cry of a toddler in a blue raincoat trying to wriggle away from his father and the hum of caged animals were interspersed with the sounds of heavy feet on wet pavement.

On the other side of the tunnel was Regent's Canal and the Snowdon Aviary. Eva paused at a glass cage full of forest, where a snowy-haired sloth was draped upside down from a tree branch with its stretched-out furry limbs wrapped around itself. She moved on, to a cage with an animal that appeared to be a cross between a small polar bear and a rat: long snout, ungainly body. Its shoulder blades undulated as it moved solemnly across the cage. Over in the distance, a yellow neck was extended in the rain, contemplating the weather for a slow giraffe moment, wondering where the uncomfortable feeling might be coming from. The giraffe lolloped under the arched doors into his covered enclosure, and Eva kept walking through the rain towards the birds of prey. There was hardly anyone around at this end of the Zoo, but human remnants were scattered on the floor: a spilt pack of Maryland Cookies getting soggy in a puddle next to a baby's sock. Eva passed fat owls and Dracula-shaped vultures, speckled curve-beaked falcons, and then came across a cage with graffiti only half-scrubbed off from its chrome bars. "FREE GOLDIE!" the scoured red paint shouted. Alone in the cage behind the graffiti was Goldie, stabbing dejectedly at a nearly fleshless rabbit carcass. His feathers looked duller than Regina's, his flat brow and hooked beak slightly paler. His yolk-yellow eyes matched a yellow spluttering of colour on the underside of his beak, which he cocked to the side every so often. He didn't have the same hooded eyebrows as his girlfriend did, so he looked a little wearier, less piercingly aggressive. His sprung neck disappeared into the rabbit's stomach while Eva watched and then came back up, bored by his solitary meal, idly looking for something else to do.

* * *

Southwark Crown Court is on the river between London Bridge and Tower Bridge, a stale taupe building with slits for windows and a low metallic awning over its front door. It faces away from the Thames, towards South London. Eva queued behind a grey-haired barrister and a plump boy with a shaved eyebrow to get through the metal detectors, then she scanned the entrance hall for signs of Luke. To the left was a Costa coffee kiosk and a seating area, where a large Indian family were sitting glumly on blue plastic chairs sharing sandwiches from a Tupperware box. To the right was an information desk, where an obese barrister in a too small waistcoat and a sweaty wig was talking on his BlackBerry, looking like a caricature of himself. It was one fifty-five in the afternoon, so Luke – who was always early for everything – must have been already in the courtroom. "Police Officer in the case of Edisa to Court Seven," the intercom said.

"Where would I find the trial of Andrew Alves?" Eva asked the man behind the curved information desk, remembering the name of Luke's client from the papers laid out in the living room. The man pointed to a television above the desk that listed all the courtrooms, but answered the question anyway: "Court Six, third floor – take the lift to the top," he said.

The barristers in the building all took wide strides, as if they were counting them, while the non-barristers, nervy, appeared to shuffle. "Lead for the case of Demisovski to Court Two," the intercom instructed. Eva shared the lift with a lanky Rastafarian wearing sunglasses indoors and two scruffy barristers, one female and one male, each with torn gowns. One of the barristers even had a stain on his court band, those white buck-tooth collars they wear around their necks. "I had the alfalfa salad with pork belly," the female barrister said to her male colleague. "What a pleasure," said the male barrister. The Rastafarian adjusted his sunglasses, eager to get out of the lift.

The top floor was a long corridor with an orange carpet lined with brown plastic seats and dusty pot plants. Van Gogh prints – a strange choice – hung at worrying angles all along the wall. A man in a leather jacket sat with his head in his hands outside Court Four, and at the end of the corridor a barrister held a baby in his arms while asking its mother and father questions about their current employment. The double doors of Court Six were closed. Eva opened the first one into a small space and she peeked through the latticed windows into the courtroom. She could see an elderly judge on a raised bench at the front, but her view of the prosecuting and defending barristers was obscured by the semi-partitioned glass dock, where she could see the slumped shoulders of the man whose photographs she'd seen in Silver Place. She pushed open the second door and it creaked slightly, but nobody turned around except the court clerk in the corner, who glanced at Eva over his glasses and then focused back on the proceedings. Eva sat down hurriedly on the wooden bench while the clerk swore in the first witness. The only other observer was a plump and leather-faced woman wearing a red silk scarf over her head that matched her lipstick. Even if Luke turned around and stared at the defendant, Eva – hiding behind two layers of glass and tucked far away in the corner – wouldn't be seen.

At the far left of the room the jury sat on a two-tiered bench, and on the far right of the court a small man in a denim jacket stood on a raised lectern in front of a microphone with his hand on the Bible, promising to tell the truth and nothing but the truth. Behind the smudgy Plexiglas box in front of Eva the defendant looked up towards the judge's podium. He was more ginger in reality than he had seemed in the photographs that came with Luke's brief. The back of his neck was speckled red, as if he were hot and he had a shaving rash under his chin. His face was soft, except for stressed veins on his temple and forehead. He was dressed smartly in a suit, and on his lap he had a ring-binder that Eva watched him open and close in apprehension, each time putting his finger in the teeth of the clasp, so that it didn't make a noise but pinched the skin.

Seen through the glass dock, the main action of the courtroom gave Eva a peculiar sense of the defendant's perspective. Between the judge and the dock were three rows of benches, with only the front one filled with the robe-lined shoulders and wigged heads of barristers. Luke was on the left nearest the jury, and an older barrister, the prosecutor, was to the right nearer the clerk. The clerk took the Bible away, and the prosecutor stood up abruptly, rolling his shoulders back under his gown and clicking a biro open in his hand. Next to Eva, the woman with the red scarf kept her wrinkled hands primly in her lap.

"Would you please state your name and occupation for the record?" said the prosecutor in a terse voice and the accent of a newsreader. The witness, the small man in the denim jacket, said "Eduardo Vargas", and from his reply

Eva guessed he was Spanish, with English as his second language. Mr Vargas said he worked as a car-washer at Fleet Cleaning in King's Cross, and the defendant was his manager. He'd worked there for three years, he replied in answer to the prosecutor's questions, and he never knew anything about the accounting side of the company. He just washed cars and sometimes fixed them, he said, *and paid his taxes*. He'd never seen any accounts for the company, but he knew that a full service for an average-sized car was £45, paint touch-ups could be anything from £50 to £100. Eva listened to the prosecutor's questions, concentrating on the curiously compulsive movements of the defendant. He was now tapping his foot on the floor as well as snapping the ring-binder closed on his finger. Inside his dock, a broad-shouldered policewoman winced every time Andrew Alves closed the ring binder on his freckled skin. As the dialogue continued – work hours, how staff were hired – Eva watched the defendant's skin squeezing and releasing, squeezing and releasing, wondering when the flesh was going to break. Alves was chewing his lip, too, rolling it under his teeth.

"Thank you Mr Vargas. No further questions," said the prosecuting barrister at last, and Eva looked back up from the defendant's finger to the judge.

"Does the defence council have any questions for this witness?" asked the judge.

"Yes, Your Honour," Luke replied, standing up in front of the court and making Eva's pulse race. She sat farther forward in her seat to squint through the layers of Plexiglas, but even then only saw him as a blurred shadow.

"Mr Vargas, can you recollect an occasion, any occasion at all, in your three years working with the defendant, where you or the other workers ever asked for a pay rise, or perhaps discussed changing the price of any of your services?" Luke said.

"We were paid fine, and it wasn't our business what he charged for stuff. I didn't know nothing about that stuff that you say Andrew did," said the witness, shrugging. "We didn't talk about that sort of stuff. We mostly talked about cars. I wasn't part of nothing illegal."

"Nobody is saying you were. But you never spoke about anything other than cars?" said Luke. "You never talked about money?"

"Objection, Your Honour – leading," said the prosecutor, and Eva frowned. The judge looked at Luke.

"Sustained. Please rephrase the question," said the judge.

"Mr Vargas, could you describe your boss's management style?" said Luke.

"Best mechanic I know," said the witness. "Great boss, for sure."

"Did he work the till ever? Run credit cards, write receipts?" Luke asked.

"He didn't do that much. Said he didn't like numbers. He'd rather wash a car."

"He didn't like numbers?" said Luke. Alves snapped the ring-binder closed on his middle finger and dug his buckteeth into his lips. The veins in the man's temples bulged. Every time the ring-binder bit shut, Eva felt an itch in her own finger. The plump woman with the red silk scarf was leaning forward in her seat to Eva's left.

"No," said the witness.

"May I please direct Your Honour and the Jury to Exhibit A," said Luke, "which is an IQ test taken by the defendant while he was embarking on a Adult Learning Course while looking for a job in the months before taking on the management of Fleet Cleaning." Luke paused. Alves snapped his binder on his skin again, and Eva flinched. "Mr Vargas, could you please tell me what Mr Alves's IQ is? It's in the bottom right-hand corner."

"It says seventy-five," said Mr Vargas.

Blood rose up finally through the torn skin of the garage manager's fingers. He wiped it on his trousers, rocking back and forth. The policewoman said something to him, but he only raised his fist in his mouth, then put his head between his knees, bowing his red-speckled neck and revealing the bumps of his spine above his shirt collar. The policewoman wrote something on an index card, which she then folded, knocking lightly on the glass to get attention. The secretary took the note and tiptoed over to the clerk at the far right-hand side of the room.

"He scored particularly low on numerical reasoning and memory, although his motor speed and social skills were normal," said Luke. "Can the jury see that number highlighted there?"

"Objection, Your Honour," said the prosecutor, rising again to his feet. "What is the defence trying to achieve here? We all know there is no evidential link between IQ and criminal activity," said the prosecutor.

"Of course not," said Luke, "but there's a common-sense link between numeracy levels and the capacity to perpetrate complex fraud, I should think. The British Psychological

Association's 2009 report entitled 'Intelligence: Knowns and Unknowns' states that an IQ of under seventy is classed as having significantly impaired mental functionality." The clerk read the policewoman's card. "I must admit I'm surprised that a man with an IQ that verges on the intellectually impaired," Luke continued, without noticing anything, "whom the witness quotes as being 'no good with numbers', would be capable of this scale of extremely intricate financial negotiations – not to mention running a multifarious and hugely profitable network of prostitution and drug businesses." Luke paused, and Eva looked back at Alves rocking in his chair with his head between his legs. The clerk passed the policewoman's note to the judge, who put his hand out to pause the proceeding while he read it, glancing over at the dock.

"As the court is aware, the defendant has a heart complaint that we must be mindful of. Are you coming to a convenient break in your questioning of this witness, by any chance?" the judge asked Luke.

"Yes, Your Honour, of course," said Luke. The plump woman next to Eva coughed into her hand and adjusted the scarf around her head.

"Then the court will reconvene in fifteen minutes," said the judge.

* * *

Eva slipped out of the courtroom just as the rustling of paper against paper and the shuffling of chairs against carpet started up. She felt, like the defendant, that she might be forgetting how to breathe, so she walked as quickly as she could down the yellow corridor and into the lift, where two girls in luminous tracksuits were applying lipgloss. It had been very hot in the court. She stumbled her way out of the building between the metal detectors into the cold afternoon air, and immediately felt better. Luke was doing a good thing in there. He'd always appeared adamantly moral about his work, eager to do right. She hoped he was achieving something he was proud of. Under the awning in front of the court building she turned left, past glass windows looking into an office, and then left again towards the river so she could see the dull waters and the anchored HMS *Belfast*. Everything was grey in front of her, the colour stolen. The air was wet, and you could see beyond London Bridge on one side and the looming arcs of Tower Bridge on the other. Across the river, the city appeared the same hue as HMS Belfast. Eva felt dizzy. She'd forgotten to eat breakfast, so she entered a café at the edge of a little arcade of shops, over a terrace that must have been pretty in summer, to sit down in the corner seat of a near-empty room that smelt of fried eggs. Eva texted Luke "Call me when you're out of court? X", then ordered a cup of tea and took out *The Pirate's Mistress* from her bag.

"Serenity's bottom lip quivered with anxiety as the ropes burnt at her soft skin, pulling her wrists forward in front of her. Silence blanketed the deck while she was walked out in front of the pirate," Eva read. Around her she heard cutlery scraping from the few occupied tables and a pop song wining in the background. She took out her red pen and focused back on her manuscript.

"'*What are you going to do to me?*' said Serenity, her voice tremulous with fear. Captain Theodore smiled calmly as he touched her white skin and flame-red hair, considering his prize. '*I will ransom you,*' he said."

It had been good to see Luke in court – she ought to do it more often. Eva sometimes felt like she'd bought the "restricted view" theatre tickets when it came to Luke. His mother had once turned to her at dinner and said that Luke used to get terrible stomach aches in middle school because he hated having to leave home so much. "Mum, *come on*," Luke had said, catching the end of his mother's comment and rolling his eyes like a teenager. "I can't help it," his Mum had said to Luke with a grin, raising her plucked eyebrows. "I see all the different versions of him like one of those matryoshka dolls. It's very disorientating. He's ten years old and a baby and a barrister and a spotty adolescent all at the same time." Eva didn't see every version of Luke – not at all. She often found it difficult to hold one version of him close enough to understand. She wasn't even sure she knew what knowing another person really meant. Were you supposed to grasp them completely, every facet of them, the nuances of every memory? That seemed to be the moral of romantic novels, at least by the end of them, and it was implied by those elderly couples who walked around hand in hand, finishing each other's sentences. Eva watched Luke a lot, could describe everything from the pattern of his profile to his smell when he woke up in the morning, but she worried that there was always going to be a gap between them where their lives just didn't quite click together and never would. Slightly unsettled at the thought, Eva glanced back at the papers in front of her, then sucked her pen and looked up from the manuscript again, just in time to see Luke's long cashmere coat step by the café, floating under the straight stick of his huge navy-blue umbrella. As he passed, she got up and went to the door without picking up her manuscript or paying for her tea, then doubled back, figuring he'd only be up the street, and left a five-pound note on the table. She bundled her pens and papers into her arms and struggled to open the café door, nearly dropping her mobile as she stumbled.

"Luke!" she shouted down the grey-stone walkway between the buildings and the water, but Luke didn't turn around. "Luke!" She took a few steps out in the rain and realized he must be wearing his earphones. He was about thirty or forty metres away now. She took out her phone. It was only twenty minutes since the judge called time on Luke's questioning, so Eva supposed court had been shelved for the day. He was striding towards London Bridge when she dialled his number, ready to laugh and explain that she was standing just up the road in the rain, waiting for him.

"Hey," said Luke, picking up the phone while still walking forward under his umbrella in the distance. "I'm about to go into a meeting – can I call you back?"

"Hi. Sure," Eva said after a pause. "Course." He walked towards the steps leading up to London Bridge and began to climb them.

"Crazy morning. I've just got to chambers," his voice came through the phone.

"Was court OK?" Eva said quietly, thinking he almost certainly was walking to his chambers – that was the direction he was going.

"It was fine, but there's a lot of work to do for tomorrow."

"Last night – with Grace – was weird, right?" said Eva.

"Yeah. Can we talk later?"

"OK," said Eva.

"I'll call you this afternoon, I might have to work late," said Luke.

"OK," said Eva, but she realized – with a lump in her throat – that Luke had already put down the phone. "See you later," Eva said to nothing.

He turned onto the bridge. The sky above him was pale, with streaks of grey. She imagined Regina flying across the sky, catching a current of air, lifting her higher and sinking her down, skimming above the Thames any way she wanted. Then she thought of the doves and rabbits and flowers and girls trapped in the Scorpio Club. Eva wondered whether this haunting distance she occasionally felt between her and Luke was a fragment of her own shadow, something that would follow her from relationship to relationship, or if it was actually connected to Luke. She couldn't tell. As Luke's figure strode onto the bridge and merged with that of other passers-by, she turned away.

* * *

Eva remained standing outside the café near London Bridge, facing out on the Thames, until she heard someone shout "Eva!" The voice made her jump. She turned quickly around, convinced that Grace would be there next to the yellow bricks of Southwark Crown Court, tilting her hips and tucking hair behind her ears. But Grace was nowhere to be seen. A boy with a NY Yankees cap was kissing his girlfriend, a man checked his reflection in a shop window and adjusted his tie, two schoolchildren were stomping in puddles – perhaps she shared her name with one of them and they were calling each other.

But the voice shouted "Eva" again, and she scanned the crowds more closely: barristers, tourists, a jogger and there, a little farther off, around the corner leading to the front of the court building, Luke's friend Catherine was making her way towards the river and laughing.

"You are in your *own – little – world*. Right?" she said, and Eva's stomach sank in disappointment. She even continued to glance around the street for a second, as if there was still a chance Grace might be there too, lurking.

"How are you?" Catherine said. "I have a case starting in ten minutes, horribly delayed, so I can't chat long. It's crazy trying to organize a wedding when court never starts when it's meant to. I already missed one dress-fitting last week." She was wearing a grey suit with high heels, a pile of briefs and papers in her arms.

"Hi," said Eva. Luke and Catherine weren't in the same chambers, but they went to law school together and saw each other regularly in court.

"Is Luke inside? You come to pick him up?" said Catherine.

"He left already, court was adjourned."

"See what I mean? Nobody can keep to a schedule. Did you enjoy my party?"

"Lovely," said Eva. "Thanks. Yes. Did you?"

"I had a *fabulous* time. Luke's lip seems to have healed now."

"He has a habit of being in the wrong place at the wrong time." Eva smiled.

"That girl was *drunk*."

"Girl?" said Eva.

"What did he say happened?" Catherine grimaced. "Was he too embarrassed to say a girl hit him? That's hysterical. He didn't tell you it was a girl?"

"No," said Eva. "Hysterical. Did you see what happened?"

"She was outside the pub. He went to speak to her – twice I think – because she kept trying to come into the party and he didn't seem to want her there. The second time I was near the door saying goodbye to people, and she just lashed at him and then walked off – bit unsteady – trying to pretend she wasn't off her tits."

"What did he do?"

"I went out and gave him my cold beer to put on his lip. I asked him what that was about, and he mumbled about the girl being insane, some friend he hadn't seen in years." Catherine glanced at her watch. "She was completely wasted. Total psycho."

"You didn't hear why it was they were arguing?" said Eva.

"I was in the pub and they were outside." Catherine shrugged. "I gotta go," she said. "We must do lunch though, yes? *Promise me* we'll do lunch?" Then she turned away without waiting for Eva to answer, quite aware that they would never do lunch.

* * *

The scar was of Grace's making. Eva felt sick at having kissed that scar: her tongue repeatedly touching Grace's memento. And Grace probably had finger-sized bruises on her upper arm from where Luke had grasped her the previous night – little shadows. Like the maps Eva used to collect as a kid, each mark was a scaled-down picture of something much more complicated. Her own skin tingled as she thought of Grace and Luke's bodies. She rubbed the palm of her right hand: a little scar sat bang in the middle where Luke had clumsily stabbed her with a sparkler one November on Primrose Hill a few years ago. She rubbed her "firework stigmata", as Luke referred to it, then touched a ridge of skin on her elbow from when Luke pushed her over in the street once during an argument.

The elbow scar belonged to the second time she had failed to leave Luke, two years into their relationship, on Halloween. They'd been at a party where she had met up with an old school friend, and she'd been talking with him in the kitchen for most of the evening. She was dressed as the Queen of Hearts from *Alice in Wonderland* with a geisha-like white face and rosebud lips, while Luke was a somewhat half-hearted Mad Hatter wearing a top hat Eva had found in a charity shop. On the bus home from the party there was a skeleton kissing a witch a few seats down and a group of slutty nurses playing their iPods through portable speakers and drinking Red Stripe at the front of the bus. Not talking, Eva and a bad-tempered Luke got off at Piccadilly Circus, near the

Trocadero and the Apollo Theatre, winding their way down Shaftesbury Avenue until they turned into Rupert Street and towards Walker's Court, past the façades of bars and empty hairdressers. Eva squinted past Luke into the shadowed cul-de-sac of Smith's Court, where there was a battered leather weekend bag in the middle of the street, tipped over as if it had been kicked out of the door or dropped out of the window. Trying to lighten the mood, Eva walked over to it.

"It's a suitcase," she said. It felt sodden under her fingers as she bent down on her haunches to open the zip. It smelt musty. "Books," she said, taking out paperbacks written in a foreign language. "And boxer shorts," she added, taking five scrunched pairs of striped cotton boxer shorts between her fingers and dropping them on the ground. "I think this must be the remnants of a lover's tiff between an academic and a prostitute." Eva peeled open the pages of one of the books, but the pages were all stuck together. "What is this, Russian?"

"Some Eastern European language," Luke said gruffly, taking the book from Eva's hand. "*Kupovina drva*," Luke said, reading the back. "I wonder what that means."

She raised herself up on her tiptoes to kiss Luke on the cheek. "I love you," she said. As far as she was concerned, she'd done nothing wrong that night, except not want to be the life and soul of the party. "Why are you angry with me?"

"More likely 'how to grout a bathroom' than '*I love you, why are you angry with me*'. I think it's a DIY manual," said Luke at the book in his hand, no emotion on his face, which appeared elongated by the top hat on his head.

"Luke, you're being fucking ridiculous."

"You don't know how guys think. Believe me, in that man's mind you were bent over a desk somewhere."

"I was just talking to him. I wouldn't even be thinking about him now if you weren't being weird. I'm here, aren't I? Not with him."

"Half. You're half here. I always feel like you're looking for other options."

"You're angry because you're imagining me being imagined by someone else? I hate you when you're drunk like this. You have no idea how dumb you sound right now."

"Don't talk to me like that," said Luke, his voice level. His shoulders were tensed under his shirt. Eva scratched her nose, white make-up coming off under her nail. She'd seen him look this way at others, but never at her. He was usually so impassive when they argued.

"Then don't act like a twat," said Eva, laughing, but falsely. And at that point Luke had reached over and put his big hand around Eva's upper arm. He held it much harder than was comfortable, which surprised her. From the other hand he dropped the DIY book on the floor, and it fell with a thud onto the cobbles. His top hat, too, fell to the floor.

"Luke, that hurts," Eva said. "You're hurting me." She wriggled in his grasp and stepped away from him, but he kept hold of her for a moment. She could feel her heart beat in her mouth. "Let go." She shivered and heat spread from his hand into her shoulder, through her muscles up her neck to her jaw. Her whole body felt as if it were moments from being crushed by him. She wanted to shake herself away from the strength of his hold on her and the smell of

145

his breath and the intensity of his gaze. "Let go," she said a little louder than before.

And Luke did let go. It was a matter of seconds, but it seemed longer. At Luke's release her body lurched backwards and hit the alley wall behind. Her head banged on the bricks and her elbow scraped along an inch before she righted herself. Once she was steady, there was a long, dizzy pause. Eva rubbed the bump on her head and sat down on the floor.

"I'm so sorry, Eva," he said. He got down on his knees in front of her and tried to put his hand on her head, but she moved it away and wouldn't look at him. An old woman with blue-wash in her hair trudged along past the alley and glanced anxiously at the arguing storybook characters slumped together in the shadows. "I can't tell you how sorry I am. That will never happen again. I can't believe that just happened."

As the dizziness wore off, Luke started to look more shaken than she did. He kept whispering that he was sorry, and he had his hand over his mouth. She'd never known him to plead with her about anything, except maybe a pass to have "one more drink, one more song". He was sitting with his shoulders tilted forward, his large nose pointed to the ground. If beauty is in the eye of the beholder, then he suddenly looked ugly: the mean curl of his mouth, piercing grey eyes, faint scars, wiry hair, grotesque big hands. Just then Eva knew that she hated him. She felt herself hardening, not even trying to understand what might have been going on in his head for him to react like that. She just wanted to be done with him, and as far away from him as possible.

"I didn't do anything to deserve that," Eva said eventually. She remembered the first time she had seen him frown, in her bedroom at Silver Place, and thought of Darwin grief lines. "I'd rather you leave me alone now," Eva said.

Eva had never considered herself a weak person. Passive at times, perhaps, but never weak. She was certainly not scared of loneliness. She saw exits as blank pages – infinity, anything you want. Having hopped through schools and countries growing up, she was fairly sure that if she was placed in a strange country as an adult she'd survive just fine. She would continue. She was not over-emotional and she didn't make superficial connections to people. Only, after the fight between the Queen of Hearts and the Mad Hatter in a Soho alley on Halloween, Luke didn't roll easily off her.

On Halloween night he walked her to Silver Place in silence and then went back to Hackney. She didn't take his calls for two weeks, or open the door when he shouted up from the street. But she missed him. He wrote her emails and letters, apologizing. He said he was going to anger-management classes. He'd been looking for a fight and he was so sorry to have had one with her. Eva tried to remember that devouring look in his eyes, that threat, but was surprised by the thump of loss in her gut once he was no longer in her life. In a way, there had been a revelation in his eyes when he grabbed her, a secret that she saw for a second – a fissure, a new face on a painting you'd been staring at for years. When he was gone Eva thought she saw him around every corner – and there was no masochistic, dreamy pleasure in missing him, either, as there had been with others. It just hurt to think of him. She was free and unfettered, but she wanted the weight of him, the pointless emails he sent during the day, the touch of him, the way he complained about her food, the smell of him when he took off his shirt, the way he smiled at her, the comfort. Eventually, she called to say that he could come and pick up a couple of records and books he'd left at Silver Place. Even as she dialled his number, she knew that when he came over she would pretend to be drunker than she was and let her hand brush against his.

* * *

Standing on the edge of the Thames outside Southwark Crown Court, Eva fiddled with her phone, looking through Google for the phone number of Spider Media. "May I speak to Grace Taylor, please?" Eva said.

"She's off this afternoon," said a voice on the other end of the line. "Are you RSVP-ing to the talk tonight?"

"Yeah," said Eva. The sky was heavy with moisture. On HMS *Belfast*, a father struggled to get his toddler back in his pushchair and a woman sipped hot coffee, making a burnt-tongue face. "My name's Eva Elliott. I can't find my invite, though."

"It's at the Phoenix Theatre on Phoenix Street, just off Charing Cross Road. Drinks at six thirty and the talk begins at seven."

"And Grace will be there?"

"Of course."

"Thank you." Eva put the phone down.

As she walked back to her office, across Waterloo Bridge heading towards Soho, Eva went through the names of Luke's former girlfriends, searching for a Grace: there was the skinny redhead with whirlpool-green eyes from Luke's photo album in his old Hackney bedroom – Mary – then an art student named Arabella during his first year at university; a PhD student – possibly named Suzie – and then a Tammie or Talia while he was doing his law conversion in London. His last relationship before Eva was a trainee barrister named Iris. They had briefly lived together in Stoke Newington. She had tortoise-shell glasses and large breasts, but Eva only knew that from a photo she'd seen on Facebook. She often met former flings of his at parties, but never girlfriends – at least as far as she knew – and never Grace. Everyone has secrets of course: unarticulated memories, gaps around the truth. Nobody tells the whole truth all the time. Eva had never even introduced Luke to her parents.

After a few hours at work Eva stood on Charing Cross Road at the mouth of Phoenix Street, Blackwell's Bookshop on one side and the theatre on the other. Huge tubs of cooking oil were lined up on the pavement outside a Chinese restaurant, a corner store advertised minicab services with a sodden cardboard sign, a black phone booth was missing its door, some kids on bikes were arguing about where one of their girlfriends was the previous night. It smelt a bit like piss. The theatre straddled the entire corner, with a basement members' club attached. A few steps farther down Phoenix Street, Eva approached a girl with a clipboard who was standing outside the theatre's doors underneath its white pilasters and little golden phoenixes. The birds had their wings outstretched, frozen in a moment of ecstasy. A sign on the gilded mahogany doors said "Private function".

"May I take your name?" the girl smiled. Behind her, in a plush gold-and-blue lobby, a small crowd milled around a mirror-backed bar.

"Is Grace Taylor inside?" said Eva, and a worried expression passed over the girl's face.

"I think she is on her way," the girl replied, although her rigid smile suggested this statement was more hopefulness than fact.

"I'm nothing to do with this event. Just a friend. She's not off sick or anything?" Eva figured Grace might still be hungover.

"She should be here soon," the girl said, shrugging, mildly relieved that Eva was a friend of Grace's rather than a guest of the author. "You coming in?"

Eva stepped into the bar and ordered a vodka tonic among smart guests holding hardback copies of a theatre director's autobiography. She didn't recognize his name, although he was apparently famous. She sipped and waited, eavesdropping: "a tour de force", a "Rabelaisian comedy", "unflinching". When the crowd began to filter through a big glass door to the right of the bar, she stayed out in the lobby.

"You're not going to hear the talk?" said the clipboard girl, herding guests without much authority.

"I'm going to wait for Grace," said Eva.

"I've called her like a hundred times now, and she hasn't picked up. Tell her I'm cross with her, yeah?"

"Will do," said Eva smiling, and the room became quiet, except for background female acoustics on the speakers behind the bar and the drone of Charing Cross Road outside.

Eva waited fifteen minutes in the theatre bar, until half-past seven, and then – bored – she stepped out under the ecstatic phoenixes again. It was still light outside, but it was drizzling now. She'd wander around for a bit before doubling back and peaking her head through the theatre doors to see if Grace had turned up.

At the other end of Phoenix Street from Charing Cross Road was a small community garden rimmed with red railings. Through layers of bushes and trees Eva could see daisies, roses, nettles. Concrete flowerpots spilled over with lavender. Wheelbarrows full of weeds. Crazy paving. A church spire, St-Giles-in-the-Fields, reared its white stone finger into the sky. Eva let herself imagine that Grace would be in that garden with her head in her hands, sitting on a bench – crying, perhaps, or smiling to herself and smoking. A noise made Eva start, but it was only a black cat with a gouged-out eye jumping out of a bush. The cat stalked past Eva's legs, leaving a flash of warmth there. A blackbird flew up to the top of a building and opened its yellow beak over London. A car alarm was going off. Eva followed around the edges of the garden, peering though the triangles of foliage. Grace wasn't in there, of course. Eva was disappointed to see that the gate was locked, so she continued around St Giles Passage. Through another gate she stepped into the grounds of St Giles-in-the-Fields, all smog-patterned white stone. Someone had drawn chalk pictures on the pavement and the colours were weeping now, hopscotch patterns smudging and stick figures melting there at Eva's feet. Raised tombs were dotted to the right of the church, but Eva continued left towards another gate and a Narnia-like lantern, huge and black with a few blobs of chewing gum pressed at the base.

The front entrance of the church led out onto St Giles High Street and the side onto the junction of Flitcroft Street and Denmark Street. Eva hoisted herself up onto a stone ridge next to a staircase and hugged her legs to her torso. It wasn't raining any more, so Eva leant back on the church walls and retrieved *The Pirate's Mistress* from her bag. The side entrance in front of her was an unattached stone doorway, massive, framing a padlocked black gate. Cigarette butts, soggy leaves, a needle, beer ring pulls and an Accessorize receipt were puddled by the mouldy base of the columns while, just outside the gate on Flitcroft Street, a torn leather office chair had a pigeon sleeping on its seat. Eva tightened her jacket around her neck and took out her red pen. Beyond the gate, a woman talked into her Bluetooth earpiece, a road sweeper rolled his dustbin. A middle-aged woman trudged in Dr Martens boots, and a blond ponytail bobbed out from a crowd of tourists. Eva expected the woman to look up and reveal an old face, or that of a teenager, but it was Grace's figure that turned the corner from St Giles High Street onto Denmark Street. Eva blinked: Grace was walking in the direction of Charing Cross Road, towards The Phoenix Theatre.

"Grace!" Eva scrambled down from her perch on the wall, dragging a wet streak of mould off the stone onto her trousers. "Grace!" She jumped onto the floor and ran to the gate, scaring the pigeon on the office chair, which launched towards the rooftops. Grace turned her head in Eva's direction.

"Eva," Grace said quietly from the other side of the road. Her lips were crimson and she wore peacock-feather earrings in her ears. She didn't step towards Eva. "This church used to be a leper colony, you know that?" A smile caught the edges of her lips for a second. "I feel like a leper this morning. I'm massively embarrassed about last night. I was so drunk."

"You hit Luke at the start of August," Eva said. "What did he do to you?"

Grace's face darkened. She tucked her hair behind her ears and stepped away from Eva. "I know him better than you do. We grew up together."

"He told me."

"Yeah? He told you what?"

"Wait for me a second, OK? Meet me at the front entrance, will you?" Eva pointed right, forty metres or so across the churchyard, where the main door was.

Grace nodded, and Eva ran over to the gate, jumping over a flower bed and around a grave. She looked over her shoulder once, and Grace was walking towards the church entrance as well, but when Eva came out onto the road she couldn't see her. Eva nearly tripped over a bicycle chained to a traffic sign. No Grace. There was a hairdresser's, a job centre, a tattoo parlour, a guitar shop, any of which Grace could have slipped into while Eva's back was briefly turned. She looked in the window of the hair salon – a woman getting dreadlocks done, another with a head full of silver foil – but couldn't see Grace. She put her head in the tattoo parlour, where a man with arabesques over his arms and neck was reading a magazine.

"Did a blonde girl just come in here?"

"No, ma'am," the man said.

Eva asked the same of a tanned hipster in Hank's Acoustic, a bar, a café and an Indian restaurant all the way down to Charing Cross Road, but Grace had slipped off. Eva went back to the Phoenix Theatre, where the clipboard girl was sipping Evian at the bar and waiting for the talk to finish, but as she walked over, the girl's phone beeped, and she took it out of her pocket. The girl studied her phone with a sullen expression on her face.

"Damn, what the hell am I going to do with the author after the talk? Grace's bailed out on me. She's gone back home. She's sick."

* * *

Eva flipped the hall light on, and a shadow flashed across her eyes from inside the flat: a moth's silhouette briefly casting shapes against the staircase wall. She sat down at the living-room table where Luke's papers were lined up at the back, his illegible Post-it notes curling slightly towards the ceiling. He had called her from his office telephone at around eight that evening, as Eva was walking home from The Phoenix, telling her about how much work there was to do for the money-laundering case, how complicated the finances were and how convinced he was that his client was innocent. They'd spoken for five minutes or so, but Eva didn't say much. She didn't say about bumping into Catherine, or what Grace had said outside St Giles. Now she flicked on his desk light in the living room, which had a broken neck and lolled over his papers. She picked up his yellow legal pad and unfolded it. On the top line she deciphered: "Wife's maiden name Aika Pakchoian, brothers Hamik, Rehan and Avedis Pakchoian. Illegal? Have Lucinda check." Lower down he'd written and highlighted the words "medical records, panic attacks, cardiac dysrhythmia", then "Brothels? Four in London, soon to close", which was underlined. Eva got up and put one of Luke's vinyl records on the turntable. The needle skated for a second on the black plastic rink and then began, throwing something dramatic into the living room. The Scrabble game was still under the coffee table so she eased it out and examined her letters. What was she going to do with T, M, E, U, E, P, T. She put down AMPUTEE against the A of Luke's SCANT.

She got up and stepped into the bathroom, where Grace's bangles were still in the sink. She sat on the edge of the bath and absent-mindedly put them on in the falling evening light. They felt heavy on her wrists. She listened to Luke's music for a moment, then continued into what used to be her room before her grandma died. Boxes of Eva's stuff still sat in the corner, but mostly it was used by Luke as a wardrobe. It smelt of cedar, mothballs and lavender in there, but moths were still braving the brew. Grace's bangles slipped up and down Eva's wrists as she scooped some of the dead bugs onto an envelope out of the bedside light next to her childhood bed and left them there like soldiers laid out on a sheet. There were more corpses splattered on the blue walls. Luke's shirts were lined up on a rail in there, his shiny shoes in a row underneath, his boxer shorts and socks kept in a chest of drawers he brought from his flat in Hackney. Eva ran her fingers over the shirts, which went from light to dark across the rail, with a hooked anti-moth contraption placed every three shirts. He stored his suits in travel bags to keep the insects away. There was a separate rail for ties, and an entire drawer in the chest was devoted to his coloured handkerchiefs.

Eva had always controlled her exits with such meticulous precision and eager pleasure. Now the palms of her hands were clammy as she put them in the pockets of two of Luke's suits. She found business cards, a pair of earphones, a single contact-lens packet. She tried the pockets of his jeans – a napkin with some gum trapped in it, a pound coin, a receipt from a pub. Every time the building creaked or a moth flew in front of the light, Eva jumped a little and then told herself to calm down. She unfolded the flaps of one of the unpacked boxes behind Luke's clothes rail to find piles of history books, then in another box she ran her fingers over the spines of law textbooks from his conversion course.

In a third box she expected more books, but instead found that it clattered slightly as she brought it out from under the clothes rail. Through a fissure she saw an uncharacteristic, un-Luke-like mishmash of objects. She eased out two "gold" cups engraved with his name, both first place in debating championships. Inside the cups were three dusty medals: long-distance running, again all of them first place. She brought the bedside lamp over to the box and read an old school report card: "Luke has been learning to occupy his time constructively this year... has been working on becoming a better listener... is intelligent and well organized, but has a habit of drawing attention to himself in class by asking the teacher constant pedantic questions". Eva smiled.

There was a handwritten history essay on the Crusades, his unframed university diploma, a precocious article he wrote in his school magazine about government education policies, and a random birthday card from his grandfather. It looked as if he'd made a pile of things he couldn't quite throw away but didn't know where to put. There was even a school tie, black and pink, which Eva unsnaked from the bottom of the box. In doing so she dislodged three postcards that were lined up with their faces towards the cardboard wall. They fanned down, and Eva picked them up out of the box to hold them in front of the light. Eva recognized the first, which said: "'Cover her face; mine eyes dazzle. She died young' – John Webster." Eva ran her fingers over the deeply indented ink as she had done the first time she saw it amongst bank statements and takeaway menus on the doormat at Silver Place. She put it down on the carpet. The next postcard said: "'The person who hurt you is also here... If you are still angry at that person, if you haven't been able to forgive, you are chained to him' – Leymah Gbowee." And the last one: "'There is a point of no return, unremarked at the time, in most lives' – Graham Greene."

Eva read all of the quotes again. They made her feel sick, an acidic twang at the back of her throat, so she turned each postcard face down on the carpet and pushed them away across the floor. He'd kept them. He hadn't given the postcard to the police, or handed it in to his chambers. Eva closed her eyes for a second and then went back to Luke's box of possessions, her hands shaking a little She took out a small photo album, the same one that she had looked through in his Hackney bedroom early on in their relationship. Some pictures she recognized: Luke on a camping trip with his dad; his mother surrounded by papers at their kitchen table with a "No. 1 Mum" mug; the geeky school portrait of thirteen-year-old Luke looking as if he were solving calculus problems in his head.

Eva peeled back the sticky plastic and took out the snapshot of his first girlfriend: red-headed Mary, with her freckled face and sad green eyes. She was snuggled up with Luke on a bench, while a boy in a football bib ran towards the camera with his fist raised. Mary looked extremely thin and timid sitting next to Luke on the bench, as if she didn't want to be seen, let alone photographed. Eva put the picture down on the carpet in front of her.

While Eva had countless albums and boxes of letters from her grandmother, bags full of old school exercise books and teenage diaries and half-finished craft projects, Luke just had clothes, his history books, his law books and then piles of paper that were organized every week and slotted carefully into lever-arch files. This single box of his childhood memories had never even been unpacked. He could have put this photo album with hers in the living room, but never had done. Perhaps it was fitting that everything related to Luke's present and future was very organized, and the few things related to the past, things that no longer had an active function, were just shoved in a cardboard box and forgotten.

Eva squinted at a picture of Luke's pretty mother, whom Eva had met many times at birthdays and holidays. In the picture she wore a red tailored jacket, while Luke's stepfather wore jeans with monogrammed slippers peaking out at the bottom. Luke's weekday childhood in London was the sort where his dentist appointments were mapped out a year in advance and marked clearly on whichever Gauguin or David Hockney wall calendar the mother received for Christmas; there was always someone to help him with his homework and listen to his debating-society opening statements.

Luke spent every other weekend and every other holiday in Devon with his father, who never remarried. He said that he had a completely uncomplicated relationship with his mother and stepfather, but he was less close to his father. Eva had only met him once, in Smithfield Market, where Mr Jones came every so often to speak to restaurant and shop buyers. Early one morning – two years into their relationship – Eva and Luke had eased themselves through the plastic-ribbon curtains at the front arch of the market into the butcher stalls' aisle, glancing on either side, behind curved glass partitions, at ox livers, wide-open rib cages strung up on metal hooks and pig heads with their eyes squinted closed. Eva had regretted spending ages creating the perfect "outfit to meet your boyfriend's father", which was a rather prim dress and patent court shoes that made her standout among the butcher stalls. Luke had perhaps looked even more conspicuous than Eva, though, a crisp pocket handkerchief sticking out of his jacket and shiny leather brogues clicking on the damp cobbled market floor. He was even dragging his trolley bag over the cobbles, packed with his court wig and gown.

Luke's father had smiled at his son and then strode over to shake his son's hand with his blood-covered plastic gloves still on, just to see him step backwards and tilt his head to the side in mock-irritation. This was clearly a long-practised ritual, the father making fun of his son.

"Hi, Dad," Luke had said, smiling. It was just before Christmas, and his words misted in the air. "This is Eva."

"Do you want to hold a pig's heart?" Luke's father had said, turning to Eva.

Afterwards Eva and Luke had gone into a Pret A Manger and drunk lattes, laughing about Eva's face at his father's words. It must have been quite a culture shock, Eva thought, being a posh little urban only child who spent his evenings doing Latin homework in his mother's lily- and sculpture-filled conservatory, then having to hold his own working on a pig farm every other weekend. Perhaps Luke just didn't like it there much, so he didn't talk about it.

Eva put photographs of Luke's mother and father side by side on the floor of Silver Place. In the rest of the album, the green eyes of Luke's first girlfriend were scattered throughout the pages: she was reading *Great Expectations* on a hammock, holding Luke's hand with a dreary beachscape in the background, sitting alone on a picnic rug with a notepad on her knees. Another image in the album was of Mary and Luke and a younger kid in a baseball cap posing around a wooden stile between two green fields, presumably in Devon. A few farmhouses dotted the horizon, white and thatched rectangles in the distance under a summertime bright sky. Luke's grinning face was in the middle of the composition, marked with some teenage acne as well as the scars. His body had that slightly ill-fitting look that teenage boys sometimes have, while Mary's fragile frame, perched a little behind Luke's with her hand on his, had the stretched-out pose of a catwalk model. She was wearing a floral summer dress with pink wellington boots that drew attention to the alarming thinness of her bare legs. On the stile steps in front of the fence was the third kid, with black frizzy hair cropped above the ears, covered in a baseball cap, and giant eyes like a manga cartoon character. It was the same kid who was punching the air in the background of the photograph of Mary and Luke on the bench. At first glance Eva thought this younger kid was a boy with a misjudged haircut. On closer inspection it was a tomboyish girl in jeans, a baggy T-shirt and muddy hiking boots. She was smiling at the camera, a gap in her teeth that she'd clearly had corrected by braces later on. This was what Eva had been looking for among Luke's things as she flicked through his memories: a photograph of Grace. Eva pulled the picture closer to the light. Grace's marked features were gawky as an adolescent, although they became sensual as she grew up. Her hair was black then, and looked like it had been cut with kitchen scissors. They were all there, all three of them together, all friends existing in Luke's life before Eva did.

* * *

Eva stared at the photograph and listened to herself breathing. She felt a rising panic, so allowed herself the relief of veering off abruptly into a thought of Sophia sitting in the growing lake of bath water and tears in the front room of the Scorpio and concentrating so hard on remembering her magician lover that all of the windows in the club smashed at the same time, cracking down their centres and splintering onto the carpet. Eva closed her eyes just for a moment: the magician's assistant was trying to recall the shape of her lover's face, maybe the smell of his hair, or the exact colour of his skin after he'd spent the afternoon in the sun rather than reading inside. Sophia tried to bring back to her mind the first time they spent the night together after she ran away from home to join the circus with him, kissing in a horse truck among the smell of manure and happiness.

In the semi-retreat of her imagination Eva saw all the magician's flowers adorning the Scorpio Club catching fire from the intensity of the magician's assistant's memories and all the white doves flapping desperately at the walls or heading for the broken windows while the snakes slithered down plugholes, and the tiger cub treaded water while Sophia, exhausted, screamed.

* * *

At around ten p.m., after leaving a note asking Luke to call her when he got in from work, Eva put on her coat. She walked into Ingestre Place towards Berwick Street, then across Shaftesbury Avenue into Leicester Square with all the tourists and the sweaty teenagers overdressed in patent stilettos and miniskirts with no tights. Aden, the academic she had broken up with on the steps of St Paul's, used to wait for her by the railings outside the Hippodrome on Charing Cross Road sometimes, opposite the Angus Steak House with the American and Spanish faces staring through the windows. She'd come through from the Tube station and pause on the corner of the street to look and see if he was there. He was always early, standing in his long coat with his hands in his pockets. Whenever she passed that corner, she could swear she could still smell him: cheap soap and Lucky Strike cigarettes. Sometimes they'd go and sit in the little park and look at the awkward Shakespeare sculpture, but usually they'd be going somewhere – to Browns for a hamburger, to the theatre, to some party. Now Eva was older, Leicester Square looked drabber. She always knew it wasn't exactly cool, but it had an appeal back then. In the square a crowd was forming in the far corner near the Odeon. A bald street performer was trying to get up on a unicycle. He had a tiny quiff of blond hair on the top of his head and he kept jumping to an elegant roll, up into the sky, and then falling too far backwards and tumbling down the other side of his wheel, but landing on his feet each time, to the squeals of damp schoolchildren and nearly drunk pre-clubbers in leather jackets.

Eva dialled Luke's mobile number as the acrobat threw himself up in the air again, spokes spinning, but Luke didn't pick up his phone and it went straight to answerphone. Then she dialled his office, and again the call went to voicemail. The moment felt surgical, somehow, as if Eva were peeling back skin and looking inside something that was unexpectedly decayed. As she watched the acrobat spin, she thought of secrets she'd never told anyone before.

She'd never told anyone that she once went back to the flat of an artist she met at a party in a gallery, purely to make another boy jealous. The artist tried to make her give him head in his dismal kitchen and he'd grabbed her hair and she'd been so full of revulsion, with herself more than him, that she almost did it – but at the last minute a doorbell rang and Eva managed to leave the flat as the artist's drunk flatmate came in.

It was a secret that she had a false tooth on the bottom right-hand side of her mouth from falling off a running machine at school once, landing on her face.

She'd never told anyone that she always checked for murderers behind the shower curtain before she peed.

Or that she cried so easily as a child that her grandmother sent her to see a therapist every Wednesday for a summer, when she was twelve.

Or that she was slightly scared of her mother, for reasons she did not understand.

She'd never told anyone that she couldn't live without them.

Or that for a few years when she was a child she used to pray every night.

She'd never told anyone that she was almost always surprised when she looked in the mirror, because that was somehow not what she ever imagined herself to look like.

Or that she still sometimes expected to see her grandmother making tea in the kitchen if she was half asleep when she crawled out of bed.

Eva had watched a magic show in the Hippodrome with her grandmother when she was ten. She wore her best blue dress, and they sat a few rows from the stage on red-velvet seats. This was five years before Eva moved to Soho. She'd been looking forward to the outing for weeks. Her grandmother had even sent a book on Houdini for her to read, which her mother had taken away after she started to talk about disappearing. ("What are you doing?" her mother asked when Eva closed her eyes at the kitchen table one morning. "I'm disappearing," Eva said.) Out of the theatre's darkness came plate-spinners and contortionists, leotarded women balancing upside down on metre-high sticks, while obese geisha-faced women sang eerie operatic songs. Warriors did back flips and juggled samurai swords, flying up on ropes to dance in the air. Eva sat on the edge of her seat as three men dressed in yellow tiger costumes carried lengths of chain and body-sized hammers onto the stage, pushing a massive water tank. The tigers also did handstands and back flips, and then three limp female bodies appeared, hanging by lengths of blue silk rope from the rafters above the water tank. The rope was tied around the women's middles, so each spine hung in a semicircle with heads and toes pointed to the floor. The tigers did a few more excited back flips and then each of them used their long hammers to hook a woman and pull their bodies towards them through the dry-iced air. The tigers sniffed and spun their captives, who hung like dead fish on a line. While dancing, the tigers began to tie chains around their dead-still women. Ankles were bound and padlocked, chain braided through and around legs, tiny wrists knotted together and fastened behind backs. Blindfolds were put over the girls' eyes, and then they were left still hanging in semicircles a few inches from the stage in front of the water tank.

Eva and her grandmother were three rows from the front, on the far left near one of the aisles, so when the tigers prowled down off the stage and began to pick out people from the audience, Eva held her breath and stared at her hands, hoping not to be chosen. A fat man hauled himself up onto the stage, hands on his thighs as he climbed, then a Chinese teenager wearing a baseball cap and a pretty young woman with spine-length hair – and then Eva's grandmother giggled at the sight of a tiger in the aisle motioning for Eva to follow him. Her grandmother literally picked her up under her armpits to push her out, and Eva found her hand clasped inside a tiger's slick, yellow-gloved paw, skipping up into the blinding spotlight of the proscenium. Once she was up there, she could hardly see the audience at all. It was hot on the stage, and it smelt of sweat and rope. Eva copied the other participants in running her hands over the chain folds and padlocks digging into the silken-spandex skins of the girls. At first she was nervous to touch them – they looked dead, but the tiger paw put her hand on the chains. She had to reach up to touch the girls' ankles and wrists, but they were definitely chained tight.

While she stood there sweating into her best dress, the tigers locked huge metal weights to the girls' ankles so that when they were elevated into the air again, gravity pulled their bodies upright and the weights hung under their toes.

The tigers motioned for Eva and the other helpers to sit down again. Eva climbed down the stairs behind the fat man and then couldn't remember where she'd been sitting. She stood frozen in the darkness, searching for her grandmother's face in the audience, until a loud splash sounded behind her, and the girls were dropped into the water tank. The passive roped women came immediately to life, thrashing against their chains as beads of air climbed through the water from their pursed mouths.

"Eva!" her grandmother whispered, so she climbed over and sat down in her seat as quickly as she could. The mermaid girls struggled in the water, and Eva felt panic rising in her gut, from her stomach upwards to her lungs. In retrospect, of course, the escape was an illusion or a trick, but she'd checked the chains herself – as far as she was concerned the mermaids were never going to be able to escape. The bodies thrashed against the glass, and Eva's chest tightened. The first girl wriggled her ankles out from the weighted block, and her fetters slid off her body as she rose to the surface gasping for breath, struggling the last of the restraints away from her wrist. Almost as the first mermaid surfaced, the second emerged gasping, but the third seemed stuck.

Before the last girl escaped, Eva found that she was sobbing quite loudly in the theatre. It was unexpected, like peeing after a car journey or falling asleep when you're tired – and she couldn't stop. It was a melting sensation coming down all over her, and she didn't even get to see the end of the show, because great gusts of air and tears were pouring out of her and the next thing she knew she was standing with her grandmother in the red-carpeted foyer. Even as her gran shook her by the shoulders and her head was jolting back and forward, Eva couldn't stop crying. She hoped the last mermaid had escaped, but she never found out.

* * *

Eva phoned Luke again on his mobile and office number as she walked out of Leicester Square, but once more she went straight through to voicemail. "Call me, Luke" was the message she left as she avoided a boy vomiting against the alley between a pizzeria and a nightclub and a pink-haired woman in a sequined dress holding a riding crop in her hand and smoking outside a doorway on Greek Street. Two bald men kissed under the awning of a restaurant as she turned left into Walker's Court, the smaller man pressing the bigger man against the building until the rain got a little stronger, coming in at an angle under the awning so that the smaller man touched the damp hems of his trousers and laughed, taking the larger man's hand to lead him back inside the bar out of the wet. Eva walked up Charing Cross Road, then left into Goodge Street, where the homeless prophet was lounging on a bench outside Echo Books wearing sunglasses with broken lenses, drinking a can of lager. "It's coming," he said as Eva passed. On the other side of the road, the Oxfam shop had two carrier bags of clothes outside it becoming unusable in the rain and the Scorpio's bouncer was sitting on his stool by the club's entrance as always. Eva unlocked the door of Echo Books next to the shut-up sandwich shop.

In the thin corridor, boxes of new books were piled on the left atop the familiar ratty blue carpet. Eva tiptoed up the creaky stairs towards her office on the top floor. The fax machine was silent, phones dead at eleven in the evening, computers black. She flicked on the desk light in her office, illuminating proofs and cover jackets to be checked, publicity copy to be gone over, Post-it notes and index cards all piled haphazardly on the large brown desk.

She noticed that advance copies of *Cleopatra's Pearls*, a book one of the other editors had worked on, had come in, and she opened it with curiosity. The book's spine still smelt faintly of glue, a sickly and satisfying smell. Eva felt calmer than she had done in Silver Place, and she tipped her chair back to read, putting her feet up on the window sill so she looked out on The BT tower winking in the darkness. Below, the hairdresser and the Chinese buffet and the dry-cleaning shop were all locked up and dark. Eva couldn't see the pavement, but she heard motorbikes and night buses, the occasional group of drunks passing below. "Abigail Blue sat alone in the antechamber of her mistress Cleopatra," Eva began. "Birds of paradise sang from vast cages hung from the ornate ceiling..."

Three hours later Eva woke from a dream about drowning mermaids and birds of paradise with a pain in her shoulders. She shivered as if she'd been touched, and then realized she'd fallen asleep leaning back in her chair. She looked over to the desk at her phone to check if Luke had called, but the screen just blinked the time, two a.m. It was pouring outside, huge slabs of rain pelting down beyond the window panes. If Luke were at home, then he would have called her. Even if he wasn't home, he ought to have called her by now. It was cold in the empty office, and Eva plugged in the space heater, spewing hot air onto the back of her thighs, then looked up out of the window and over at the Scorpio. All of the windows were lit up brightly from the inside, but the green curtains were still closed, squeezing light out in chinks at the sides except for the top floor, where through a gap in the curtains of the top-right window a naked girl could be seen being held up against a wall at the back of the room. The club had never been illuminated before, but now Eva saw the corner of what looked like a mattress in the room and the blur of a shadow, perhaps a plant. It was just a chink through the curtains – a man's back was visible, the girl's feet arched around the lower tail of his spine perhaps, a butcher shop of raw body bits muddled by reflections bouncing off the surface of the window itself. The disembodied limbs moved into a different position and were gone for five or ten minutes, until they came into frame again, horizontal on a mattress. Beyond the blur of glass, it looked like the girl was face first into the mattress. Half a second later, both figures were invisible again, and then a flash of plump body appeared – perhaps the man's whale-vast thigh or stomach or backside – blocking the gap in the window before the bodies disappeared again. A few minutes went by, and the shapes did not reappear. High up in the sky, above the chimneys and TV aerials, an aeroplane floated overhead in the darkness, the flickering fairy lights of its eyes blinking in the dark, and Eva imagined that Dante the Mysterious had finally come back to claim his lover. The bony-faced girl (if it was the bony-faced girl, or any one of the other girls who presumably worked in there) was running her fingers down the spine of her long-lost lover, not some lonely punter who could only get laid if he paid for it. It wasn't a brothel full of trafficked teenagers. In the Scorpio behind the curtains were glitter-encrusted tuxedos and bowties that spun – there were bunches of magic flowers and doves erupting from top hats as the magician's assistant talked about her childhood and made love to her magician.

Eva woke up in her office again, this time to the sound of a ring tone. She didn't know what time it was, but she blinked away her sleep and picked up her beeping phone, its screen flashing with an unknown number. Eva could feel the stamp of her desk's mottled texture on her cheek. The windows of the Scorpio were black again, as if they'd never been illuminated, square dark holes in the red brick surrounded by peeling white paint. At this early hour, the Scorpio's bouncer wasn't at his post – the awning was rolled in and the door was closed. Luke's voice came clearly through the speaker. "It's me," he said. "Sorry to wake you."

"Where are you?" Eva cleared her throat.

"University College Hospital. Grace took some pills and called me in a panic to take her to A&E." An ambulance roared in the background.

"Shit," said Eva, and her heart beat hard against her rib cage for a second. The clock on her phone gave the time as nearly six a.m. "Is she OK?" Eva thought of Grace's bright eyes at the casino, the excited way she tilted her face up from the cards to the croupier.

"I found her half-unconscious with a bottle of Temazepam and a quarter-litre of rum on her kitchen floor at around midnight," said Luke. "She couldn't stand up."

"Did she mean to?"

"Justin broke up with her a few days ago. My guess is she meant to drown her sorrows, not to throw up on herself under her kitchen table and have her stomach pumped by a first-year med student named Donald."

"What did the doctors say?"

"That she's got a mild concussion and an almighty hangover, but she'll most likely be fine." Luke inhaled on the other end of the phone. So Grace had gone home, after

171

bumping into Eva near Charing Cross Road, and taken an overdose.

"Are you still there at the hospital?" Eva said.

"Yeah, still here," said Luke. "She called around eleven thirty, and I've been here since a bit past midnight. They had to keep her awake to check she's not concussed. They're not sure when they can release her."

"I was worried about you," said Eva.

"I'm fine. A bit shaken."

"Of course," said Eva, quieter now, watching the homeless prophet asleep on the bench, some pigeons pooled by the rubbish bin pecking at crumbs in the beginning of sunlight.

"I'm sorry I didn't call," said Luke eventually. "I left my phone at Grace's when I went to pick her up. It's been a terrible night."

"She must be in real trouble to do something like that," Eva said.

"I'm really sorry," said Luke. "For tonight and the other night when Grace turned up at your place blind-drunk."

"Do you want me to come over to the hospital?"

"No, I'm just going to go back up and see what the doctor says. I need to get my phone from her anyway."

"You sure?"

"There's no point in the two of us losing even more sleep. Anyway, they said she could probably go home soon." His voice had a high-pitched edge.

Eva sat at her desk for a while. She put her pens methodically into a jam jar to the right of her lamp, then arranged a small puddle of drawing pins so they all faced spike up on her computer-screen stand. From a book cover tacked to her corkboard a pretty blonde model gazed post-coitally down at her. Eva blew her nose on a Pret A Manger napkin and picked up her thumbed and annotated copy of *The Oxford Style Guide* to distract herself. "Compounds that contain an adjective should be hyphenated when they precede the noun," she read. "When a comma would assist in the meaning of the sentence or helps to resolve ambiguity, it can be used." She crinkled a Dairy Milk wrapper and nudged it underneath the base of her desk lamp, then turned to her computer and Googled "Temazepam". "Approved for the short-term treatment of insomnia, Temazepam has anti-anxiety, anticonvulsant and skeletal-muscle relaxant properties." Then she Googled "Dexedrine", the pills Grace offered her in the casino: "Dextroamphetamine is a psychostimulant drug known to produce increased wakefulness and focus as well as decreased fatigue and decreased appetite." Eva had a sudden desire to see Grace. She thought of how her fingers had felt on the soft area between Eva's thumb and forefinger when Grace had touched her in Chinatown. She got up off her desk, shut down her computer, turned off her space heater and left the room. She wanted to see Grace tuck her hair behind her ears.

* * *

It was a ten-minute walk up Tottenham Court Road to the revolving doors of UCL Hospital. Eva went up the granite front steps through the frosted-blue-glass entrance ("the trendy place to die," Eva's Dad had said when his

mother was ill) and stepped into the already bustling reception with its glass lifts and flashing screens. "Please
store medication out of reach of children!" one screen
admonished. "Infection!" warned another screen. "Don't
be the one to pass it on." A man in a limp green dressing
gown appeared, pulled along by the momentum of his
drip stand while a teenager wrapped in blankets wheeled
himself in a chair. Broken legs jutted out among bunches
of flowers waiting on the shiny floor. Eva walked over and
asked one of the women in blue fleeces behind the yellow reception desk where she might find a patient named
Grace Taylor, who had been admitted a few hours ago
with a concussion and possible overdose. The woman
typed into the computer.

"Looks like she's been signed out. Were you coming to
collect her?"

"Do you know when she left?" Eva asked. She had the
sense of being on the fringes of someone else's story.

"It went in the system about ten minutes ago. She was
signed out from the Acute Observation Unit. Is there anything else I can assist you with?"

"So that means she's OK?" said Eva.

"Means she came into Accident and Emergency, then
stayed for observation but was fit to leave."

"Thanks for your help," said Eva. She knew the hospital
well from when her grandmother was there. She turned
away from the reception towards a corridor that led through
a skin-coloured hallway, past the pharmacy and the chap-
lain's office towards the hotel cafeteria, where she'd had a
cup of tea with her father the morning her grandmother

died. She could go there and wait, she figured, then call Luke again in twenty minutes, when he might have retrieved his phone. She didn't want to call Grace's phone. She watched a baby crawl on the floor and get scooped up into the folds of his mother's burka and carried out of the revolving hospital doors, down the steps into Euston Road. Outside the hospital, a blond man smoked a cigarette on the steps. He was near the external entrance to A&E, doing up his shoelaces with both hands while his cigarette hung limply between his lips. Eva stepped out of the hospital, and Justin looked up at her as she came over to him. He raised his eyebrows, squinting against a rising column of smoke.

"Hi there," he said, taking his cigarette from his mouth and exhaling.

"Hi," said Eva, giving him a half-hearted smile. An old woman bent over a fag nearby, about the same age as Eva's grandmother was when she had died.

"How is she? Did you see her?" asked Eva, sitting down next to Justin on the cold stone steps and staring ahead at the buses and cars on Euston Road.

"She'll be fine," said Justin, glancing at Eva.

"You didn't take her home?"

"She didn't want me to. Luke went instead."

"That was good of him," said Eva. She took a deep breath. "I suppose she can't be in such a bad state if she could leave the hospital."

"Cigarette?"

"No thanks," Eva stared at Justin's smooth, pretty profile, the opposite of Luke's broken features. He wore a preppy navy V-neck sweater and black-leather deck shoes. "Has she done anything like this before?"

"She's always been fond of her oxy-whatever and Dexe-something and Quaaludes – and anything else she can get her hands on," Justin said, adjusting his glasses on the bridge of his nose and placing the cigarette between his lips again. "She only takes things she's been prescribed at some point in time – for depression and insomnia and panic attacks or whatever – as if that makes it legitimate to self-medicate off the Internet."

They sat in silence for a minute. Justin pushed his glasses up on his nose again, an uneasy movement quite different from the Zen-like economy of energy he showed at dinner in Chinatown. Eva had then thought he'd appeared almost irritatingly calm, but perhaps that was only in comparison to Grace's hyperactivity. It was clear he was anxious now. He ground his cigarette into the bottom step of the stairs and then smudged the ash mark with the heel of his leather deck shoes.

"Are you OK?" said Eva. She fiddled with the cuff of her jacket, trying not to lift her fingers up and bite her nails. "You guys broke up?"

"I didn't think she was particularly upset about it," he replied after a short pause, then looked at Eva.

"She must have been putting on a brave face to you," said Eva, thinking of how nervous Grace had been at the casino. Justin shrugged, looking at the increasing rush of traffic on Euston Road.

"She seemed pretty sure about it. Not that it came as a surprise. Once Grace has something, she doesn't want it any more."

Justin smiled for the first time since she had sat down, a slow sideways smile in her direction. He looked exhausted and took off his glasses to rub his eye sockets.

"So she broke up with *you*?" Eva said.

Justin raised one eyebrow. "Hard to believe, I know."

"I just thought you were the one who ended it."

"Is that what she told you? God forbid she'd seem anything but sympathetic. She didn't love me – not really. I'm not sure she ever loved me, actually."

He adjusted his glasses again and took out a squashed pack of Benson & Hedges from his trouser pockets. He ducked his neck to light his cigarette, and Eva noticed a shaving cut on his neck.

"She called Luke," Eva said.

"She and her sister were close to Luke when they were kids."

"Her sister?"

"Mary." Justin paused. "I really hope she finds a way to be happy," he said, ashing his cigarette and staring at the mound of grey where it fell. "Strange to think it's not my responsibility any more."

"I hope she's OK too," murmured Eva. Traffic buzzed around them, an ambulance siren came to a halt, a man rushed out of a taxi up the steps of the hospital with a look of horror on his face.

"I should get to work now. Are you going to be all right?" said Justin, then drew from his cigarette and picked up his bag.

"Sure," Eva said, frowning as she visualized Grace and Mary from the photograph in Luke's album. She had thought Grace was a boy at first, masculine in comparison to Mary's figure in pink wellington boots and lip gloss. She wanted to ask Justin to stay with her for another moment, give her more information, but he was looking around and seemed eager to be gone from the hospital.

"I hope everything works out the way you want it to," he said, touching her shoulder.

"Same for you," Eva said.

Justin turned left onto Tottenham Court Road, while Eva went and sat in the hospital canteen, whose floors were made of shiny plywood, layered with so much varnish that it appeared wet. Around the edges were pink or blue panels of wall, which only made the room appear more depressing. There was a smell of burnt lasagne, and fake daffodils in frosted-glass vases on each table. Perhaps it was the waiting, or the faces caught between impatience and submission, but that hospital canteen had something of an airport lounge about it. Everyone was thinking about exits.

* * *

On one of the two TV screens in the corner of the room, the news flashed with footage of refugees – dusty, screaming children's faces – then back to the studio, where a red-lipped presenter gave a broad smile and said: "*Yesterday afternoon Regina, the golden eagle escaped from London Zoo, was spotted flying out of Regent's Park. She was seen over rooftops flying south towards the river, and she finally landed in Trafalgar Square at around four p.m.*"

Eva raised her eyebrows and smiled as the screen flicked to footage of Trafalgar Square, with Regina perched on the bronze head of a sculpture in a far corner of the square, Nelson's Column in the background.

"*As the rain continues in the wettest summer in Britain since 1925,*" the presenter's voice continued, "*the Zoo has been desperately trying to recapture their prize bird, but she has so far eluded her keepers.*"

On the screen, Regina rippled her shoulders against the cold and peered down at the umbrella arcs below her, the nervous pigeons being nudged out of the square by a swelling throng of humans flashing their cameras.

"*In Regent's Park she attacked two small dogs and killed three ducks, including one from the pond of the American ambassador's garden, which almost caused a diplomatic row.*"

The camera panned past smiles on the balcony to the right of the steps: a grinning man with long dreadlocks, a serene pregnant woman, a goofy teenager with the stone spire of St Martins behind her, an attractive wide-eyed blonde who tucked her hair behind her ears while a dark-haired man with broad shoulders held a blue golf umbrella straight above both their heads. Eva blinked. She wasn't sure of what she'd just seen – really not at all. The TV screen was not large and the camera only passed over the blonde and her companion for a moment, but it was enough time for Eva to imagine that the man was Luke, the collar of his cashmere coat turned up against the rain, his skin pasty next to the butterscotch colour of Grace's long neck and the scarlet of her lipstick in the crowd. The camera moved back to Regina herself.

Eva got up and stepped closer to the television, nearly tripping over the legs of the table as she craned her head upwards at the screen. She was tired. She'd slept in her office chair, waking up from dreams of mermaids to the sight of torrential rain and figments of her imagination fucking in a window across the street. Around her the canteen buzzed: fridges, a throbbing heating unit, the tapping of a fat woman's fake nails on plywood, footsteps. She stared up to see if they'd play the Regina footage again, but the screen flashed back to the studio.

"Wasn't that *something*, James?" said the female newsreader to her male colleague.

"It *certainly* was, Louise."

She must have imagined what she'd just seen: Luke holding his umbrella protectively over Grace, both staring up at Regina. She thought of the magician's assistant face down on the mattress opposite Echo Books, the beer-bellied man's hand on the back of her head. Eva had a strong sense that she needed to see Luke or Grace. She was slipping away from her surroundings – colours a little too bright, light a little unreal. She wanted to touch Luke, or Grace. She wanted someone to be near her.

"I'm about to go into a meeting," Luke had said to Eva the day before, as she watched him walk towards London Bridge, over a mile from his office. "I'm just walking into chambers," he'd lied. "I might have to work late." It had been three o'clock in the afternoon when he came out of court. If it had been him staring up at Regina, perhaps he had walked west all the way along the river in the rain, past Blackfriars Bridge and across Waterloo Bridge, down along the Strand towards

Charing Cross. Perhaps Luke had picked Grace up from her office, or they arranged to meet somewhere else, in a café or a restaurant, or a pub looking out on the Thames. Eva felt sick. She imagined Grace and Luke whispering to each other as they watched Regina from the edge of the square. They'd spent the afternoon together, that's why Grace was late for her event at the Phoenix Theatre. Perhaps he took Grace to the rooftop restaurant in the National Portrait Gallery, where he'd taken Eva for her birthday the previous year. Maybe they had shared a bottle of wine, then wandered a little tipsy through the galleries, pausing in the miniatures room on the first floor, neither of them paying attention to the inch-high painted pendants of Thomas Cromwell or Catherine of Aragon, the oil-on-copper portrait of Henry VIII or the eerie, blue-eyed Sir Walter Raleigh with a ruffle around his neck and a gold oval frame. Eva used to visit that room when she was younger, after school or on Saturdays, peering at the painstaking smallness of the miniatures. She tried to think what Grace's and Luke's expressions had been like on the screen. Had Grace been open-mouthed? Was Luke smiling? Eva couldn't remember. It was such an extraordinary thing to see – a golden eagle in Trafalgar Square.

Eva walked home from the hospital in a daze and lay in bed to read that day's newspaper headlines on her computer, searching the photographs for the faces of Luke or Grace: "EAGLE EYED IN TRAFALGAR SQUARE," announced *The Guardian*. Eva zoomed in on the faces of children and smiling women, but couldn't find either of them. "ZOO EAGLE SPOTTED IN CENTRAL LONDON," said *The Times*, but there was no Grace, no Luke. "HUNT FOR ESCAPED ZOO EAGLE INTENSIFIES," read The *Independent*. Eva closed her eyes on the photographs of Regina on her majestic bird stand, Nelson's Column and the National Gallery in the background, and sank back on the bed exhausted.

She would have liked to map the moments when her relationship with Luke intensified, a little graph like the ones school kids make in exercise books. That first kiss in King's Cross, the first "I love you" after he seizured in Silver Place, that day when he hurt her after the Halloween party, and their first holiday together, when she had watched him reading *The Economist* by a dirty swimming pool in Spain and felt oddly timeless. The airline had lost his luggage that holiday. He spent the week wearing lurid Bermuda shorts, plastic flip-flops and giant dictator-style fake Dior sunglasses acquired, at the airport, from a shop that also sold fridge magnets and inflatable pool crocodiles. Perhaps it was the effect of the heat, or the bells constantly in the distance, or the smell of chlorine and jasmine that filled the humid air inside and outside the guest house, but that holiday she'd realized that it wasn't normal love she felt for him – at least not love as she had known love before. It wasn't need: she didn't need to touch him or be looked at by him. It was a stillness, almost, as if she hoped to be watching him just like this, beyond a garden next to a swimming pool in the middle of nowhere, in twenty, thirty years' time. It wasn't desperate or urgent.

"Eva?" said Luke. "You awake?" Eva sprang her eyes open and saw Luke looking down on her, holding the tip of his tie to his chest so it didn't fall on her. He smelt of sweat with a slight twinge of sweetness. She glanced sideways at her clock: eleven a.m. She sat up.

"Our witness didn't turn up," he said, "so court was adjourned. Looks like I'm going to get him off though."

Despite everything, Eva was relieved to see him. There he was, within touching distance. He didn't touch her, though. There were so many questions in her head, but instead she said:

"How?" She rubbed her eyes, coming out of her dream.

"His brother-in-law gave him the job and did the accounts. Our guy's not the brightest bulb. The brother-in-law owns a bunch of dodgy businesses."

"Like what?" Eva said, closing the computer that was still open on the bed.

"Internet scams, nightclubs. I have to go in for the afternoon, but just wanted to check you're OK. I'm sorry about last night."

"How is Grace?" said Eva. She thought of the eagle perched in Trafalgar Square, the silhouetted frown of the bird and the sculpture.

"She's a bit shaken." Luke took off his jacket, and his shirt, underneath, was wrinkled. He loosened his tie and then eased it off from around his neck, laying it carefully on the back of a chair. He undid his trouser buttons. It felt good to be near him, but the hairs on Eva's fingers were standing to attention, and she found herself noticing tiny details of Luke's appearance – the exact angle of his forehead, the way one of his eyebrows was slightly higher than the other – almost as if she were memorizing him. "Did you spend the afternoon with her?" Eva said.

"Of course not," said Luke.

"You only saw her *after* she took the pills?"

"She called me from her kitchen floor after she fell, at about 11.30." He bent down to take off his trousers and revealed blue striped boxer shorts with ridiculous matching peacock-blue Pringle ankle socks. He smoothed his trousers over the back of the chair and came to sit down on the bed at Eva's feet. "She called me when I was finishing off at work," he said. "She was almost incoherent. She said she'd taken pills and couldn't move. I had to help her out, right?"

"Of course you did." Eva dragged the cool hem of her duvet between her fingers, staring at Luke's socks. "She's Mary's sister, though," said Eva. "Do you still see Mary, too?"

"No," Luke said, and he turned his head away from Eva.

"So you and Mary were childhood friends, too?"

"Yeah. You knew that."

"I didn't."

"Well, yeah. Our fathers were neighbours, in Devon. They lived in the next-door farm and I spent a lot of time there, growing up."

"Did Grace make your lip bleed at Catherine's party?"

"I'm sorry I lied, but I made it pretty clear that I didn't want to see her, and for some reason I thought she'd do as I asked. I just wanted her to go away. I didn't want to talk about it, even to you."

"She hit you because you said you wouldn't see her?"

"She'd been trying to contact me for a while, then I bumped into her at Catherine's do and she lost her temper. You would have thought she'd have grown out of all that."

"Of all what?"

"Tantrums. She was a ferocious kid. A proper little bully, always getting in fights."

"Were you?"

"What?"

"Always getting in fights?"

"Sometimes. Grace and I played football and fought and all that. Mary was more reserved. More thoughtful and mature. They lived in a house full of people and games, neighbourhood-watch meeting in one room and boy scouts learning knot ties in the other. There were always a million people flooding in and out of the house. Mary kept herself to herself, while Grace was leader of the gang."

"Were you ever in a relationship with Grace?"

"No. It was always Mary, even when we were little. Mary was magic." Luke touched Eva's foot and the contact felt uncomfortable, too hot. She wished he wasn't sitting so close to her. "Grace was just the sister of the girl I'd always been in love with, that's all. I'm not that keen on hanging out with my ex-girlfriend's sister. It's not so unreasonable."

"But she's keen on hanging out with you."

"We bumped into each other. She kept asking about you, about my life now, and trying to get me to agree for us to have dinner, and I said I didn't want to pick over the past – and I don't know, at some point she just, sort of, launched herself at me."

"There must have been an argument, then or before?"

"Like I say, we never really got on. Lots of arguments, as children and teenagers. We argued that night, because she was drunk and difficult, and we'd had a hundred arguments before that point. I thought she'd slink off after she hit me, that she'd be embarrassed and disappear. I really thought she'd fade away again."

"You smell of perfume and vomit."

"She's always been a mess. Even as a kid, she was a mess."

Eva pushed the duvet away from her fingers and turned her face from Luke as if turning away from his smell. He didn't look at Eva, just stood up from the bed and picked up a towel from the chair.

"I can't talk to you when you smell like her," Eva said, and brought her legs up against her torso to rest her knees on her chin.

"I smell of hospitals. I spent the night in one. Helping an old friend. A family friend."

Eva paused, studied his face briefly in their bedroom. He looked tired, creases reaching from his nose to the edges of his mouth, darkness under his eyes.

"Go take a shower," said Eva.

While Luke was in the shower, Eva glanced sideways at his BlackBerry from the bedside table. She picked it up. For a moment she pretended that she would put it back. She didn't let herself think, but held it in her hand and scrolled, her heart speeding up, over to the "messages" icon. She thought: the eagle, up there in the sky, with Grace and Luke staring up at it amazed, either in reality or in her imagination. She listened to the sound of Luke's shower pounding against the bathtub, and thought of Luke's body in the bathroom just beyond the bedroom wall, his face upturned to the shower head. Eva didn't have to look very hard to find a mention of Grace on the phone. The last text message sent to Luke's phone that day was from Grace. It read: "U want to meet at Shepperton Road or Poppins? One OK?". Eva took her finger off the cursor, her head throbbing. The shower stopped on the other side of the wall. She put the phone back where she'd picked it up, and a moment later Luke came into the room with a towel around his waist. ("I went to a psychic this morning and he told me that keeping secrets was bad for my health," Grace had said during her game of two truths and a lie.) Eva's head was still throbbing.

"I have to go back to court," said Luke. "Are you OK?"

"I'm fine," said Eva, and she watched him get dressed without speaking.

"I'm sorry I didn't call you last night. It was just so hectic."

"It's fine," said Eva, not looking at him now.

"It's your go at Scrabble?"

Eva didn't reply, and he left the room. All she could think of were nonsense words, her grandmother's mournful exit haikus: "Longly and go on, so," she would say, "I'm perfectly the opposite of right." Or: "I'm scooped out. I want not to be here, caught here. It's all to be gone soon."

* * *

At one p.m. Eva sat at a window table in Starbucks, opposite the black-marble arched entrance of Luke's Fleet Street chambers. She felt the tingle of doing something wrong, a raw feeling in her gut, but she wanted to be sure of herself. She took a sip of coffee and kept staring out of the window. She'd Googled "Poppins" earlier and found that, assuming they weren't meeting at a kindergarten in Woking, a household-staff recruitment agency in Leeds or a cake shop in Newcastle, they were probably having lunch at a café near Fleet Street. She figured that since Luke needed to be in court later he'd opt for lunch in town rather than Shepperton Road, which was in Islington. He'd obviously been to Grace's flat before, and they'd clearly had lunch in Poppins before. Perhaps they had lunch there before walking to Trafalgar Square under a single umbrella in the drizzling rain and seeing Regina amongst the statues.

The sun had come out, and the rain had paused for the first time in weeks. Everyone seemed happy. People laughed and talked to each other as they smoked outside cafés and office buildings, rather than hiding under awnings, puffing quickly with haunted faces. Men in pinstriped suits came out onto the pavements, hands in their pockets and sunglasses on their heads. Women in stilettos strode to lunch meetings with papers under their arms.

Eva analysed every figure that trouped out of the arch, waiting for the flash of coloured handkerchief that always peeked out of Luke's suit pocket, or the familiar hunch of his shoulders. But none of the men were Luke – just anonymous people with frowning faces, squinting against the unexpected sun. It was already a quarter past and the dregs of Eva's coffee were cold when she glanced up with a start to see Luke on the other side of the zebra crossing and coming directly towards her, shoulders tense, looking at the floor. He wasn't wearing his coat, and he had his sunglasses on his head.

Eva turned her face from the window, but Luke seemed deep in thought as he crossed the road towards her and then turned to his right. Eva got up from her window seat once he'd passed by and stepped straight out into a man talking on his mobile phone just to the left of the door.

"Sorry," Eva mumbled, and a little of the man's coffee splashed on the front of her jeans (just what you want while stalking your boyfriend, Eva thought, *coffee stains*). She stood still for a moment to watch Luke walk another two blocks, heading in the direction of St Paul's Cathedral's sunlit balloon head, which appeared to be lifting off behind the jumble of Fleet Street buildings. Luke turned left into an alleyway between the shiny blue cross of a Boots chemist and the front awning of a Wagamama restaurant.

Eva knew she shouldn't be watching him. But she couldn't stop thinking about his face – and Grace's – as they watched Regina in Trafalgar Square. On the far side of the alley was Wagamama's staff entrance, then an old-fashioned barber shop, then the Poppins café where, through the two large windows that formed the front of the place, Eva watched Luke's figure sit down on a corner table behind a window-sill pot plant that partially obscured her view of him. She took another step into the alleyway, which was entirely in shadow and much colder than Fleet Street. She edged forward, as close as her courage would allow. If he had looked out of the window he might have seen her, since she was perfectly visible to him from there, but Eva almost thought that would be OK – and anyway Luke just looked straight ahead at the blonde figure sitting in front of him. Luke wasn't a man for sideways glances. Grace – it must be Grace, wearing a long-sleeved white shirt with the collar turned up at her neck, her flash of blond hair loose – had her back to Eva, so she could not see her standing there. Eva thought back to Luke's flamingo-bodied "sister" when he'd turned up the first time at Silver Place, the woman in the red jacket outside the pub near Old Compton Street, the publicity girl tucking hair behind her ears at the Brooks's club party: all incarnations of Grace. Like seeing the shadowy magician's assistant at the Scorpio window, it was all shards and pieces.

When bad things happened to her, Eva often felt almost separate from them. Yet she didn't feel that way at all while watching Luke lean over and cup his hands on top of the smaller ones already resting on the Formica café tables. She was absolutely present in the moment. She didn't feel the touch as if it were on her own skin, or imagine what she might say to Luke the next time she saw him, but was just standing there in a Fleet Street alleyway staring in at the mime of Grace and Luke holding hands across a café table. She hugged her jacket around herself and followed Luke's lips moving beyond the glass partition, then dipping his head and whispering something to the girl sitting in front of him. After that, Luke withdrew his hands and Grace leant forward as he leant back, like bodies in a boat, so they both remained parallel for a second. The firework stigmata on Eva's hand and the scar on her elbow both stung. She couldn't see Grace's face. Luke remained leaning back in his chair, while Grace straightened up. A waitress seemed to break the moment by coming over with two mugs and two plates of sandwiches, and the three of them chatted for a while, before Luke and Grace were left to themselves again.

Eva couldn't tell what was happening after that. Luke's mouth moved quickly, then closed as he listened to whatever Grace was saying, interjecting with occasional bursts or taking a bite of his sandwich, or putting his hand on Grace's hand and then taking it away again. Neither looked happy. They talked for about twenty minutes, and Eva moved around a bit, keeping her head down so it didn't look as if she was just staring through the window of the café. She kept thinking Luke would turn and see her there, a hundred yards at an angle from the window, but his eyes didn't stray from Grace. She almost wanted him to turn and see her, but he didn't.

Luke's black hair was sticking up in all directions. She'd been so preoccupied with leaving him that it hadn't occurred to her that he might be the one to leave.

She ought to have been angry seeing him there with Grace, but anger wasn't exactly what she was experiencing. She felt loss – a hungry, sorry, sure feeling. She wiped at the stains of coffee on her jeans. Luke had one hand flat on the table now. When he lifted it and hit it back down again, saying something sharp, Grace pushed her chair back and stood up. She disentangled herself from the chair and paced out into the aisle between the counter and the tables. Eva started and rushed back to stand behind the corner of the alley, back in the sunlight of Fleet Street as Grace stepped out of the café, followed a second later by Luke. He took her wrist in his hand, and for a moment there was a hint of threat: fragile Grace held still by Luke's strong hand. Eva tried to breathe as Grace allowed Luke to drag her into his arms. They folded together not quite in a kiss, but certainly in an

191

embrace. He hugged her, and she seemed to sink into his body. It was tender.

Eva looked away. She didn't want to see. When she lifted her eyes again Grace and Luke were disengaging themselves and then stood opposite each other, not speaking for a moment. Luke disappeared inside the café, presumably to pay the bill, and when he came back they turned towards Fleet Street, walking in Eva's direction. Eva stepped away from the grey-brick corner and turned backwards on herself, sneaking through the automatic doors into Boots.

She stood near the window, by the make-up counter, in air that smelt of face powder. Grace walked straight past the front window of the chemist shop, alone, wiping her eyes. Somewhere after coming out of the café she must have started to cry. Her pretty face was briefly visible to Eva: she could still see the tomboy child in her – the hair was blond now, the gap in her teeth was closed, she no longer wore a baseball cap backwards or grubby tracksuit bottoms, but she was the same girl as in Luke's photo album. Luke strode past the window a minute later, his shoulders hunched, sunglasses on his head, looking at the pavement as he had been thirty-five minutes before when he had walked in the opposite direction.

Once Luke and Grace had gone, Eva continued to pace around Boots in a daze. When the security guard started to give her funny looks and she'd walked through each aisle at least twice without touching anything, she retraced her steps and went back to Poppins Café, taking the table Grace and Luke had shared twenty minutes ago. The place smelt of stale coffee. Somehow the café had seemed eerily empty apart from Luke and Grace, but in fact there were many people, mostly men, spread out on the tables. A businessman in pinstripes was reading *The Financial Times* and checking his BlackBerry every few seconds, two executives wearing more casual suits were talking and occasionally jotting down notes on a shared pad of paper spread between them at a right angle. Eva ordered a coffee from the waitress but didn't drink it, because her stomach was already clenched in knots. She paid the bill and hailed the first cab she saw to take her back to Fitzrovia.

* * *

Back in her office, her hands still shaking, Eva looked across the road to the Scorpio. To calm herself down she tried to imagine Sophia and Dante behind the window. She imagined the girl's tiny mouth like a pebble dropped in a puddle, her high cheekbones and wide forehead, her bony shoulders as she kissed her lover inside the sea of tears she'd cried before he appeared in the limbo of the club to reclaim her. A pair of pink frilly knickers floated by in the waves of Sophia's tears, and a sodden rabbit was slumped in a boat fashioned, perhaps, from a lampshade. Clothes and magic wands and flower bouquets and playing cards all bobbed on the flood of Eva's imagination as Sophia and Dante made love again in the water. Only, Eva kept loosing concentration and filling the water too high, so the lovers would have trouble breathing, or blinking and forgetting about the water altogether, just seeing the girl lying face down and naked on the mattress with her hair all matted to one side.

Above the Scorpio, beyond the chimneys, the sky was the colour of wet papier mâché. An aeroplane flew over. Perhaps it was because of the sky, or a creeping sense that all this was her fault for not asking the right questions, for being lost in her own world, but Eva had a fleeting mental image of her mother sitting alone on a beach in Singapore. The memory belonged to a day Eva had spent with her parents watching aeroplanes pass across Changi Beach in Singapore when she was seventeen. When she left for London at the age of fifteen, her parents had moved into a compound of bungalows near a golf course on the north-eastern edge of Singapore, near Changi International Airport. Their little red-brick bungalow was a short drive from the beach, so on the fourth day there her mother prepared an elaborate picnic of scones and egg sandwiches while her father packed beach chairs and binoculars for plane-watching (as well as his mobile phone, frisbee, two newspapers and a hand-held DVD player just in case he got bored, which he invariably did on days when he wasn't working). Up until the afternoon at the beach, the holiday had been bearable, if slightly unnatural, each of them doing a reasonable job at pretending to enjoy themselves. In the evenings they had dinner together and watched TV. When her father was working, Eva went to the market with her mother, or sightseeing by herself, even to a giant mall one morning to buy a spare part for her mother's Magimix. She had seen her parents sporadically in London for the previous two years, but this was the first extended period of time she'd spent with them since moving to Silver Place. Her mother didn't seem too bad: routine-driven perhaps, but then the whole living situation – with the bungalows and golf courses and man-made beaches – had a mechanical quality about it. Perhaps she was simply born for a doctored existence, making cakes for charity raffles at golf-course gala dinners, and everything before had been a mistake – which was fine by Eva, as long as her mother had found some sort of peace. But on the day of the beach picnic, once they'd eaten their egg sandwiches, the sky began to cloud up and her mother soon followed.

"There's going to be traffic jams up there tonight if that storm breaks," Eva's father said in a jovial tone, lying down on the sand to watch the aeroplanes passing over as he lit his umpteenth cigarette: he still had the same habit of smoking half a cigarette, putting it out, and a moment later lit another one. He wore beach shorts and a Panama hat, while his wife wore a faded sundress with little daisies on it. Eva watched the aeroplanes with her father for a while, sharing the binoculars and letting him tell her where each plane was heading, and then Eva opened her copy of *Romeo and Juliet*, which she was meant to be writing an essay on for school. Her mother began to clear up the plates, while Eva clicked her biro and underlined key passages. "Oh, do you think we'll ever meet again?" Eva said in her head, memorizing Juliet's words. "I have no doubts. All these troubles will give us stories to tell each other later in life," replies Romeo, leaving Juliet's bedroom their first night together.

"You know this beach is haunted?" said her father all of a sudden, and Eva looked up.

"Please don't talk about that," said her mother in that whispery voice of hers.

195

"Why? It's living history right here, maybe she can write about it in one of her reports or whatever she does at her school. Thousands of Chinese were tortured and killed here during the Sook Ching massacre of the Second World War. She can write about that."

"Please don't ruin this," her mother said, so quietly it was almost inaudible.

"Ruin what?" he said. "I'm just talking."

"I'm going to go for a walk."

"Tell us if you see any ghosts." Her father went back to his binoculars.

Eva read for another hour as the clouds built up in the sky, but soon it was obvious that they should pack up and head home before it rained, so she stole off to find her mother. She wasn't far up the beach, sitting alone beyond some tidily planted palm trees with her chin on her knees staring out into the sea with that same expression Eva remembered from when she was a child: her mother appeared both intent and distant, as if involved in a world that was not the one around her. Eva experienced a flush of heat at her mother's solitary and sad appearance, not only because she recognized it from unpleasant moments of her childhood, but because she suddenly acknowledged something of it – a remoteness, an aloofness – in herself. She desperately wanted to back away as she'd learnt to do as a child when her mother looked this way, but instead she told herself that things would be different this time. Her mother's shoulders looked so frail under the faded cotton of her dress, her face old.

"Is everything OK?" Eva said, sitting down in the sand next to her mother.

"I'm fine," she said, not looking at her daughter. "Just fine."

"Are you and Dad OK?" Eva said.

"Oh yes," she said. "We're fine." Then just as Eva was about to ask another question, her fingers itching to put her arm around her mother's frail shoulders or touch her hand, she turned her head and looked coolly at Eva with her brown eyes: "Please, I think perhaps I'd like to be alone just now."

Eva's palms started to sweat. She got up again as quickly as she could.

"We should go soon though," Eva mumbled, wanting to be as far away from her mother as possible, flushing from the memory of being a child and ignored. The look her mother had given her was impenetrable, a selfish look of complete isolation that Eva remembered so clearly from Bali and Hong Kong. Eva walked back to where her father was smoking near the deck chairs.

Eva was not always present – she knew that. Grace was present, Grace existed centre-stage. Luke, too, lived for the moment.

* * *

"Wearing her best green-velvet dress with the white rim, Lady Serenity Azure pressed her back to the wall in the darkness," Eva read from *The Pirate's Mistress*. "She could hear the men eating the wild boar they caught that afternoon, the smell of meat and the sound of guitar music washing over the beach. Lights from the fire danced in the darkness and Serenity knew it was now or never." At four p.m. Serenity was lost in the island wilderness pursued by pirates, and Eva stepped out of the office to buy a pack of ten Marlboro Lights from the newsagents next to Le Pain du Jour, a few doors from her office. Eva had not smoked for a year, but she crossed the road to where the Scorpio's bouncer was puffing away on his perch. She held the cigarette shakily between her fingers.

"Do you have a light?" The man looked at her for a long moment as if to say, *obviously*, before passing over a plain silver Zippo. Eva lit and inhaled, tasting something nasty and nostalgic, like memories of being drunk.

"You work across the road, yes?" the bouncer said. "I see you sometimes."

"Yeah. It's a publishing company. We publish romantic novels," Eva said, still sensing that there might be a punch or a scream or even some tears in her, but swallowing the feeling in a surplus of cigarette smoke.

"*Romantic* novels?" the bouncer said, frowning at her under bushy eyebrows.

"You know, um, love stories?" Eva said. "With pink, shiny covers?"

"Ah," the bouncer nodded, with that grin that men often produce at the mention of such novels. "I see, those. For the women, yes?"

"Yeah." Eva smiled and inhaled, feeling giddy. The corridor went back at an angle, its red carpet like a tongue. "Would you like some? For the people who work in your bar?" Eva said with nonchalance. "The dancers?" she added, worried that he'd turn her away or clam up if she said the wrong thing about the girls. The man gave Eva the once-over: her knotted boots, torn jeans, the faded crease of her T-shirt peaking down under the rim of her jumper, an ancient leather jacket she had bought from a charity shop.

"To keep to read?" he asked, cocking his quadrangular head to the side.

"The place I work in," Eva pointed to the Echo office across the road, "is packed with books. I could just bring you some, if you like."

"OK, yes. The girls like the stories I think, to read. Why not, huh?"

"OK," said Eva, continuing to smoke her cigarette. At least this was something; it wasn't centre-stage, but it was something.

Eva went down into the basement of Echo Books to rummage around stacks and stacks of novels – hundreds of fantasies of ultimate love. Brown cartons piled up to the ceiling like damp bricks, full of copies of *Flirting with Sin* from the Noughties (a moderate bestseller, which Echo massively overprinted at the height of its success), preserved in the hope that it may come back into fashion. *Sacred Fury* propped up a wonky work desk in the corner, where ancient post-office weighing scales sat coated in dust, all the prices long out of date. *The Diamond Girl* spilt up over another tower of brown cardboard bricks. Eva emptied a box and, as footsteps plodded over the corridor above, filled it with as many examples of escapism and far-fetched romance as she could find. She then folded the flaps, waited until there was silence above and made her way up past a broken piece of mirror, more posters, a ladder and a space heater.

She grabbed a copy of *Cleopatra's Pearls* as she stepped out of the front door into Goodge Street. Nobody was likely to notice these missing books, and Echo would be none the poorer for their disappearance.

Outside, she smiled at the bouncer, and he raised his eyebrows, leaning forward to peer into the box. She had a horrible feeling he was going to ask her to leave the box in the hallway, but instead he said: "There's no one down there, but get Dominik to make you a drink if you like – you tell him Adam say it's fine."

Eva smiled.

* * *

She stepped through into a narrow corridor. Up close the carpet was a faded blood colour with bits of dust and fluff around the edges. The wall was lined with mirrors. At the end of the corridor was the sort of glass cubicle you get in banks. An arched-shape fissure in the reinforced glass was just big enough to put a hand through, and behind it were papers, files and calculators. To the left was a staircase with one wall covered in pleated red silk. Three cardboard boxes were stacked at the top of the stairs. A ladder was slung against the wall, near a door on the first-floor landing. The staircase continued downstairs, disappearing into a basement where the low fizz of jazz music could just be heard.

Eva walked down the steps and turned the corner into a dark room with a bar right in the middle, almost tripping over another box, full of women's high-heeled shoes in all shapes and colours. She entered the basement and looked around her. As her eyes adjusted to the darkness, she saw that at the far end of the room was a black painted stage with two gold poles and on the wall closest to the staircase were DJ decks. A massive flat-screen television had been taken off the far wall, and wires hung out of some broken plaster. The television, on its side, was half covered in bubble wrap. The carpet was brownish leopard print, trampled so flat that it almost looked like unvarnished wood, and around the edges of the room were leopard-print sofas and chairs. A ribbon of miniature light bulbs, slightly thicker than fairy lights but similar, wound all the way around the basement and a circular shelf of drinks in the middle of the bar was mirrored and illuminated Barbie-doll pink with odd knick-knacks on show: a few cans of a drink called "Pussy", a novelty Coca-Cola bottle with a tattered label naming it "Cock", a Malibu bottle in the shape of breasts, a porcelain doll wearing a T-shirt saying "Boozer". As Eva stepped over to put her cardboard box on one of the stools around the bar, a man appeared from the other side with cocktail tumblers in his hands. He had a horse face with shadowy eyes. He scrubbed a dishcloth around the rim of a glass and looked Eva up and down.

"Adam outside asked me to bring these in," Eva said, opening the box and taking out the azure-blue beachscape cover of *Cleopatra's Pearls*. She noticed that in the far corner of the room a tall blond woman wearing jeans, a big hooded peppermint-coloured jumper and five-inch clear-plastic wedges was coiled up on one of the sofas reading *Hello!* magazine. There were no doves in here. No bunches of flowers or top hats of giant playing cards. The low ceiling was black and the place smelt sharp, of cleaning fluid masking body odour.

"Should I put them somewhere?" said Eva. "They're books."

The barman shouted something in what sounded like Polish to the woman on the sofa. She was probably around thirty, with long nails, big lips and lines around her eyes. She uncoiled herself up from the sofa and reluctantly walked on her plastic stilts to the bar without making eye contact with Eva. She was a full ten or eleven inches taller than Eva. In a way she did look magical, another species, perhaps a pornographic centaur with plastic hooves. She picked through the books, nails tapping on the covers as she looked at them and then smiled at the barman. It was a strange smile, her swollen lips seeming more suitable for pouting.

She said something in Polish to the barman.

"For her?" said the barman, pointing at the blonde.

"For anyone," said Eva, and the barman nodded at the woman, who nodded at Eva. "But they're in English."

"For us," the woman said, "to make practice with reading the English."

"Yeah, I guess," Eva said, smiling. A saxophone played in the background. The fairy lights on the ceiling reflected off the mirrored wall on one side of the room. At one side of the stage were some stairs going up to another room.

"This one's the best," said Eva, holding up *Flirting with Sin*.

"They free?" The woman took the book and turned it over in her hands.

"Yeah," said Eva. "We publish them, just across the road. We printed too many."

"You want a drink?" said the barman, motioning to his mirrored pink bar.

"A vodka-and-tonic would be great, thanks," Eva said.

"Lemon?"

"Sure," said the man as the woman took *Flirting with Sin* back with her to the sofa.

"Do you want me to take them upstairs or something?" said Eva.

"Upstairs?" the man said, pouring vodka over ice and eyeing Eva sideways. "No." Just then a great fat man clomped down the stairs, wearing a short-sleeved white-chequered shirt, shiny suit trousers and huge, rapper-style trainers. He shouted something over his shoulder and then, noticing Eva at the bar, he stopped. The lines reaching from his nose to either side of his mouth created a pronounced triangle on his chubby face. Eva hoped this wasn't the man she'd seen naked in the window, the man she'd imagined to be Dante.

The barman replied something and handed Eva her drink.

The fat man exchanged a few more angry words with the barman in their foreign language, then motioned for the tall blonde to get up and made a dismissive gesture at Eva.

Eva didn't know where to look, so she lowered her eyes to stare at her drink, finishing half of it in a single gulp and then getting up off her seat.

"*Teraz!*" shouted the fat man, and both Eva and the barman jumped. Only the blonde woman stood still and expressionless on the stairs. Eva could hear her own blood beating in her ears. The fairy lights made shapes in the dark mirrored wall to her right. The mirror wobbled, almost like a horizontal puddle.

The fat man shouted again, and then both he and the barman looked over Eva's shoulder to the staircase that she had come down ten minutes earlier. She turned and saw the magician's assistant there at the doorway. A momentary glance was enough to see that she was a child – maybe fifteen years old in her leopard-print strappy top and basketball shorts. Eva had noticed her deep-set eyes from a distance, the tiny, knotted mouth, but not how the features fitted together into an unformed face that might one day be pretty. She had a mercurial look – a woman merged with a half-dazed child searching for her mother at the school gates.

"*Wracają Anya!*" the fat man hollered over Eva's shoulder, and a woman appeared very briefly behind the girl. The woman was older and plumper, with leathery skin, possibly the same one she had once glimpsed in the Scorpio Club corridor retrieving the escaped white bunny from Adam's arms. Eva had the impression she knew her from somewhere else – maybe Southwark Crown Court. Could the woman have been there, in trouble for something, or supporting someone who was in trouble? The older woman and the magician's assistant withdrew from the doorway. *Anya*, Eva said to herself. The character was not called Sophia, but Anya. There was a similarity between the names, the soft vowels of their endings perhaps, although Sophia was more of a whisper than Anya. The fat man nodded in Eva's direction and went back upstairs, into the VIP area of the club, followed by the blonde centaur in the plastic hooves. For a moment the barman and Eva were still, then he said to her:

"You go. Business no good now, there is problem for him."

"Oh," Eva said. "Well, thanks for the drink."

"Thank you, too, for the books," he said.

Eva slipped one copy of *Flirting with Sin* into her bag and walked up the red-carpeted stairs back into the hallway. She scribbled her phone number on the inside jacket of the book and wrote: *"For Anya, from Eva, the girl from the office window across the street. Call me on this number if I can help you."* The book was just slim enough to be pushed under the door at the top of the stairs and then Eva rushed out of the club. She felt slightly outside herself, as if she were the heroine of one of her novels.

It was nearly five by the time Eva got out of the Scorpio, so she didn't go back to work but walked away through Soho. She stepped down Goodge Street into Mortimer Street, then left down Regent's Street, towards West End Central Police Station on Savile Row. There was a drunk smoking a rollie on the steps; a bearded man in a suit stomped out as Eva walked into a small waiting room. Three chairs were lined up along one side of the room, and a female police officer sat at a desk behind a streaky pane of glass. Next to a door marked "PRIVATE" was a corkboard with posters of "missing" people, grainy images of men and girls staring straight ahead. Eva waited in line behind a man in paint-splattered overalls who was describing how he was at the receiving end of a hate-mail campaign. He was given a form to fill in and went to sit down with a morose expression on one of the plastic seats, while Eva stepped forward to the woman, who yawned. Eva was sweating.

"Good evening," the constable said to her.

"There's a place on Goodge Street called the Scorpio Club," said Eva through the glass. The constable nodded, a yawn quivering again on the corners of her lips. "There's a girl living in there who can't be more than fourteen-fifteen. I think her name is Anya."

"May I take your name?"

"My name? Eva Elliott," said Eva.

"A child," mumbled the constable. "The Scorpio Club," she said, nodding to herself and reading something off the computer. "We are aware of the Scorpio Club. There is an ongoing investigation at the moment." Eva could feel the man in the paint-splattered overalls listening to the conversation from his seat, along with an old woman with a perturbed, possibly senile smile on her face, who kept scratching her scalp.

"Are they closing the place down? They looked like they might have been packing up," Eva said, and the woman looked up at her from the computer.

"I'm going to need your contact details. We'll be in touch if we need any more information from you," the police-woman said.

Off Savile Row was New Burlington Place, where Eva stood and looked up at Justin's office building. "Bluetone Productions", it said on the buzzer, which Eva remembered from her conversation with Grace and Justin in Chinatown. One side of the back alley had big glass windows framing white rooms with Macs on clean desks, while the other was a semi-crumbling wall of restaurant and café back entrances. Eva rang the little chrome buzzer of "Bluetone Productions".

"Is Justin around?" Eva said, dipping her neck to speak into the intercom.

"Which company?"

"Bluetone," Eva said. She looked through the window into a nondescript reception area with a security guard sitting behind a desk. Everything was white, with white-leather seats and white-framed posters on the wall, advertising documentary films.

"Do you have an appointment?" said the security guard.

"Could you just tell him that Eva's outside?" she said.

"Wait a moment," said the voice, and Eva shivered, hugging her jacket to her body. The security guard punched some buttons into his phone and nodded a bit, then spoke through the intercom without getting out of his chair. "Come on in," said the guard, and the door buzzed open. Eva shook out her umbrella and folded it up as she stepped in.

"He'll be down in a moment," said the security guard. "Please take a seat."

Eva put her umbrella down and sat on a white sofa. She picked up a copy of *Variety* and flicked through it without reading it, then got up to get a cup of water from the cooler near the window. The room smelt of central heating and Febreze.

"Eva," Justin said, coming out of the elevator. He was wearing the same preppy navy V-neck sweater and black-leather deck shoes as that morning. There was something comforting about the wrinkles around his mole eyes, his only slightly thinning blond hair, his residual suntan. He was very pretty. She could at once imagine him as a child making sandcastles, and how he would be in the future as a middle-aged man playing tennis every Tuesday and holidaying in the South of France with his future wife and charming blond children. In contrast to Luke's fragments, all versions of Justin appeared tied together. He'd choose a nice girl now, after Grace, and marry her soon.

"Sorry to bother you at work," said Eva.

"I was just finishing. What's happened?"

"Do you want to have a drink? Do you have to be anywhere?"

"Grace called to say she was OK," said Justin, stepping closer to Eva across the white reception room. She put her plastic water cup in the bin and turned away from him, even though she would have quite liked him to put a hand on her shoulder.

"Has anything else happened?" Justin asked.

"Nothing," she said.

"Let's go have a drink – yes, of course," he said. "Of course."

Eva and Justin ended up in the lobby bar of the Grange Holborn Hotel, where Justin was staying. They drank bottled beer in a bar decorated as if meant for the out-skirts of Las Vegas, with golden lamps and chandeliers and replica Greek jewellery on sale behind display cases. Sitting on low leather armchairs, businessmen ordered sandwiches and house white. The floor was black-and-white marble, and the partitions between seating areas were made of patterned frosted glass.

"I've been here the last two nights," said Justin. "I'm letting Grace stay out the month at our place."

"Nothing beats a room-service hamburger and crap TV," said Eva, faking good humour and taking a handful of salted peanuts in the palm of her right hand.

"So what's new since this morning? You look like hell," Justin said. He took a sip of beer without breaking their gaze.

"He moved in with me at the start of the summer, in May," Eva said, rubbing warm peanut salt between her fingers. "He alphabetized our books together."

"He alphabetized them? Modern romance." Justin paused. "And now?"

Eva shrugged. "Where would you meet Grace during the Apocalypse?"

"I'd walk in the other direction," said Justin, nodding his head.

"No you wouldn't," said Eva.

"No. I'd probably go to the St Paul's side of the Millennium Bridge and pretend I didn't expect her to turn up."

"He's been lying to me," she said. "He's been seeing Grace. Did you know?"

"I know they bumped into each other at some party."

"And after that?"

"She told me she wanted to 'have a chat with him about old times', but he wouldn't see her, wouldn't return her calls."

"Do you know why?"

"She said she just wanted to be friends with him again," replied Justin, then spoke a bit quieter, as if softness could temper the meaning. "She told me he came over at our place a few days ago while I was away filming, if that's of any help." Justin took off his glasses and rubbed his eyes as he'd done outside the hospital earlier that morning.

"I spent a lot of our relationship thinking about leaving him," Eva said, looking away – at fingerprints on the glass table, fake flowers on the reception desk, Justin's clean nails. "I always knew it wouldn't last."

"Had you decided on a method?" Justin said, trying to lighten the mood. "A girl once tipped a plate of spaghetti carbonara on me when I broke up with her."

"Rookie mistake: always clear the area of portable objects before a serious ending."

"In primary school a girl broke up with me in a Valentine's Day card."

"Harsh," Eva said.

Justin shrugged. Eva wondered if he knew about Luke and Mary being together once, but decided not to mention it.

"Are you hungry?" said Justin.

"I guess," said Eva, although she wasn't.

"I'm hungry," said Justin, not keeping her gaze. "Shall we order room service with some stiff drinks and not talk about Grace and Luke?"

Eva raised her eyebrows, about to interject. Justin continued: "And I mean that innocently," he hastened to say. "A hamburger – and I might even let you chose the movie."

Later Justin was leaning forward on a chair and Eva sat on the tip of the hotel bed. There were socks and scrunched up T-shirts and books all over the mustard-coloured carpet, shirts and boxer shorts piling out of two suitcases on a red sofa in the corner of the room. Justin's house keys – Grace's keys – sat next to a bunch of magazines – *New Scientist*, *Wired*, *National Geographic* – along with some unopened post and an invitation to a film screening from the day before. A room-service tray covered in hamburger fragments was now pushed near the door. Eva tried not to think about Luke, but he kept sneaking back into her mind. She and Justin had a game controller in their hands and were concentrating, neither of them with much enthusiasm, on a game called *Dragon Blood II* on the television in front of the bed. She was controlling an avatar with horns growing out of her blond hair, almost a centaur, with hooves instead of shoes, and Justin was a bald man with heavy eyebrows and skin-tight trousers. The game was set around monster-infested cathedrals and ancient ruins, where the aim seemed to be to kill as many dragons as possible. Creatures of all sorts came out of nowhere, bats or birds swooping out of the sky.

"Fire!" Justin said. "Get that dragon over there in the corner."

"I am," Eva said, pressing random buttons, wishing it would all stop. She pressed something and, through some unknown cause-and-effect chain of events, a mauve dragon exploded on screen, taking out a few other coloured animals in the process. The screen splattered with purple blood, and Eva's mind, as soon as it wasn't occupied with buttons and dragons, reverted to thinking about Luke and Grace hugging outside the café earlier,

Luke holding the umbrella over Grace as they watched Regina in Trafalgar Square, all the small sharp puzzle pieces nudging around in her head. Eva tried to push the thoughts away again.

"Do we get to go to another level now?" said Eva.

"No, we still have to vanquish Radar – he's the prince of the dragons in this area," Justin said. "Another vodka tonic?"

Eva kept her controller on her lap while he put his down and set about making her a drink from the minibar. He opened a Corona for himself. They clinked glasses a little mournfully and, after a second's hesitation, Justin sat on the bed with her.

"So is this what you do in your swanky hotel room every night?" said Eva, resting her feet on the floor.

"Pretty much."

"It was a good hamburger."

"It was."

Eva slipped her finger up and down the side of her drinks glass.

"Did you ever play the polar-bear game?"

"No," said Justin.

"You have to sit in silence and not think about a polar bear. The first person to think about a polar bear loses," said Eva. They both paused.

"How are you doing with the polar bear?"

"Badly," said Eva. "You?"

"Grace had it tougher than most," Justin said. "They were a very close, eccentric family. All that happened with her sister was hard on Grace." He put his glasses back on the bridge of his nose, adjusting them with his finger. Outside, traffic was huffing past on Southampton Row, and droplets of rain were thickening on the window pane.

"Her relationship with her sister was tough?" said Eva, imagining this might be because of Luke, despite what he'd said about never being with Grace.

"Well, yeah," said Justin, looking at Eva's blank face. "Luke didn't tell you?"

Eva thought of the photograph of the timid girl with thin legs: her slumbrous, fox-like face and sad eyes, Luke's protective arm around her.

"Grace thinks you look like her," said Justin.

"Like Mary?"

"After we had dinner in Chinatown, Grace was all freaked out. Said you had Mary's mannerisms. I don't know. The expression of her eyes or something."

"Do you think so?"

"I never met Mary."

"You've never met Grace's sister?"

"Mary was anorexic – she died when she was seventeen," Justin said. The hotel room pulsed. "I guess maybe you look a bit like her, from the pictures I've seen."

"What happened to her?" said Eva.

"A problem with her heart," said Justin, tilting his head to the side. "Because she wasn't eating – hadn't been eating properly for a while."

"Fuck," said Eva. That was all she could utter, that inexact syllable, the sharp exhalation of its ugly sound.

"She had a blood infection, I think. She came out of hospital, and they thought she was fine, but she had a heart attack at the farm. She'd been ill for quite a while by then. Grace was sixteen when it happened."

Eva and Justin fell silent, and then a motorcycle exhaust backfired on the street outside the hotel, a pop like an exclamation mark on the conversation. She had a bitter taste in her mouth. It was strange how emotion *tasted*. Adrenalin was metallic, boredom was cotton-woollish, fear was bitter. Eva felt the panic dripping down the back of her throat. She thought of that look she sometimes saw in Luke, that struggling expression he got in his eye when he thought nobody was watching. That look, perhaps, was Mary.

Eva and Justin tried not to touch each other as they put spare covers and pillows on the hotel-room sofa for Eva to sleep on. He offered to sleep on the sofa himself, but she declined. He lent her a T-shirt, and she got changed in the bathroom, sitting on the bathtub to check her mobile.

Eva didn't want to talk to Luke, but he didn't want him to worry either. She had three missed calls from him, so she texted: "Staying with a friend, back tomorrow." Then she crawled inside the covers on the sofa, and Justin got in the bed and they said goodnight and switched off the lights, but neither of them fell asleep. Eva's blood throbbed at her temples and at her wrists, and her mouth still tasted of panic. The energy was all pent up, tightly wound. She kept tossing and turning under the covers, trying to find a position that was comfortable.

"Eva?" said Justin, after fifteen minutes. "You awake?"

"Sorry, am I keeping you up?"

"That sofa is clearly uncomfortable. Why don't we both sleep in the bed? We're not teenagers. We can handle it. Climb in," said Justin – and she did, slipping under the duvet with her back to him. They lay awake for a while, listening to each other breathe. At one point his hand reached over and rested on her upturned hip. If she'd turned that hip towards him, even slightly, they would have released tension and anger together, but she didn't move. Eventually his hand fell off her hip as if it had just been there to comfort her.

In that hotel bed, falling asleep next to someone who wasn't Luke, Eva felt very much as if she were falling. She wondered what Anya was doing, in her room looking down on Goodge Street: perhaps sitting on her mattress reading *Flirting with Sin*. Perhaps the girl didn't have access to a phone and couldn't call Eva's number. Perhaps she'd find a phone and call, though, but then what would Eva do? Why would the girl call her, anyway? Why call a stranger who leaves notes in badly written romantic novels?

Eva took a quick shower in the hotel room and got dressed in the semi-darkness. As she did so, she noticed Justin's key on his bedside stand. He stirred and turned towards her.

"You off?" he mumbled.

"Thanks for letting me stay," she said. "I need to go home and change before work. Thanks again."

"No time for breakfast?" he said.

"I'm already late. You can sleep a little longer."

"OK."

And as Justin turned away from her, she slipped his keys into the pocket of her jacket, along with a copy of *Wired* magazine still in its plastic wrap, with Justin and Grace's Shepperton Road address on it.

Eva sat in a café on Warren Street for an hour after leaving Justin. At 9.30 she called Echo Books and told them she wasn't coming in until later. Her boss wasn't impressed. Then she called Grace's office and put the phone down when one of her colleagues confirmed that she was back at work and not off sick. Eva had thirteen missed calls, seven new messages and four texts from Luke, staggered throughout the previous night, but she didn't call or text him back. She put her phone on vibrate, hoping that Anya might call from the Scorpio, then took a taxi from Fitzrovia to Hackney.

Twenty-five minutes later through rush-hour morning traffic, Eva's taxi eventually pulled up outside a red-bricked building on Shepperton Road, perhaps a converted school, with tall arched windows on the top floor and smaller white-rimmed windows down below.

She looked up and wondered if Luke could be in there, even though it was a Thursday, and as far as she knew he had never missed a day of work. "Justin and Grace" was written on the buzzer next to flat 3A. The front door opened with an electronic button that hung on Justin's keychain, leading to a small reception area that still had rubbery flooring particular to schools and hospitals. You could imagine paintings of stick people and bulletins about parents' evening on the walls. Eva couldn't see a lift, so she walked up the stairs to the third floor.

She knocked first. Nobody answered. She stood in the landing for a moment, listening for any noise inside the flat. Then she heard a creak on the staircase behind her, so inserted Justin's key into the chrome handle with a click and stepped into Grace's flat.

It was bright, and so immediately clean-looking that even with sunlight pouring in through the windows no dust was illuminated in the squares of sunlit air. No smudges on the windows or on the furniture. Half the furniture was made of glass: the dining table, chairs, coffee table and TV bench all appeared more like solidified light than objects. It was a high-ceilinged studio loft with a spiral staircase leading to a small balconied bedroom above the main living area. Big arched windows with off-white blinds filled up one of the walls, a mirror covered the other. It wasn't a big flat, but the oversized windows and mirrors gave an illusion of space. A yellow silk dress was draped over a black leather sofa, a pair of costume-jewellery earrings and some of Grace's trademark bangles were abandoned on the coffee table – the rest of them were still at Silver Place. Eva took off her shoes and put them carefully in the corner next to the front door, almost as if she didn't want to sully the flat with her scuffed ankle boots.

She took a step inside. The kitchen cabinets were against the back of the room, with a freestanding island separating it from the rest. In the taxi her hangover had hit, so she opened the cabinets looking for a glass to put some water in: pasta and muesli were kept in plastic Tupperware on the top shelf of one cupboard, herbs were stored on a spice rack; coffee, couscous and rice were all in glass jars with air-tight lids. The glasses were in rows according to style – champagne flutes, wineglasses, water glasses. She took a cut-glass whiskey tumbler and ran it under the tap. She leant on the sink to drink it down gratefully while staring around at the minimalist modern art on one wall of the flat, the bookshelves behind the spiral staircase, the brick arched loft windows.

This was just the sort of flat she had thought Luke ought to be living in when he first turned up to look around Silver Place. She hadn't ever imagined where Grace and Justin lived, but she would have placed them somewhere more bohemian than this empty white loft. She put her glass in the empty dishwasher and opened a cupboard. With embarrassed interest, she opened the fridge: vitamin capsules, probiotics and nail varnish; some salad, organic-turkey slices, half a cucumber and a paper bag from Wholefoods with some sort of takeaway salad in it. Eva closed the door again.

In the middle of the room, a few cardboard boxes were already in the corner ready for Grace or Justin's packing. A single tall bookshelf was hidden behind the spiral staircase: it almost went all the way up to the ceiling, so you'd have to climb a few steps to get to the top shelves. Fat volumes by Jilly Cooper, Jackie Collins, Danielle Steel were interspersed between novels by Milan Kundera, J.G. Ballard, Graham Greene, Truman Capote, *The Oxford Guide to Film Studies*, *100 Greatest Films of All Time*, *Film Posters of the 90s*, critical theory, a thesaurus. Eva picked out an illustrated book called *Fashion* from the bottom shelf, inside which Justin had written "For the most fashionable girl I know, on her birthday". Then she opened a photograph album packed full of nicely arranged pictures of Justin and Grace on holiday in

Cyprus or Italy or somewhere. Grace looked younger, her face ever-so-slightly plumper in the pictures, and her hair black as when Eva first noticed her outside Silver Place and as she was in Luke's photo album. Justin looked younger too, and in every photograph he hovered affectionately over Grace – a hand on her shoulder or arm, a protective glance from the side or from above.

While Eva was looking at Grace's almond-shaped eyes in the photographs, her big mouth with oversized teeth and that fringe cut, as it was all those years ago outside Silver Place, bluntly across her forehead like an expensive doll's, she heard a sound outside in the apartment-block corridor. The footsteps got louder, until they were outside the door, but to Eva's relief they continued. There was a low scratch of metal scraping metal, then a muffled click. A door creaked in the distance and closed, leaving silence.

Eva put the holiday album down where she'd found it and felt her knees weaken as she came back up to a standing position. She walked across the flat and sank down on the sofa in the middle, opposite the coffee table and the small television in the corner. She ought to leave – put on her shoes and go.

She touched the cool silk of the yellow dress laid out on the edge of the sofa. Grace had probably been horrified by Silver Place and its stratified layers of chaos. No single, elegant silk dress and a bit of stray jewellery constituting mess in Silver Place.

She shut her eyes, her head aching. She took her phone out of her jacket. Fourteen missed calls from Luke. She imagined him sitting where she was sitting now, on the leather

sofa, perhaps watching Grace potter around the room getting dressed or laying the table for dinner when he'd told
Eva he was working late or when she hadn't bothered to
enquire about his whereabouts at all. Perhaps they'd had
dinner on that glass table, perhaps there'd been candles and
music, things she never really thought of doing for him. She
blinked Luke's image out of her mind, wiggled her feet on
the floorboards, her toes just touching the bleach-white
rug under the coffee table. Next to Grace's bangles was a
spiral notebook full of scratched out "To Do" lists. "*Call
Alix Walker, confirm interview time,*" one of the pages said
in girlish handwriting, the words all crossed out in purple
glitter pen. "*Follow up with Psychologies magazine about
Louie. Patent red shoes to match red jacket – Top Shop at
lunch? Pick up dry cleaning. Call Mum about weekend.
Finish Marlen's press release.*" On the other side of the
room, a leather weekend bag sat on the glass table, next to
three folded T-shirts, a slick Clinique make-up bag and a
pink toothbrush.

Grace and Justin's bed was just visible on the mezzanine
above the main room. She wasn't sure if she wanted to go up
there. Maybe this was enough, now. She must leave. Only, it
didn't feel as if there was much to lose just then. This was
not the goodbye she had been dreaming of since the first
time she and Luke kissed.

She got up from the sofa and climbed the spiral staircase
in the left-hand corner of the room. There was a low black-
painted bed at the top, the kind with big storage drawers
hidden underneath. She opened one drawer gingerly with
her foot – there were little cotton storage combs inside, each

with a different knicker and bra set folded inside. She almost laughed. If Luke were a woman, he'd keep his underwear in storage combs like these.

In a big built-in wardrobe opposite the bed, one of the panels slid open on dresses and dinner jackets, stilettos and chinos. It smelt of perfume and laundry. Two more photo albums were kept upright with a Selfridges hatbox in the corner of the wardrobe. One was labelled "New York" and the other "Family".

Carefully, Eva took out the photo album labelled "Family". She recognized Mary's timid face on the first page. Luke's first girlfriend was maybe sixteen in the photo and, like Eva, Mary was pale with freckles. Her hair was poker-straight and red, though, while Eva's was dull brown and messy. She couldn't see a great resemblance. Had Grace touched her hand in Chinatown, dragged her for lunch in Piccadilly because she looked like a person she missed? If Eva had felt ghostly before, she felt inconsequential now.

She studied the photographs: Mary and Grace holding hands with other children around them, Mary in a ballet tutu and Grace in dungarees with her cap on backwards; Mary, gauchely adolescent but not too thin yet, reading a book with a solemn and determined frown on her face; Grace with her head completely shaved; a kitchen table piled with food, family and laughing guests.

On subsequent pages Eva studied a twelve-year-old Grace with her black hair just growing back, pouting from the seat of a tractor; a rounder-faced Mary with braces on her teeth and shiny pink lip gloss: she was thin, but looked much healthier than in later photos.

221

He obviously didn't fall in love with her when she was anorexic. That came later.

A teenage Mary wrinkled her nose for the camera; Mary and Luke holding hands on a stormy English beach while Grace and a whole bunch of other kids sat on a towel in the background.

And then there was another photograph, of Mary in a hospital bed, her skin pulled tight as a fist against the bones of her skull and her half-smiling lips like a pinch of ever-so-slight colour in an otherwise white face. Her dry eyes had a haunted look. There was nothing mischievous or young about her in that photo. She was cradling a bunch of lilies in her arms, and there was a pink-and-purple "Happy 17th Birthday!" balloon tied to the bedhead behind her. Eva, who was never particularly connected to her body one way or the other, could not understand the compulsion to cause the body pain. That, certainly, she did not have in common with Mary.

Eva sat down on Grace's bed and put the album on her lap. She noticed a pocket on the back page of the album. She opened the pouch and took out rows of negatives couched in faded yellow paper, a ticket stub for a school performance of *A Streetcar Named Desire*, a pressed flower taped to a piece of cardboard and three chalky newspaper clippings folded several times that clearly hadn't been opened in a long time. Eva unfolded all of the newspaper clippings and pressed them out on the bed. They smelt of dust, and she had to be careful to stop the edges disintegrating as moth wings might under her fingers.

NORTH DEVON GAZETTE – 23rd September

LOCAL GIRL MARY TAYLOR was found dead near her family's farm in Little Torrington on Saturday, having suffered fatal injuries after a fall. Ambulance crews were called to the farmhouse at 11 p.m. on Saturday, where paramedics pronounced her dead at the scene. Family and friends are left devastated by Mary's death, aged just seventeen, and have paid heartfelt tribute to an "angel" who will be "missed and never forgotten".

Her father, local farmer and union activist Bob Taylor, told *The North Devon Gazette*: "Mary will be forever missed by her parents, siblings and friends. She was a thoughtful and intelligent girl, a good student who loved reading and spending time with her family. She shall always be loved and remembered."

A funeral, for family and friends, will be held at St Edmund's Parish Church later this week.

NORTH DEVON GAZETTE – 28th September

HUNDREDS join funeral procession for much loved local Torrington girl Mary Taylor. Mary died after a heart attack at her parents' farmhouse on 7th November.

School friends from Torrington High gathered outside her home in Little Torrington to join the funeral procession to St Edmund's Parish Church.

Mary's boyfriend, Luke Jones, who grew up on the neighbouring farm to the Taylors, read 'September', by Ted Hughes, while Mary's sister, Grace, and two brothers, Max and Tim, who are regulars in the church "a cappella" group, sang a song from *Cabaret*.

The parish church was packed for the funeral service, led by the Rector, the Revd Jeremy Hummerstone, and a sound system was set up to relay the service to others outside in the churchyard.

NORTH DEVON GAZETTE – 22nd September

All are welcome to the annual gathering at St Edmund's Parish Church on 23rd September to light a candle and say a few words in remembrance of Mary Taylor, beloved daughter and friend, who died three years ago today.

As she reread the three articles, Eva heard the scratchy metal sound of a key in the door. She waited for the noise to subside. A click and slide as the handle turned, then a tap of heels on the floorboards inside the flat.

Eva remained still, the newspaper clippings in her fingers, heart thumping so hard that she could feel it in the back of her throat. She didn't exhale.

"Look, I have to go, the taxi's waiting, I have a bunch of errands before I catch the train," Grace's voice came clearly from downstairs, and for a split-second Eva thought the words were directed to her, but then realized that Grace was talking on the phone. She didn't move. Grace paused, putting her toothbrush and make-up case inside her bag. "I haven't heard from her, no," said Grace into the phone. "No."

Eva's shoes were by the door. If Grace hadn't seen them on the way in it was because the door hid them as she opened the door: she'd surely see them on her way out – ancient boots with knotted laces, out of place in the clean whiteness of her flat. Eva sat stone-still.

"Oh come *on*," said Grace, picking up her bag, "clearly she's pissed off at you and she's staying at a friend's house, Einstein. I don't blame her."

Eva tried not to shift her weight on the bed.

"Fine, fine, calm down," Grace said, and her heels clicked back across the room underneath the mezzanine where Eva was sitting. "I haven't," Grace said. "I won't."

Grace had taken her bag from the dining table. When the apartment door clicked closed Eva's heart was still beating so fast she felt dizzy. She put her hand over her mouth. The room was quiet. She could hear the creak of a water pipe behind the walls, the stir and buzz of traffic outside the windows. Alone again, she put the newspaper clippings back into the photo album and the album back where she'd found it on the top shelf of the wardrobe. She looked at her phone and saw nineteen missed calls from Luke, with one from two minutes ago, so he must have finished talking to Grace and immediately called her. She put her phone back in her jacket pocket and rubbed her eyes. She climbed down the spiral staircase and stared over at her shoes sitting right there by the door, apparently unnoticed by Grace in her rush to get back to her taxi. She dragged her shoes on, unlocked the door that Grace had double-locked, then double-locked it again from the outside with Justin's key.

* * *

On the Number 73 bus from Essex Road Station, Eva tried to think of herself as a Lilliputian. Her grandmother used to tell her stories about an army of giants vanquished during a skirmish with Olympian gods and buried in the middle of the earth, whose occasional convulsions caused earthquakes. She used to lie in bed at night as a child and feel dizzy, imagining the giants asleep underneath her. The traffic lights at Euston Square Gardens blinked red and as the bus heaved to a pause, a blond woman outside a flower shop reached out to touch the deep-pink tropical petals of a tall cone-shaped flower, leaning over a bucket of lilies. But of course it wasn't Grace – not one of her incarnations. When she turned, the woman looked nothing like Grace.

The Scorpio Club was still there, sitting unchanged between the hairdresser's and the £3.50 Chinese-Thai buffet. She wasn't sure what she'd expected to happen. Storm troopers? Immediate closure as soon as she pointed out what was going on? Adam was still smoking calmly under the awning and he gave a faint smile at Eva as she stood on the opposite side of the street and looked up at the darkened windows. On the first floor she could see the beach-blue spine of *Cleopatra's Pearls* with an ashtray on top, and next to it what looked like the yellow spine of *Flirting with Sin*. One floor up, she thought she could see a green spine, a red spine and a navy-blue spine, all nicely lined up next to a coffee mug. On the top floor – at Anya's window, where the curtains didn't quite close – there were no books. Eva let herself into the Echo Books office.

"Eva?" said her boss through the door as she trudged to the first-floor landing, past old publicity posters flaking off the stucco wall. She was turning up for work gone midday, and she'd been even later the day before. She knew she was taking the piss. The office was lax, but not so lax that nobody had noticed all her absences that month. Perhaps they'd fire her, but right then Eva didn't care. Two paint cans kept her boss's door slightly ajar, so she popped her head around, into the cloud of cigarette smoke that lingered constantly amongst the book dust and stench of space heaters in that room. Instead of curtains, the publishing director of Echo Books had a strip of cross-hatched plastic sacking stapled against the window behind her desk.

"Hello, my dear," her boss said from behind her desk. Piles of proofs and manuscripts formed a jagged skyline around her. "Someone came by earlier for you." Eva's pulse jittered at the thought of Grace.

"Is she here?" Eva said. "Did you let her in?" Her fingers, strangely, tingled. She remembered staring at Grace in the pockmarked mirror of the Brooks's Club bathroom, thinking this talkative stranger had an elfin profile, as if drawn with a very soft pencil.

"God no," her boss said, eyebrows dancing, perturbed by the thought, looking back at her computer. "I assume you're not *just arriving* at work?"

"*The Pirate's Mistress* is almost finished," Eva replied. "Just putting the last touches to it. When did the girl come?"

"An hour ago. She said she'd return. Do try to get *The Pirate's Mistress* to me at some point, will you?"

"Of course." Eva slunk out of the office and went upstairs to her office at the top, peering out at the dark daytime windows of the Scorpio.

"Serenity smoothed the reddest of dresses over her body and smeared a touch of perfume, just a touch, behind her knees and her earlobes," Eva read. "The sky above them as they tussled on the beach was the deepest of blues, scattered with brilliant white stars." The Echo Books doorbell didn't ring again until four p.m. Eva put her pen down on the pirates and opened the window to stick her head out into the spitting rain, expecting Grace's blond hair on the street below. Instead there was a large fuchsia baseball cap with a tiny stick figure wearing a miniskirt underneath it. Eva frowned. She looked across the road at Adam, who was watching the Scorpio girl. Eva clattered down the stairs two steps at a time past the publishing director's office, down into the hallway, opening the front door into the street. Before her was the magician's assistant in the flesh, wearing a shell-fabric bomber-jacket hood pulled over the top of her cap. She had a quilted plastic mushroom-coloured handbag over one shoulder and her hands in her pockets. She looked at Eva with stern eyes and didn't smile. Eva stepped aside, and the girl entered the hallway without a word, looking around at the light bulbs on the ceiling, the half-clothed women lounging on posters from the walls. From the other side of the street Adam was observing them, smoking a cigarette, but he didn't get up off his stool when he caught Eva's eye. Eva turned to face the girl in the hallway.

"He's watching you," said Eva, unsure what you were meant to say when you meet a figment of your own imagination. She was solid, or almost solid: flesh and bone to be sure, although slight and placid. Eva could smell the girl's breath: stale cigarettes and toothpaste.

"Is OK," said the girl, not holding Eva's eyes but glancing down at the floor. She had the tiniest of skirts over bare white legs and blue plimsolls on her feet without socks.

"Come upstairs?" said Eva. The girl's eyes were set far back in her skull, as if her eyeballs were stones sinking slowly into some viscous anaemic substance. She followed Eva up two flights of stairs, her plimsolls hardly making a noise as they pressed the worn carpet of the stairs and landing. The only person in the higgledy-piggledy office Eva couldn't avoid was the accountant next to her office at the top of the building, whose open door she had to pass to enter her own. The accountant frowned at her as she smuggled Anya past, but she shut her office door before he said anything.

The two girls stood clumsily in the office for a second once the door was closed. The air was too hot from the space heater under the window, which had no half-settings: just full pelt or nothing.

"Do you want to sit down?" she said to Anya, moving a pile of papers from one of the three office chairs and spinning it around for the girl. Anya was looking past the chairs, the desk, the books, the ancient computer, and out of the window, towards the Scorpio.

"They are closing it," Anya said. There was something both aggressive and babyish about her. She pursed her lips as if her gums were dry. "Is no good any more."

"How come?" Eva said.

"They in trouble. With the policemen. They say we must move."

229

"What are you going to do?"

"There's a new place near, an apartment." Anya looked at Eva from under the rim of her cap. Her brown eyes were bloodshot. "I could leave if there was money."

"Did you get the book I left?"

"Yes," the girl said wearily, not smiling. She pushed her hood down from her head. Without that extra shadow around her face, Eva noticed that the girl had a blister on her slim upper lip, a little beetle-fat mound of skin about to burst there, and a bruise on her neck underneath her ear. This was no soft figment of anyone's imagination. With her severe mouth and thin face, she was probably more a part of reality than Eva would ever be.

"If you had money would you leave the club?" Eva said. "Not go to the next place they've organized for you?"

"The barman, he's quit because of police. Before he go he went and got passports from safe. He and Adam, they not the boss, they say we have choice now, but not really. Because no money." Anya gave a pointed look at Eva again.

"Where would you go?"

"Back to Croatia. My mother is not OK."

"What's wrong with her?" Eva said, wishing the girl would sit down, but she remained teetering near the closed door as if ready to escape the office.

"Ill," Anya shrugged her shoulders, which Eva imagined were skeletal under the shiny bomber jacket.

"I'm sorry."

The girl didn't offer any more information, but stood there as if bored.

"Your English is good," Eva said, trying to put the girl at ease.

"I learn from a school book. Is no problem."

"Are you going to read the novel I gave you?"

"I do not think it is much truth," Anya said, and Eva might have laughed if the girl hadn't looked so very grave. Anya still had her coat on and her handbag over her shoulder and she'd put her hands back in her pockets. "You say in note that you help me," she said, abruptly doing away with the small talk. "You buy me ticket to Croatia?"

"You want an air ticket?" said Eva.

"Expensive," Anya pointed out.

"How much?"

"Thank you. Soon," Anya said. Eva sat down at her desk and began searching for flights. The girl made her nervous. Anya took a single step forward into the office, so that she could see what Eva was doing. Eva glanced sideways and saw that the girl's hands, momentarily out of their jacket pockets, were so thin-skinned that veins were visible. It was as if the girl had been superimposed on her box-piled, book-lined, paper-drowned office. Having watched Anya through two panes of glass for so long, she felt edgy now she was so close.

"Where in Croatia?" said Eva, wanting to get this done and turning to Anya. "There's an airport in Dubrovnik or Zagreb."

"Zagreb," said Anya. She dug around in her bag for her passport and put it on the table.

"OK," said Eva, flicking through to the right page on her computer screen.

"You pay that?" Anya said, looking at the screen.

"Sure," Eva said, as the girl fidgeted at her shoulder. Eva didn't have a lot of money in her bank account, but she had enough to buy the girl a plane ticket. "I'd be glad to."

"Good," said Anya, without a smile, squinting at the screen. "Flight eight o'clock."

"That's it," said Eva.

"Today," said Anya, impatient, near-insubstantial fingers making fists.

"You don't have any luggage?" said Eva.

"No," said Anya, putting her fists firmly in her pockets, burying them in.

"Can I ask you a question?" Eva said, taking out her debit card to complete the booking.

"Yes," said Anya, waiting, watching Eva press "Confirm" on the screen.

"Is there a bunny rabbit in the Scorpio Club?"

"A what?"

"A white rabbit?"

"A rabbit?"

"Yes?" said Eva, typing in Anya's passport number.

"No."

"You've never seen a rabbit in there, with black paws? Maybe the pet of a woman who wears a red scarf on her head?"

"No," said Anya, throwing a cautious sideways glance at Eva. "There is Maria with a scarf, but no animal." Eva finished, printed a receipt and took some money from her wallet to hold out for the girl.

"Thank you," Anya said. She folded her fingers over the money and flung her hands into her pockets again, eager to get away.

As Anya's gaudy cap turned into Tottenham Court Road, Eva stared at the empty window across Goodge Street, with the curtain that didn't quite open. Perhaps she had just imagined the rabbit. She couldn't remember now, it seemed a long time ago. She thought that the bony-faced girl of her reveries was still in there, nothing to do with the knowing child in the shell-fabric bomber jacket with an ill mother in Croatia who had just left Echo Books and disappeared from view. Then Eva changed her mind and imagined that everyone inside the Scorpio was disappearing – the magician's assistant, Dante, the lion cub, the tiny albino rat, the bunny rabbits, the fugitive doves, the butterflies and all the other magician's assistants – they simply woke up that morning with their slightly translucent skin after the flood subsided, and knew that they were on their way out of existence. The magic was vanishing. The charm was broken, and soon all the creatures would be no more, there'd just be the hint of a few silhouettes in the air, the faint sound of paws on carpet, the outline of a body fading away in the darkness. As Sophia sat on her bed and began to disappear, she remembered how on late summer evenings, at home, before she met Dante and ran away, the cherry tree in her garden hung with fat red fruits. Sophia's mother perhaps worked all day at a dress shop or as a secretary in town, so it was always in the evening that they'd go out with lanterns to pick the fruit and boil them on the stove with lemon juice and sugar. Sophia's favourite moment was when the sugar started to thicken and glisten on the pot, changing form. The summer when the circus came to town and Sophia fell in love for the first time, the cherries tasted particularly sharp on the back of her tongue. Eva imagined that Sophia left the jam boiling for a minute too long, while she watched a firefly jump at a lamp, so when the jam set that last time it tasted of burning. It was a strange thing that after all Sophia been through since then, all the cities she'd travelled through with her magician, the limbo she'd lived in, all the years she'd spent tearful and angry and missing him while trapped in at the Scorpio Club, when everything finally disintegrated like a figment of someone else's imagination, all the magician's assistant could think about was the taste of burnt cherry jam.

* * *

When Eva left the office that day – after finally emailing her boss *The Pirate's Mistress* – Grace was sitting on the bench outside Echo Books with the leather weekend bag at her feet, along with a growing scattering of cigarette butts and an empty cup of coffee. Eva couldn't help feeling relief and anticipation. Grace wasn't wearing any make-up, and without it she looked almost childish: soaped-clean with her big eyes resting on Eva. Over her bottle-blond frizz she wore a woolly hat, and the collar of her blue raincoat was pulled up against her neck. A young man wearing a vintage Rolling Stones T-shirt was asleep on the bench next to her. Two women eating baguettes cast a vacant stare out of a café window. Adam still sat on his perch outside the Scorpio, and the pubs on Goodge Street were beginning to fill with after-work drinkers rolling up their sleeves and slipping off their ties. Grace had clearly been crying, and her hands shook a little as she placed the cigarette between her chapped lips, in her own world until Eva stepped forward.

"Grace," Eva said.

Grace's pupils dilated slightly as she squinted at Eva and then sideways at the man asleep in the Rolling Stones T-shirt. "Lives with his mother, don't you think?" she said, instead of saying hello. "Sleeping it off before he goes home. He's been here for an hour." She paused. "I've been here nearly two."

"You should have rung the bell." Eva stood above Grace while she remained seated. She almost pouted, as if Eva had been tardy.

"I didn't think you'd want to see me," said Grace, crossing her arms and then uncrossing them, putting a nearly finished cigarette to her lips for a last drag.

"I wouldn't have done," said Eva. "But I would have come down to tell you that."

"Luke said you didn't go home last night."

"No."

"Sorry about my silly overdose attempt," said Grace. "Did it upset you?"

Grace dropped her cigarette on the floor but didn't stub it out, so it continued to leave a trail of smoke. Eva had thought Grace was raw in Brooks's, easily exposing herself to a stranger in the bathroom as Eva wouldn't have exposed herself to her best friend. But of course Grace

ANNA STOTHARD

hadn't revealed anything that she didn't mean to. Now
though, standing in Fitzrovia with tearful eyes and drawn
skin, she looked torn open. "You'd think I'd have come up
with something to say to you, after all this time waiting out
here," Grace continued. "But I'm not sure why I'm here. I've
known Luke for so long..." She smiled, but it didn't look
like a real smile: it was like she'd pulled up one side of her
mouth by a string and held it there quivering for a moment
before dropping it back down again. "I've tried to care about
other people, but when it comes down to it – they're not him,
they're not him and me – us." She pulled her knees up on
the bench so that she was knotted in a sort of cross-legged
position, one knee over the arm of the seat, still peering up
at Eva. "We were quite competitive growing up, you know?
He was always over at our house when were kids. I told
you, right? Big family, always taking in strays. Well, Luke
didn't get on great with his dad and he was always over at
ours." She rubbed her eyes with her hand. Eva swallowed a
build-up of hot, panic-tasting saliva in her mouth and had
an urge to trace the edge of Grace's cheekbones, down to
the creases of her wide mouth to their cracked edges. "We
played football, dared each other to go winter-swimming
while Mary screamed at us to stop. Our parents just let us
get on with things, let all of us be – our brothers, too, running around the farm like feral things. As long as we turned
up at church we were free to do what we wanted. We had
a game with the neighbour's crazy dog – he was always
chained to a post – seeing how close we dared get while it
pulled at the end of its chain. Once it wasn't tied up. Luke
was in hospital for a month."

"Was Mary there too?"

"She didn't play the game. It was me, Luke, my brothers."

"Were you jealous, when Luke and Mary got together?"

"No," said Grace. "We were kids making swords out of tree branches, and she'd turn up in her ballet uniform and he'd go all quiet and blush. There was never any question – that was always going to happen."

"But were you jealous?"

"No," said Grace. She almost grimaced. "It wasn't like that. He was my friend. They made each other happy. She was quiet, but she lit up when he was around."

"And now?"

"Now it's complicated," Grace licked her lips and held Eva's gaze. "It's only natural that I miss him. Those were the best years of my life. Before she died and Luke stopped coming to Devon." At their feet a shifty pigeon stared at a piece of sandwich crust and then decided to go for it, pottering forward, and spiked the wet bread with its beak, flipping it with rare pigeon elegance to a safer bit of pavement. She tugged at the collar of her raincoat with one hand, while the other hand hung loose at her sides, as if she wasn't sure what to do with it. "When I saw him with you at that party a month ago, I felt like he'd erased the past – or I'd found a parallel universe. There was something about you, about the two of you together."

"I don't look like her. I've seen her pictures." Eva shivered.

"It's just the way you move, the way you talk, I'm not sure. But there's something of her in you. I once saw a girl who had Mary's exact hair colour – just hair colour – and I followed her from Bank station to Wimbledon Common."

"The way I move?"

"I was just passing by the pub a month ago and saw him through the window. I hadn't seen him in years. I stood at the edge of that party. I saw you and Luke that night, and I felt like I'd walked into a wormhole. You were laughing at something he said and he touched you on your ear – and just for a moment I thought: this is what it would be like if Mary hadn't died. I wanted to come in and talk to you – I wouldn't have made a scene, I wouldn't have said anything – but he wouldn't let me join in. I miss her."

"And him?"

"I miss him too. He didn't even come to her memorial last year. I miss the three of us. I try and love other people, but I always go back to when we were kids and happy. Before we all grew up and Mary opted out of life, we were just happy. You don't know him like I do, that's all."

In the afternoon din of London, as Grace paused, Eva reached over and put the tip of her finger, just briefly, on Grace's hand between thumb and forefinger, in the same way that Grace had touched Eva's hand in Chinatown.

"You couldn't ever love him like I love him," said Grace quietly, looking at where her tanned skin touched Eva's white fingertips.

When Eva took her hand away, both girls could still feel the slight sting of the contact on their skin. Grace turned away, and Eva let her.

* * *

Eva could still almost smell Grace's breath on her face, and feel where their skin had touched, as she walked slowly up the red-carpeted communal stairs of Silver Place, then into her flat, up the white zigzag of the internal stairs towards Luke.

"Eva," Luke said from the living room, getting up from his desk as she appeared in the doorway. She had that ache in the back of her tongue that precedes tears.

"Where have you been?" he asked. She couldn't work out what to feel or where to look as they stood, closer than she would have liked, in the small room at the beginning of their exit scene. Luke was wearing jeans and a white T-shirt, clearly having come back from work earlier than usual. There was a half-eaten sandwich on his desk and a wineglass stained red on the coffee table next to their Scrabble board. Her letters were face down on the table, and his were arranged on his wooden tray, ready to be played: A, H, M, Y, R, B, R.

"Myrrh," Eva said, nodding at the words.

"I was going to do 'barmy'."

"Barmy?"

"Like 'insane'. I can't remember whose turn it is, though."

Eva already felt giddy – not strong or weirdly eager as she had been during other exit scenes in her life. There is always a moment, in goodbyes, when a person who has been a part of you peels off back into the crowd, and even though they're standing right there, they are becoming strangers again. The body in front of you stiffens into something you only recognize from before you knew them well. It's like a first kiss in reverse, moving backwards from intimacy to isolation while staying in the same place. It has the buzz of renewal, similar to the first time you let someone take off your top, run fingers along an inner thigh, kiss behind your ear. It's a chemical change of form, a shedding of shape.

"You're back early from work," Eva said.

"The jury went for 'not guilty' this morning. My girlfriend didn't come home last night, so I gave myself the afternoon off to worry about her."

"Was the money in your fraud case from clubs in London?" On the surface of the living-room window, the last rays of sunlight revealed patterns of fingerprints and dust.

"And Internet scams. They're closing everything down."

"Is one of the businesses that's being shut down the Scorpio Club on Goodge Street?"

"Is that near your office?"

"Just opposite."

"I think it is one of them, yeah." He frowned. Eva didn't tell him about the magician's assistant or the Croatian girl with the fuchsia cap, or about Grace turning up outside her office. Luke rubbed his shoulder with his hand as if searching out a knot. Eva looked at his scars, the one on his eyebrow, the one across his cheek, and the little slash on his lip, almost invisible now, from the engagement party at the start of August.

"I'm sorry Mary died, Luke," Eva said. "I wish I'd known."

Eva thought about how he'd looked beyond the café window when he was talking to Grace and then embracing her on the pavement outside, and how she had regretted spending so much of their relationship with her foot half out of the door. Everything she could never grasp about Luke – his history, his nightmares – Grace could clearly understand.

"Yes," said Luke, staring at the wonky tiles of their kitchen floor. She thought of her grandmother saying once that kissing was a trick to get people so close together that they couldn't see anything wrong with each other, but Eva didn't think that was true at all. It's not flawlessness that makes you fall in love, surely, it's the belly buttons and how their sweat smells and body fluids and seeing scars other people don't see.

"I saw you with Grace outside the café yesterday afternoon," she said, and before he could come any nearer she stepped past him and walked into the bathroom, closing the door behind. She looked at her own face in the mirror and smoothed her eyebrows with her finger – a little salute. She shuddered at the freckles over her nose, her green eyes and colourless lips.

"Eva," Luke said outside the door, without trying to open it. "Grace used to be my friend growing up, I was like a part of their big family." His voice was only slightly muffled, a relieving distance between them. Eva could feel herself flexing with the desire to leave, no longer to be near him, similar to how your tongue lifts at the thought of a sour thing before it reaches your mouth. She rubbed the back of her knees, covered in her jeans, then started to untie the laces of her boots.

"Please open the door," said Luke. The daylight was just starting to be replaced with the globed street lamps underneath the windows, the flashes of Soho neon making patterns on the walls and illuminating the bathtub and sink in dusky colours. Eva stood up from the bath and put her hand on the brass doorknob. She opened the door and looked through it at Luke in the dark hallway, leaning back on the wall with his knees slightly bent and his big shoulders tensed.

"Growing up, Mary was the one I spoke to on the phone when I was in London during the week, and the person I hoarded up jokes and anecdotes for, waiting to tell her, ever since I was a kid. I was at an all-boys' school all week, then every other weekend was with my dad, but I spent a lot of time at the Taylors' next door, where everyone was welcome. I remember sleeping over in Mary's bedroom when I was eight and my dad joking with hers about who would pay for the wedding. It was that sort of thing."

"And Grace?"

"She was Mary's little tomboy sister. Mary had two younger brothers as well, I put them all in the same category, sort of, although Grace was closer to mine and Mary's age than her brothers. We played baseball sometimes, we were on a football team together, one summer we rebuilt this old tractor my dad got in an auction; we didn't exactly get on, and we fought a lot, but we hung out." Luke's BlackBerry rang in his pocket. He took it out and stared at the screen, silencing it with his thumb.

"Her?" said Eva.

Luke nodded his head and put the phone back in his pocket. Eva turned her shoulder to the right, towards their bedroom, and Luke reached out to put his hand on her arm as she took a step forward. She stopped, staring down at his rough knuckles in the half-light, until he withdrew his hand by his side. She watched him search for words. He crossed his arms, then uncrossed them. His eyes flicked to Eva and then away again. His limbs seemed to be on separate strings to his body just then. He appeared to be getting smaller, pieces of him separating from other pieces, at least in Eva's head. There was his nose – Roman, broken, a little scar on it; his jaw – square; his eyes – grey, narrowing nervously; and a mouth that was tightened into a hard, speechless frown.

"Did that change after Mary died?" she asked.

"About a year after Mary and I started going out she developed anorexia," Luke said. "She'd been ballet-dancing since she was ten, so at first nobody really noticed, but by sixteen she was in and out of hospital all the time. The evening she died, their parents were at some church fête or something. I was meant to be at a football match with Grace, but stayed home to look after Mary, who'd just got back from hospital. She was so tiny, like a bird body, you know? That feeling when you hold a small bird? You could feel all her bones. She wouldn't touch me any more. She used to look after me because of my epilepsy, but obviously once she was ill I tried to look after her."

Eva bit a hangnail on her thumb and dug her toes into the worn hallway carpet.

"Grace came back from the football match all sweaty and excited in her football kit and shouted up that they'd lost the game from being a man down," Luke continued. "Mary was watching a film in bed, and I was doing some homework on her desk."

Luke cracked his knuckles, stretching them out. His forehead puckered with frown lines. "Grace came into Mary's bedroom and said she'd petition to have me chucked off the team for poor attendance. I shrugged and said that was fine.

"I stood up from the desk and Grace pushed me on the chest. Mary was still watching the film in bed, she didn't even get up, cos Grace kicking off like that was so common. Grace and I used to fight properly, but now I was so much bigger than her, we couldn't go at it like we used to. I took her arm and twisted it just a little, not enough to hurt her, just to walk her out of the room. I think Mary said 'stop it' or 'please be quiet' or something. None of this was strange, though: Grace and I had been play-fighting and bickering all our lives."

"Grabbing her wrist was normal?"

"It was how we'd always interacted, though, since we were toddlers almost. Outside the room, in the hallway, Grace started laughing and stamping at my feet. I tried to jump out of the way and stop her, but she kept pushing me and giggling like a crazy thing – and then I don't know what came over me: I slapped her across the face to shut her up." He paused. "That wasn't normal. Mary came out of her room and stared at us."

"Did she say anything?"

Luke paused for a second, his mouth tight. He took a deep uneven breath and crossed his arms.

"She said something like: 'For God's sake Luke, don't humour her – just leave her alone when she's like this.' I wasn't looking at Mary, though. I was watching Grace, her big mouth, her cheek, which was red where I hit her. She stank of sweat from the football game, a little bit of pulp in her teeth from oranges at half-time. She continued to laugh after I slapped her, like it was something funny."

"Sometimes, when I can't sleep, it's all still slow-motion in my head: Grace is laughing, her mouth is wide open. We are all at the top of the stairs. I slap Grace again – I just want her to stop laughing – but she laughs even louder and pushes me back as hard as she can. That's when Mary steps forward to try and separate us or stand between us. I'm not sure what Mary wanted to do, but she stepped forward."

He kept his eyes fast on Eva and said, after another long pause: "I pushed Mary away with my left hand, without even looking at her. It was Grace who screamed then, not Mary. I just wanted Mary to stay out of the way, but I'd pushed her off balance. She didn't make a noise. One minute Grace and I were fighting and the next Grace and I both lunged after Mary as she fell backwards down the stairs."

Luke stopped again. Floorboards creaked in the building.

"A healthy person wouldn't have fallen," said Luke. "Neither of her brothers would have done – Grace wouldn't have. They would have easily held the banisters. I wasn't even looking at Mary, wasn't even thinking, and I certainly didn't mean to do it, I was just irritated with Grace and..." He trailed off, then added after a short silence. "Her brothers ran over, screaming, Grace called the ambulance but..." Again he could not finish the sentence and put his hand over his mouth. Eva imagined pieces of Luke flying up into the sky and hovering for a moment, then settling again in a pattern she couldn't recognize. She stepped over to where Luke was standing in the middle of the kitchen and put her hand on his.

"The paramedics said she died of cardiac arrest," Luke continued, almost whispering. "Maybe her heart gave out as she fell – and that's why she didn't grab the banister or my hand. Maybe it happened when she hit the floor. I was meant to be looking after her. I would never have purposefully hurt her."

Eva closed her eyes for a second, then opened them again. In the darkness of the hallway, Eva thought of blustering, flippant early love: breakfast-at-lunch love, love full of revelations such as "I take my tea black" and "my middle name is Patricia", which amaze and confuse and shift your perception and make you, somehow, fall deeper, as you begin to understand a person and therefore possess them, a little bit more each day. She had spent years sewing together Luke's likes and dislikes, his references and foundations, but as she stared at his red-rimmed eyes, it was all unravelling and it all felt too much, too novel, too frantic. She felt weightless thinking of this hole in the story he'd presented of himself, such an unspoken grief in the middle of it.

"After that, Grace grew up fast – drugs, boys – she got expelled from school for fighting, and her parents sent her to some residential boot camp where she tried to slit her wrists. I saw her from time to time, we got drunk together in London on and off, but it always ended up in an argument." Luke frowned. "We saw each other at Mary's memorial most years. I'd missed last year though, so it had been two years since I'd seen her when she turned up at Catherine's engagement party. I'd been avoiding her calls and she was angry."

"Was it her sending you the strange postcards?"

"Yes. She sent that three times before Catherine's party, trying to get my attention, because I wasn't returning her calls. We used to be friends. She found it difficult..." he faltered, looking away from Eva again. "I find *her* difficult," he said. "She's Mary's little sister. I feel ten years old again when I'm with her, like nothing has changed and we're still fighting for the TV remote or arm-wrestling for the front seat of her dad's pick-up. I feel so guilty, Eva. Every moment. It's why I became a lawyer. To try and understand."

She tucked her hair behind her ears and then stopped herself.

"You would have liked her. Before she got ill. You could have got on."

They stood in silence. She wished she could take away that look in his hawkish grey eyes. A moth flew past between them, and neither of them moved. Grace might as well have been there in the room with them. Footsteps clicked on the ceiling above the kitchen. All summer, the story had been intersecting with her only occasionally – in casinos, Chinese restaurants, on the news – but she was a walk-on part in a narrative where the opening chapter happened years ago. It was Grace and Luke, since they were children, battling dogs in the fields outside their farms. Eva wasn't strong enough to be the story's heroine, perhaps. Already at the edges, Eva could step right off the pages. To leave would be no terrible thing. She could step away from the tangle and feel less trapped, less caught and worried. As Luke squeezed her hand, she thought of white sky, cold air, the click of her own boots receding on the pavement, new beginnings. She considered her tingling fingers where her skin met Grace's an hour ago. Pretty, vicious, haunted Grace. Her heart sped up not because of Grace's fading touch or Luke's thumb pressing at her hand, but with the thought of one day *remembering* this last night with Luke. She already had a sense of nostalgia.

He'd chosen to keep that sadness, that jolt of violence and passion, as a private conspiracy between him and Grace. He had elected to remain at a distance from Eva.

Eva thought of the magician's assistant in the Scorpio, surrounded by rose petals and bunny rabbits and playing cards, but she couldn't hold the image in her mind for long: her imagination turned to Anya peeking her head around the door of the bar and then running back upstairs again, her sullen face under a wide-brimmed fuchsia baseball cap. She thought of her grandma – "wish to be gone now little girl" – and she herself wished to be gone. Holding her breath in the hallway, she tried to think of the strange pleasure she found in saying goodbye to people, the fun of it. She reminded herself that leaving was the most truthful moment of any relationship and as you walked away all the mistakes you made and the things you became with that person simply disappeared, allowing you to start again and be whatever you wanted to be. Leaving was powerful, it was a shedding of skin.

"Say something?" said Luke, his fingers on her naked shoulder.

"I used to cry all the time as kid," said Eva, giving a faint smile. "All the time – it was humiliating. I had to go to therapy every Wednesday for a whole summer. I have a false tooth from falling off a running machine, and I'm sorry I've never introduced you to my parents. I should have done."

"There's nothing except history between Grace and me. I didn't mean to hurt Mary. I loved her. I wish I'd had the guts to tell you what happened before now." She stared at Luke, and could see what he would look like when he was old, with the crazy deep pinch lines between his eyebrows having set in, and what he might have looked like when he was young, scar-free, eager to please. She could see him reading at Mary's funeral, his voice cracking a bit, but holding it together till the end. She could see him in a business meeting, in a lunch meeting, doing paperwork, calling his Mum. She could see all of it in that moment. She remembered him appearing in the bedroom doorframe a month ago, naked apart from one sock wrinkled around his ankle, with his stubble wet from drinking out of the tap and a little bit of blood visible on his top lip. She thought of how he sat on her bed six years ago and his perfect grey suit wrinkled around his arms as if he'd melted there in front of her.

Eva thought of the humid winter in Bali, then the swimming pool on the Spanish holiday, and she tried to remember the thrill she felt at the sight of aeroplanes in the sky, the fun of guessing where they were going.

She watched a moth dancing in a wash of fake sunshine from the kitchen window. He must have known she would leave. He knew her better than anyone. We all do what we know, trapped in tightening circles. Childhood habits: of violence, or exit strategies. As he leant forward to give her a kiss, she closed her eyes and thought about the relief she would find in walking away from him.

* * *

Under the buzzing phosphorescent ceiling of Singapore's Changi Airport, Eva saw her father pacing behind the arrivals barrier, staring at the floor around him while women bundled grown men in their arms and girls embraced returning lovers across the white Arrivals floor. He wore khaki board shorts, a blue shirt and grey socks poking out from the leather of his sandals. He was clearly gagging for a cigarette.

"It's been a while, kid. Welcome back to paradise," he said in his booming voice. He had beads of water on his wrinkled forehead. He put a hand on his daughter's shoulder and led her away from the crowds of families craning their necks and tour guides and taxi drivers holding laminated boards with names on them. "Did you know Singapore was recently voted the least corrupt country in the world?" he said.

"Wow," Eva said, exhausted. "That's great."

"Isn't it just. No suitcase?" her father said, frowning, looking around the airport as if someone else might have stolen it from her.

"No," said Eva, but she didn't explain how she'd only extricated her passport while Luke slept the previous night, and hadn't packed anything else.

They walked through the large Arrivals hall, past leggy Chinese lettering on advertisements and signs, past rows of foreign newspapers, strange colours and food smells surrounding them from the various kiosks. She felt at home in the airport's immersive soundscape of intercoms and machinery, its shiny floors. Nimble women clicked back and forth in the crowds, men dragged wheelie suitcases in careful zigzags.

"For how long will we have the pleasure of your company?" asked her father.

"I'm not sure."

She followed her father through automatic doors, and a wet sheet of hot air arched towards them. In the car park, her father took a deep drag on a cigarette and proudly tapped the bonnet of a brick-red, mid-life-crisis sports car. Eva squeezed herself into the passenger seat. The moment her father turned on the engine, a blast of air-conditioning gave her goose bumps.

"How's Mum?" Eva asked.

"Fine, fine. Made a damn fine birthday cake for our friend Tony's seventieth at the club the other night." He checked his wing mirror, began to reverse, squinting in concentration. "Took her best part of a weekend," he said, and they revved up a ramp into Singapore's wide, clean streets, swamped with bright sunshine. Her father did not appear to have aged since their last meeting at Heathrow airport. If anything, he seemed younger.

"How's life?" he said. "Work good?"

"Fine," said Eva, yawning, although after emailing Echo Books that she needed a month off for personal reasons she didn't think her job would be waiting for her when she returned.

"Didn't sleep much on the plane, I suppose?"

"No," she said, staring out of the window as the city's tall buildings loomed up over her. In fact, she hadn't slept at all on the plane. As the aeroplane's wheels lifted from the runway and London became smaller underneath, Eva had felt so good to be disappearing. Everything that was important shrinking and dissolving.

"You were never much good at sleeping on planes," said her father. "You only quietened down if your mother walked you up and down the aisles."

For the rest of the drive, they remained in silence. Her parents had moved into a gated estate a little farther from the airport, and they belonged to a new country club. Their bungalow looked very much like the previous one Eva had visited years ago, only this one was white rather than red-brick. Her mother was sitting in the living room when they arrived, a smell of cinnamon and sugar filling the humid air. She kept a meticulous house, full of pastel colours and polished glass. A frilled bunch of chrysanthemums sat on the coffee table.

"Sweetheart," her mother said, standing up from the sofa and giving off a smile that looked – as Eva remembered thinking so often as a child – ornamental.

"You look well," Eva said.

"Oh, and so do you, darling," she whispered in her slow cotton-wool voice, with a slight frown at Eva's red-rimmed eyes and greasy brown hair. Neither parent asked about the abruptness of their daughter's arrival or the vagueness of her plans. She'd emailed them from an Internet booth at Heathrow Terminal Three saying she was on her way, apologizing for the late notice, hoping they didn't mind. Her mother showed her to a spare room with floral pink lampshades that matched the curtains. Doilies, cut-glass water tumblers and a bowl of potpourri sat between two

THE ART OF LEAVING

single beds with dusky-peach sheets on them. Eva declined all offers of angel cake and tea, preferring instead to lie down immediately on top of the pink sheets and fall asleep with the smell of baking in her nostrils. In the few minutes before slipping out of consciousness, she tried not to think of Luke, who would have woken up in Soho the previous morning to an empty flat hoping, at least for a while, that she was out buying milk at the newsagent's.

When she opened her eyes again, it was morning in Singapore. She had to count backwards to realize what morning it was. She must have been asleep for at least fifteen hours. She stretched under the pollen-coloured light coming from the edge of the curtains, a single finger of sunshine pointing across the bed as if wanting to prod her awake. It was three mornings, she decided, since leaving Luke asleep in Silver Place, although it seemed like longer since easing herself out of their shared bed and listening to piano music quietly in the living room for three hours, thinking everything through in the half-light. She hadn't felt angry exactly, just lonely. Her head had been throbbing as she wrote a quick note on his yellow legal pad, saying she was going to stay with her parents for a little while. She did know it was cowardly, this constantly repeated instinct to jump away from the centre of things – like she'd talked to Luke about meat cuts and acid rain after seeing him with another woman in the dark outside the pub at the start of August, like she'd stayed awake next to Luke without talking the morning after Grace turned up drunk. Closing the front door on their home at five a.m. with shaky hands, she'd walked along the cobbled pavement with a flat feeling of relief: not thrilling or full of possibility, but a yawning, gritty emptiness. The sensation of leaving was, at least, full of adrenalin, familiar if not pleasurable.

She shut her eyes on the memory of walking away from Silver Place. Outside the spare-room window came the sound of children in the street below. She got up off the bed and opened the curtains a crack to watch some kids playing chase around the gated complex, all wearing blue-and-white cotton school uniforms, their rucksacks and lunchboxes flung in a pile near a flower bed. Her parents' house was surrounded by a cluster of identical stucco bungalows with tidy front yards. A girl in a white cheesecloth sports shirt raced down the street with her head thrust out in front, her long black hair nearly horizontal behind her. A child with the stain of some red fruit drink forming a smile around his lips was panting on the corner. Giddy screeches in the air. *One o'clock, two o'clock, three o'clock, four o'clock…* a kid was counting loudly near their bungalow. A wild, barefoot boy laughed, his shoulder bones bouncing, and Eva imagined Luke, Mary, Grace and their two brothers playing tag together in some flower-blooming garden, Grace laughing rowdily and Luke rolling on the ground while Mary, quieter, watched. A girl in the far corner of the street pushed another girl over. The next few months were going to be a concentrated effort of un-thought, focused mental absence. She closed her mother's floral curtains on the children and sat back down on the bed.

Eva stayed in Singapore for just over a month. Her mother played bridge at the country club most evenings, while her father watched sports in the shadowy mahogany-lined club bar with lots of other sun-scorched expats. Nearly every evening she watched movies in a cinema inside a big shopping mall, twenty minutes' walk from the club across the golf course. She would drive there with her parents (crammed in the tiny back seat of her father's car) and then amble across to the shopping mall. She'd coil herself in a small velvet seat at the back of the room to watch whatever was on. She sat in the salty air-conditioned cinema for hours, through unsubtitled romantic comedies in Tamil, low-budget Chinese dramas, children's stories, action adventures starring Nicholas Cage and Steven Seagal. Sometimes she watched the same film on consecutive nights. She read a few of her father's airport thrillers while lying on her mother's sofa, and she swam laps in the country club's small indoor swimming pool, which was mostly empty except on Wednesdays, when wrinkled women in colourful bathing caps did water aerobics to the tinkle of new-age music.

"In books it's all about exits and entrances, isn't it? But in life it's all about the middle," Luke had said the night she left him. He had touched her neck as he said it, and she'd shivered right down from her tongue to her toes. It had been the sort of touching that was half – perhaps more – an attempt at repelling. Afterwards she had sat on her own in the living room until morning, listening to his record player very quietly while he slept.

For the first three weeks in Shanghai Luke sent her emails that she didn't reply to or even want to read. She scanned their subject headings, and her fingers twitched over the messages, but she had no desire to step back inside the story. It was better off the page, in her parents' sunlit country club.

That was the mood for a while. Soft, hopeful question marks. Pliable sentences. Eva might have written back to him that she kept dreaming of Regina perched haughtily in Trafalgar Square, and Grace's ribcage in the bath. She might have written that even before this summer she would watch him at parties, or bent over the living-room table reading witness statements, and feel only the slightest connection, like he was someone she knew she ought to recognize but couldn't quite place. She could have written to tell him that she'd watched him walking over London Bridge the afternoon Regina went sightseeing, and she'd wondered whether the distance she often felt between them was a part of her own shadow or if it was him. She could have written that she did in fact miss him, that he was the only person that she'd ever found it unpleasant to leave. But she didn't open his messages.

In the second week, his subject lines went up a notch, *demanding* that she call him. But she didn't. Eva did not write back to him, but swam lap after lap in the country-club pool until she was exhausted. She started smoking again, and shared packs of cigarettes in a hedge garden with an ancient leathery woman named Marjory, who used to be a nurse. In the third week, Eva sat in the country club's sweaty-smelling business room and read: "I need to talk to you" and "there are things I need to say" and "I've moved out and I need to explain". The only emails she opened were work queries, and one from Justin saying that he was coming to Singapore to get footage of a print of the Chinese Solar deity Tai Yang Xing Jun at the National Museum. Justin had heard from Luke that she was in Singapore, and wondered if she'd like to meet up. She said she would.

* * *

On a humid afternoon in the middle of September, Eva found all her childhood toys in a big box under the stairs. She had woken up after a long unsatisfying nap and was looking for a screwdriver to fix the spare bedroom's cupboard when she saw a beige plastic hand waving for help from a transparent storage box. She took the lid off and stared down at dolls with knotted frizzy hair and sweet little pent-up smiles, chubby-cheeked porcelain faces with ringlets and lace bonnets, a loose head with a hole up its neck, the body long lost, probably in some airport or schoolyard. She hauled the box up the spare room and unpacked the musty creatures from their cocoon of stale air. The inch-high dollies were called "worry dolls" or "trouble dolls", she remembered, their puny bodies made out of wire wrapped with scraps of material or coloured yarn. You were meant to put them under your pillow at night and tell your worries to them – but she never used them like that. She used them for stories about kidnappings and unfair imprisonments. The girls in skirts would be trapped in castles by evil kings. The boys swam shark-infested waters away from haunted islands marked on one or other of the dozens of maps piled neatly in the box by her mother at some point. Eva pulled out Barbies, Cindys, porcelain-headed children in Victorian dresses who spent Eva's childhood looking for the Holy Grail, the golden fleece, the pot of gold. Eva slipped one of the maps out from the pile, her fingers on the corner of the dried-out paper. She opened it on the floor of the spare room. She felt "scooped out", as her grandmother would have said, "all tied up". It was strange to think that her mother had kept these remnants of her early years. She assumed they'd have been thrown away long ago in one of the family's many moves. They weren't in some damp garage being eaten by mice, or abandoned during that sad winter in Bali.

In front of her on the carpet, Russia was a tangerine-orange colour, Brazil canary-yellow, China, Libya and United States were coral-red. Antarctica was a white puddle at the bottom of the page, a splash rising up from the seams of the world. Eva thought of Luke running his fingers over her belly button the night before she left London, the way he held her wrists against the bed covers, making Eva shift, wriggle, shiver, glance up at the misted window in their bedroom. She'd wanted to be anywhere but there with him in the damp sheets. On the world map laid out now at her knees, she put her thumb on Singapore and walked her fingers over the Bay of Bengal, little scissor steps across India and Pakistan – Iran, the Caspian Sea – veering left over Europe and then landing on London, which she covered with her thumb. She pressed her thumb as hard as she could over England and tried not to think about Luke.

She heard a creak outside the room. The door opened, her mother's tanned face peering through. She was wearing a cotton dress with beige pumps, her blond bob set in the shape of a horseshoe around her face.

"Oh I'm sorry, I thought you were out," she said. "Would you like a cup of tea and some cake?"

"You kept all my maps," Eva said, smiling.

"Have you left Luke?" Her mother put one of her long fingers to her mouth and began to bite the nail there, just as Eva had a habit of doing.

"Yes," Eva said, still sitting on her knees, which ached slightly. She had to strain to hear her mother's soft voice, her underwater intonations.

"Even when you were tiny you were so *compact*," her mother said.

"Compact?" said Eva, rubbing a worry doll between her thumb and forefinger and looking up at her mother. She had an urge to bite her nails as well, but didn't.

"Composed, self-contained, sort of." Her mother shrugged. "Making your drawings, playing your games, telling yourself stories. You'll be OK, whatever you decide. I used to look at you when you were a toddler and think that even then you were somehow stronger than I was." Her mother had never spoken to her like this. "You know, I'm not too bad now," she added.

"That's good," said Eva, wishing she had something better to say, but tongue-tied.

"Your father and I always thought the next place would be better, we'd be happier somewhere new," her mother said, glancing around the room at the floral patterns and pink shades. "He thought I could leave sadness behind like you leave old objects you don't need any more. But it was never like that."

Eva still couldn't think of anything to say, although she wanted to say something. "Can I get you a slice of cake?" her mother asked again, filling the silence.

"I'd love a slice of cake, thanks," said Eva.

* * *

Eva searched for a map of North Devon on the Internet to look for St Edmund's Parish Church, finding it above a slim section of the River Torridge. The surrounding roads had story-book comforting names like "Rolle" and "Mill" and "Rosemoor". There was some woodland labelled Never-Be-Good Wood and Darkwood, where bad story-book characters might live in opposition to the goodies in Churchford Wood and Parsonage Wood. Eva stared at the map and wondered where the dog attacked Luke, where Luke and Mary's farms might be on the green-and-blue patchwork of map. Was the memorial she had read about in Grace's photo album held in the church every year, or perhaps at Mary's grave, or just in Grace's parents' living room, with plates of sandwiches and cups of tea in pretty porcelain? Looking back, Luke tended to go to Devon late September each year. He had told her once that it was his father's birthday that weekend, but presumably it was for Mary's memorial.

On the day of Mary's commemoration service, but a long distance away from the church or farm or grave where it would be held, Eva saw Justin before he saw her, standing in the long glass-ceilinged entrance hall of the National Museum of Singapore. He was wearing a linen suit a bit

THE ART OF LEAVING

too small for him, and he was cleaning the lenses of his
glasses with the end of his tie as he leant against the walls.
Crowds bustled up and down, school children with drawing
pads sitting on stone benches down the middle of the hall,
tourists mulling over their guide books.

Justin put his glasses back on and Eva walked towards
him. They both smiled and said uneasy hellos – *lovely to
see you, how are you, you look well*. Then they fell silent
and glanced around with taut smiles on their faces. Eva
thought of organ music playing somewhere in Devon, except it was late afternoon in Singapore: eight hours ahead
of England, so the memorial probably hadn't started yet.
They were most likely tying their shoelaces, brushing their
teeth, boiling eggs on the AGA.

"There's a Singapore 'entertainment' gallery?" said Justin
after an uncomfortable pause. "It's only *mildly* entertaining,
but very Singapore. Or we could go to the café?"

"Let's do a gallery," said Eva.

She turned and followed Justin through a white-marble
arch and up some stairs into a dark room with a huge
illuminated glass case of Chinese opera stage costumes
with intricate beads and threads woven into the shapes of
dragons and flowers. They stared through into the case,
then turned and continued towards three screens with nervy,
silent black-and-white footage of theatrical performances.
Jangly music played over the top of all three displays. Huge
operatic smiles filled up the screens, dancing heads with
big painted eyes.

"How is the documentary on the sun going?" asked Eva.

"Good, good. Fascinating subject."

"I'm sure," she said, although neither of them sounded fascinated. She thought of his hand on her hip as they fell asleep the last time they saw each other. She wondered if he'd turned his hotel room upside down looking for the keys to his flat. She doubted he'd have suspected her of stealing them.

"Did you see the two suns in the sky at the end of August? The supernova?"

"No, no," said Eva. "I missed that. Was it good?"

"Wasn't very visible, actually," said Justin.

"Everything's good with you?" said Justin, watching two women dance on a screen, their gloved fingers making beak shapes, snapping the sky behind as they moved. Illumination from the screens flashed over their faces. St Edmund's Parish Church would be full of light falling through stained-glass windows later that day. Mary's family would be getting ready now, perhaps holding flowers or photographs in their hands. Grace's mother, Eva thought, might already be tearful. Luke might put his arm around her.

"Sure. Fine. You?"

"Not so bad." Justin glanced sideways at Eva as a flash of white went over their faces from stage lights coming up on one of the screens. "I saw Luke. He helped move Grace's stuff out of our place."

"Grace not up to the task?" she said, and she turned away from the cinema screens. She imagined Luke turning away from Grace in the church, staring down at his shiny shoes. But no, they could not be at the memorial yet. Grace might be coming up behind Luke and kissing his shoulder in the bathroom mirror while he shaved, and Eva experienced a physical jolt at the image. She blinked it away, sickened. In the next museum room there were shadow puppets pinned up against light boxes all over the red walls: gremlin silhouettes with whiskers, masked armies with elaborate hats and flared sleeves. Skinny monsters were stuck in mortal combat against bears wearing feathered headpieces or snake-like men.

"Grace went to a rehab clinic for a while," said Justin.

"Is she OK?"

"She took more pills a week after I saw you. Luke says she seems a little more stable now, though. They're spending a few weeks in Devon."

"A few weeks?" said Eva, her shoulders tense with the thought of Grace's shaking hands touching Luke's.

"He took time off. It's Mary's memorial, too. I think he feels he has to look after Grace." He paused. "The three of them were very close, growing up," said Justin.

Eva imagined herself standing at the back of the church in Devon, watching Grace and Luke together, and a cold chill swept over her again, as it had at the end of August when she was sitting in the bathroom, listening to Luke speak.

Footage of moving shadow puppets played on the screens. The background was flat yellow light and a man with a forked hand and the face of a monkey was fighting a hooded skeleton holding a stick. In the foreground you could see the silhouetted heads of children in the audience, getting up here and there, fidgeting.

"Were they together?" asked Eva.

"It seemed that way," said Justin. "He was distraught after you left. He didn't think you'd leave." Justin paused.

263

"And Grace was there. They have so much history. She needed him."

Eva imagined Grace in a black dress standing at the front of the church, head bowed, hands primly caught together at her waist. Luke, in his morning suit, perhaps glancing out of the church window. She wanted to cry.

She considered going back to Justin's hotel, asking him to come with her for a drink, getting obliterated in some clean Singapore bar, kissing him in the street and laughing, holding him tight so she wouldn't think of Luke or Grace – but she didn't say anything. Instead they continued round the musty exhibit, looking at old record players and puppet stages and headdresses, talking about cities, and sun-worship, their parents, their plans, anything but the people they cared about and were not with.

* * *

On the fifth of November Eva walked from Silver Place up Poland Street, passing closed pubs and the backs of council-flat buildings. Two months after leaving Singapore, her freckles were fading again and her skin was winter-pale as usual. She crossed Noel Street into Berwick Street and Oxford Street, curving into Wells Street to veer left onto Mortimer Street so that she could walk past All Souls Church on Portland Place, all the time thinking of how the two-dimensional street patterns would look on a map. The church's circular steps and columns reached up to the stone dunce's cap at the top spiking out over the rooftops of

London and appearing to glow. As if the clouds had decided that they'd expended enough tears over the summer, in the second week of September the rain in England had stopped and there hadn't been a drop since. "Worst drought for thirty years," warned BBC News. "Save water," demanded billboards on the Tube. Eva walked past British Broadcasting House, under the blue scaffolding tunnel of building works and out in the direction of Regent's Park Tube.

Eva passed over York Bridge towards the Inner Circle of Regent's Park. The early-evening sky was nearly white, and the trees made bony silhouettes against the clouds. Eva hugged her coat tighter to her and didn't step through the gates into the rose gardens. She continued along the curving main path and turned left when she saw the open-air theatre, making her way onto the boating lake with bobbing rowing boats. She crossed the bridge into the main expanse of patchwork football fields. Three games were going on at the same time – some disorganized teenagers, a puffing group of thirty-somethings and schoolgirls in coloured bibs.

She'd cried in early October when she sat on the sofa in front of Luke's TV and watched the balding zookeeper recapture Regina after over two months of freedom. The newspapers said that the keeper had camped out in the park all through several nights and lain out rabbit carcasses in the grass early every morning. After her brief mid-August sojourn in central London, Regina had come back to Regent's Park and settled there quietly for the next month, eating food the zoo laid out to trap her and killing the occasional duck. One morning she came down from her sky-high perch in the trees where she'd made her home above the courtier crows and pigeons. She landed directly on the zookeeper's rabbit, and ruffled her mosaic of brown feathers. She didn't even glance up at the keeper as he snuck up behind her this time and put a blanket over her face. Perhaps Regina had become tired, or perhaps she'd visited her former home in the zoo one evening, alighted on the pavement outside the "birds of prey" enclosures and patched things up with Goldie through the cage bars. Eva wondered if the courtier crows thought of warning Regina of her balding stalker with a raised bag behind her, or if the crows and magpies wanted their queen gone, wanted their patch back from that intruder with marble eyes and a squat neck sunken into powerful shoulders. In the end the keeper picked the bird up with his bare hands and deftly wrapped wire around the poor creature's little legs without much of a struggle at all.

"We're very pleased to have her back, and so is her mate of five years, Goldie," the grinning zookeeper had said. There was footage of Regina back in her cage with Goldie, both on the same branch of a fake-looking tree with a brown grill visible both above and behind the two birds, sawdust and scrub underneath them. "Goldie is thrilled to have his girl back," said the chirpy voice-over of a news reporter, and Eva didn't think the voice was meant to sound sarcastic, even though the smirking and haughty beaks of both birds appeared far from thrilled, there in the zoo cage. Regina looked like she was pretending that this broadcast humiliation wasn't really happening, her face held high, eyes darting around her tiny new kingdom. Eva hoped that Regina was remembering the thrill of killing ducks in the

American ambassador's garden and the coddled taste of pet-poodle flesh, the powerful happiness of sitting on the bronze sculpture in the middle of Trafalgar Square while crowds gasped. In the zoo, Regina and Goldie preened themselves in unison, rubbing their beaks against a tree branch as if they were sharpening their knives.

Still, the crows and magpies in Regent's Park seemed happy now without the eagle shadow to worry them from above. The birds teetered above Eva against the white sky, some falling away from the pack and joining from a different angle. Others bounced gleefully out the trees with sunshine hitting their feathers. Eva went and sat on the bench nearest the south entrance of the park to watch pigeons eating bread laid down by an elderly lady wearing a striped bobble hat. Luke's books were still alphabetized with her books and DVDs in Silver Place, but while she was in Singapore he'd taken his classical-music records, the bottle of red wine his father had given him for his eighteenth birthday that Eva had been so scared she'd drink by mistake, the carefully folded suit bags and the box full of shoes she'd been so horrified by when he first appeared on her doorstep. He left his TV, but took his shoe-cleaning kit and his Gordon Ramsay cookbook and his vegetable steamer and his record player. He'd left his Japanese painting that explored different shades of "white", but Eva had taken the painting down and stored it with its face to the wall of the living room. Once she was home and Luke was gone, his key in her desk drawer where he used to keep his sunglasses, Eva fell back to keeping her clothes mostly on the floor, eating toast and instant coffee for dinner and going to bed at eight p.m. if she happened to feel like it – which she often did in the months after he left. Life had been extremely calm since she'd returned from the humid air of Singapore, without Luke bustling in late at night with his papers tied in pink ribbon, waking up early for court. He called her a few times, and she would almost pick up the telephone each time, wanted to pick up (her thumb twitching over the "answer" button), but at the last minute she'd push the phone away across the table or bed or desk. He called from work sometimes, so she knew he was in London, although not where he was living. She was lonely, perhaps, but it wasn't a terrible loneliness. She would surely be lonely, too, if she picked up the phone to Luke and found out he was still with Grace. She wondered if he and Grace still shared their secret, or if he'd now told anyone else the truth.

Eva watched the gates of the park as people folded in and out in the falling darkness. She fished a copy of yesterday's *Times* out of the rubbish bin next to the bench and flicked through it looking for any mention of the Scorpio Club, which had finally closed down completely and now had a notice of eviction posted on its closed red door. Adam was gone from his stool, and the romantic novels had disappeared from the window sills along with the pot plants, magazines and wineglasses. There was still no mention of the Scorpio in the papers. It was almost as if the place had never existed. The sign was gone, replaced with nothing, so the gap above the door appeared like a toothless gum. The people in the hairdresser's next door said they didn't know what happened, but had come to work one day, as Eva had, to find the place locked up and empty, all the noise gone from the basement and bedrooms. A postcard from Croatia had been waiting for her at Echo Books when she returned from Singapore, though, and Eva had pinned it among the jackets on her chalkboards: "Is OK here, got job in Zagreb now, in café. If you in Croatia ever you can visit me. Thank you. Anya." Somewhere on the north coast of Cornwall, *The Pirate's Mistress* was being printed and bound and glued together, ready for release. Echo Books hadn't fired Eva, but she had an interview with a magazine soon. She was going to move on.

Eva looked up from the paper to find with a shiver that the London skyline had darkened, as if a lid had been put over the park. Two of the football games had finished and the last was just about to end as Eva folded the newspaper on her lap and began to bite at the hangnail on her thumb. The sky was shifting from blue to black and gobbling up the ragged fingers of trees reaching up towards the clouds. The moon was big and wet-looking. Eva stared at it and then watched a second explosion of light, a firework bursting blue legs beyond trees and buildings in the far distance. A dog barked somewhere in the park and another firework came from the dripping first. Behind her, a bulb of white threw itself in the sky and then three little pellets of furious colour erupted and rained down on the tips of the surrounding trees. Something hissed, maybe a Catherine wheel, and a group of crows flew abruptly away over the grass and down in the direction of Soho. A huge blue explosion, the metallic blue of nail polish or car paint, split the sky in two from just beyond the wall of trees in the distance that separated her from Primrose Hill. A family marched down the path with a little blond girl waving a sparkler in one hand and tugging at her father's hand with the other, and then a couple, all wrapped up in gloves and scarves, shuffled in the same direction around the Outer Circle of the park towards London Zoo, presumably aiming for beyond, over the Canal and across Prince Albert Road into Primrose Hill.

It was quiet and frosty now in Regent's Park, but there would be thousands of people up on the hill, all packed together, bustling against each other, necks craned to the sky. When one firework ended another started up again. It all appeared to be continuous, one moment on top of another, endings crashing into beginnings and starting all over again. More people were joining the path from the St John's Wood side of the park and little ant-sized coats and scarves from the Camden Town side. There was green rain, white rain, a sudden smoky burst of light in the black sky, and Eva knew that Luke would be up there in the crowds of the Primrose Hill fireworks, as he was every year. Perhaps he was holding Grace's fingers in his hand, or standing shoulder to shoulder with her. Eva imagined hawkish grey eyes set too deeply in his face, his oversized tongue, the scar on his eyebrow, the sense of a burden.

She thought of the weight of Luke's big hands on her shoulder. The sound of him snoring in bed. The sound of him coming home late, or getting up early and pottering around the room in the dark, trying not to wake her. He'd be just beyond the canal, beyond the zoo, making conversation in the dark. She imagined the sight of him cooking in the little kitchen at Silver Place. The sight of his body as he seizured. The joy he took in yawning. The way he only took a moment to undress and so watched her like a ringmaster while she performed a faux-nonchalant dance around him, angling herself behind cupboards and doors to avoid him seeing her at unflattering stages of nakedness. The look on his face when he wanted to stay at a party for one more drink – *one more song, Eva, just one more*. The scar on his lip. The scar on his jaw. All Luke's jagged seams, where he'd been sewn back together as a kid. Eva imagined the gaps, the fuck-ups, hints of the things she didn't understand, as she sat alone on the bench in cold Regent's Park.

Perhaps all that was enough. It wasn't so much that she wanted the moment of reunion with Luke, just that she wanted to be standing idly next to him in the cold. Eva bit the hangnail on her thumb and wondered if it was worth walking past the zoo and over the canal, to have a closer look at the fireworks.